Sunvault

Stories of Solarpunk and Eco-Speculation

edited by Phoebe Wagner & Brontë Christopher Wieland

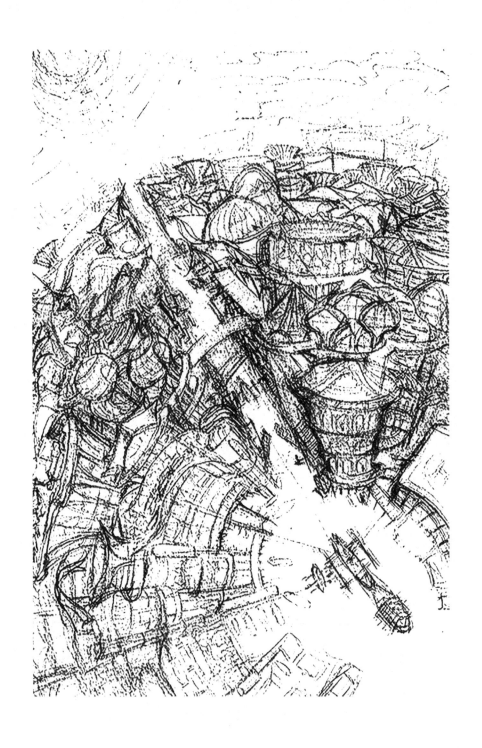

Table of Contents

Foreword: On the Origins of Solarpunk

Andrew Dincher

As a genre, science fiction (SF) has a contentious history. Some would argue that the genre began with the utopian narratives of Early Modern Europe such as Sir Thomas Moore's *Utopia*, while others argue that it began with Mary Shelley's *Frankenstein*. On the other hand, some would argue that SF was a unique creation of the late 19th century, beginning with the works of Jules Verne and H.G. Wells, then skyrocketing (pun intended) to popularity in the 1930s with the creation of magazines like *Weird Tales, Amazing Stories,* and *Astounding Science Fiction.*

Regardless, SF has a unique ability to speculate on the future of human, and in some cases other than human, existence. Though it would be a mistake to say that all SF examines the negative outcome of human civilization in dystopian and post-apocalyptic narratives, many of the most widely-read SF stories highlight the struggles of humanity in an already apocalyptic or dystopian world.

In steps solarpunk, a new movement in SF that examines the possibility of a future in which currently emerging movements in society and culture such as the green movement, the Black Lives Matter movement, and certain aspects of Occupy Wall Street coalesce to create a more optimistic future in a more just world. In the words of Sir Isaac Newton, however: "If I have seen further, it is by standing on the shoulders of Giants." Like Newton, the solarpunk movement stands on the shoulders of giants—giants of science fiction.

By its very nature, SF pushes the boundaries of the imagination; speculating on the future, altered pasts, and wildly discordant presents. Throughout the 1950s and into the early 1960s, an era commonly referred to as the "golden age" of science fiction, SF writers speculated on possible worlds and, in a more general sense, adhered to plausible hard SF stories. Authors such as Arthur C. Clarke, Robert A. Heinlein, Isaac Asimov, and Alfred Bester all wrote hard SF with an emphasis on the possibilities of the future. Throughout the 1960s and 1970s, however, SF began focusing more on the soft sciences with a movement now known as the "new wave."

Authors such as Samuel R. Delany, Philip K. Dick, Harlan Ellison, James Tiptree, Jr., and Joanna Russ (just to mention a few) were some of the forerunners of the new wave. They wrote stories that focused more on the human condition in technologically advanced worlds and focused less on science and technology. This is not to say that authors such as Heinlein and Clarke didn't also discuss the human condition and that authors such as Delany and Russ didn't think about technology. But rather there was a shift in the overall tone of SF moving towards the social sciences.

Several pivotal SF novels, however, focused heavily on ecological and environmental themes. Frank Herbert's *Dune,* a transitory novel that fits somewhere between the new wave and the golden age, explored the idea of a galactic struggle for "Spice," a substance that expands consciousness allowing for precognition and faster than light travel. *Dune* also dealt with the ecology of an entirely desert planet and the struggles of human civilization to survive and adapt in a harsh and unforgiving world.

Similarly, other SF authors have dealt with ecological and environmental issues in their fiction. Ursula K. Le Guin, a new wave writer, deals with environmental and ecological topics in several of her works. "Vaster than Empires and More Slow," for instance, is a short story that discusses the possibility of an alien planet covered with vegetation that is, in and of itself, a single thinking, living, sentient being. Kim Stanley Robinson, who is currently writing environmental SF, in his novel *2312,* sets up a dilemma in which humanity is able to terraform other planets such as Mars and Venus, but is yet unable to heal the wounds done to Earth through climate change. All of the ice on Earth has melted and New York—a still functional city—has been flooded, making it a "Super Venice."

These authors also tend to deal with social issues involving the environment. *2312* follows many of the conventions that will be used by solarpunk authors by dealing with environmental justice and imagining a solar system in which humanity has found a way to be responsible with its environment. It could almost be considered a solarpunk novel, but since it pre-dates solarpunk, its place in the canon is unclear. Regardless, *2312* is a perfect example of what solarpunk embodies.

Out of these various incarnations and phases of evolutionary twistings and turnings, solarpunk has emerged. As a genre, it sits atop the shoulders of past science fiction visionaries. No one can know exactly what this new genre is destined for, but its origins are clear.

Editors' Note

Phoebe Wagner & Brontë Christopher Wieland

In the fall of 2015 when we first met, we immediately bonded over a love of genre work in all its forms. But something was missing from the work we were reading. While discourse on the environment dominated the media and our thinking (we had just begun Iowa State's MFA in Creative Writing and Environment), we didn't see these global concerns addressed in the SF we were consuming. Often, the environment was an antagonist, already destroyed to the point of no return, or simply not a consideration. So we began our search for work that treated the environment as a central concern and attempted to find solutions to environmental needs.

We found many burgeoning styles of environmental SF, but none fit our sensibilities like solarpunk. The term traces back to a small, inspired Tumblr community around 2014, but the movement has since blossomed. Solarpunk emphasizes innovative interaction with both our communities and our environment; socio-environmental thought and creation, rather than merely survival in a decaying world, inspire the solarpunk attitude. When we discovered the genre, no unifying collection existed to introduce solarpunk to the wider SF community. We wanted a venue where artists of all brands could convene to share their ideas and interpretations of the environment in their communities and beyond, and that's what we hope *Sunvault: Stories of Solarpunk & Eco-Speculation* has facilitated.

The stories, poems, and art gathered here represent this effort to offer solarpunk to the world for interpretation and dialogue. We didn't know what to expect when submissions opened, and that's what excited us. To be the first to witness the birth of a new wave of solarpunk and solarpunk artists is a great honor. After reading over two hundred submissions from across the world, we have done our best to select the most interesting, inventive work inspired by solarpunk and the changing, growing world around us all. We are happy to see these stories represent a vibrant spectrum of ideas, solutions, and places.

If there's one thing we hope *Sunvault* accomplishes, it's that these selections inspire artists to interact with their environments in novel, creative ways while inspiring readers to seek out solutions for social and environmental problems in their communities. May the conversation continue to bloom from here.

In true solarpunk fashion, this project has been a community effort from start to finish. The generous support of the SF and online communities, as well as families, friends, acquaintances, and more, made *Sunvault* possible by funding the book's Kickstarter campaign, providing resources and kind counsel to two budding editors, spreading the word about our submissions, and so much more. Thank you all.

Our gratitude finds life in these pages.

Hand Over the Future

Clara Ng

Sunvault

Please

Chloe N. Clark

Mother says remember
she says the Earth was once an hourglass
and we kept turning and turning
it until its shape twisted,
formed something strange

Mother says be witness,
as she plaits our hair, she says
spread these stories out into the wilds
of planets far beyond the stars we
know, the ones we name easily

Mother says dream deep,
taste the edges of the rivers
that no longer run, their bodies
thick with sludge, mouths
coughing up refuse

Mother says honor the dead
but don't be lost in them,
those birds whose skeletons
spread across shores, those
landscapes left wanting

Mother says push
forward, promise to keep
moving, seeking, dreaming,
imagine that there is something
left that we have to give

The Boston Hearth Project

T.X. Watson

Arrival-Date: Wed, 16 Mar 2022 20:17:37 -0400 (EDT)
Query: Application essays
Hi Kim,

I'm writing to ask a few questions about my application; I've written an answer for the question "When have you worked well as part of a team?" but I'm concerned about the legal consequences it could have for certain people involved if information in it were made public.

I'm applying to X.S.U. in large part for your record of support for digital activism and human rights, and I want to confirm that your reputation is reflected in your administrative policies.

My questions are:

Is the application evaluation process confidential?

How seriously do you take information security at X.S.U.?

Do you retain a database of applications after you make your decision?

Thanks,

Andie Freeman

Zie/Zir

halogen@fmail.com

§

Arrival-Date: Mon, 21 Mar 2022 11:19:06 -0600 (MDT)
Re: Query: Application essays
Hi Andie,

Thank you for writing. In response to your questions:

Yes, the application process is confidential, and our evaluators are strictly instructed not to share any details. Furthermore, the identities of evaluators are as a rule not connected with specific applicants, so there would be no way for a third party, for example a court, to compel an admissions staffer to speak with certainty that they could get specific information about your application. We take this confidentiality seriously, and the consequence for breach of confidentiality is termination.

X.S.U. takes information security very seriously, and will match the level of security you prefer. If you would like, we can receive your application through encrypted email rather than the form on our website.

Normally we keep full applications on record for 5 years after they're received. At your request, we can expunge the majority of that data and retain only a basic set of necessary administrative information and our decision.

I hope these answers cover your concerns.

Best wishes,

Kim Ellis

kellis@xsu.edu

844-387-6962

§

Arrival-Date: Mon, 21 Mar 2022 16:08:09 -0400 (EDT)

Re: Re: Query: Application essays

Hi Kim,

My application is attached.

Thank you so much,

Andie

attachment: 20220314-XSUapp-Andie-Freeman

[abridged]

Essay question: When have you worked well as part of a team?

§

When I was 15 I won my first national gaming competition. This was not team-based. I played LiveFire 2190 competitively for most of my teens, and I got very good. As a result of my performance in the 2017 Nationals I was invited to try out for a position on an e-sports team who were going to compete in a new hybrid e-sports game called FREON. It was a quasi-alternate-reality arena puzzle-and-shooter game that involved one or more players per team in a complex physical arena, and a player at a control panel. The arena players wore Augmented Reality kits (they called them F.A.R. kits, for FREON Augmented Reality) and the control players would operate the kit's display to give our arena players detailed instructions on how to solve dynamic problems. Control players always had access to more information than arena players, so the communication element was vital.

There were three of us on the team: me, the control player, our arena player Conrad, a kind of sketchy white boy who got picked because he was good at gymnastics, and our team captain, Kay St. Anne, who apart from playing e-sports was an activist for homeless queer youth in Boston.

By the time things played out we had been able to practice with the equipment for several months, and played a few matches, but FREON got cancelled before the end of its first season due to poor viewership. Conrad threatened to sue the network, which was embarrassing for everyone involved. After that, he went home.

At this point I had already committed to a gap year after high school, and I had nothing to do. Fortunately, Kay offered to let me stay with her and do activist work so I had something to put on my resume for the space I'd reserved for "E-sports championship."

Kay lived in an old retrofitted church, with a windmill on the spire and transparent solar panels in front of the stain-glass windows. There were always eight or nine people living there, though the specifics varied. Kay and some other tech geeks used the basement as a hacker space, and she let a group of other volunteers use the kitchen to make food to give away almost every day. They fed us, too, but I'm pretty sure Kay paid for a lot of the supplies.

What I did with Kay was the most rewarding and important thing I've done so far in my life. To explain why, I need to establish two things:

1. The rate of winter deaths of homeless people in Boston has been increasing every year since climate change has made weather patterns more and more erratic. The city was never equipped to protect the homeless during polar vortices, and it was getting worse, not better. There had been no new construction of homeless facilities, and two closures, in the last five years.
2. The city of Boston built, and was about to open, a new living building: the Hale Center. It was a big fifteen-story Art Deco Revival temple with a custom-engineered closed ecosystem. It was basically a first class hotel, set up so that business people and politicians wouldn't have to go around interacting with the actual city. And it's the most thoroughly self-supported Smart Building to date in Massachusetts.

We thought it would go to better use as a house for the city's homeless, so we decided to take it over.

If you want to confirm, google the Boston Hearth Project. For mainstream news my favorite write-up about it is on *The Guardian*'s website, but overall the news is only really good for confirming that it happened. You won't see my name in any articles, although I am credited in the Hearth Project website as a volunteer.

We were going to do it like we did FREON matches: I'd run an A.R. panel and guide a teammate.

Kay had taken apart the F.A.R. kits and put them back together several times, and she basically knew how to make one. She used an open-source A.R. platform called AugR to build our kit, and made it mimic as closely as possible the gameplay-style interaction that FREON had used.

She was managing probably three or four teams of people on this project, so after building the system she did one last thing before leaving me pretty much in charge of the plan:

She introduced me to Juniper.

Juniper Berg is an "urban explorer," which means she's very good at breaking into buildings. (She is also applying to X.S.U. this year. You should let her in. Also, you shouldn't hold "she's good at breaking into buildings" against her.)

She's a traceuse (she does parkour) which is a much more versatile athletic skill set than Conrad had. That took a lot of getting used to. When we trained, it took a long time before I stopped failing to notice what she saw as the most sensible way to achieve an objective, which usually included getting into places that looked impossible to reach.

Practicing with AugR was like learning to operate another body. I learned new limits for what was physically possible. I know how far back Juniper's arms can go before they hurt, and how much farther before they'll keep hurting afterward. I know how high she can jump. I know how soft she can land.

Two days before the night of the show (that's what we were calling it in case we were being recorded), we moved my kit to a hotel room up the street from the building, where Juniper and I stayed to be ready. It was a very expensive room and it felt less safe being so physically close, but we needed the fast response times through our own ad hoc wireless network, which was made of signal-carrying bugs Kay and her colleagues had stuck all over shadowy parts of buildings on this street and around the Hale Center. My signals had to get to Juniper fast. The potential consequences of a bad lag spike ranged from getting her caught to getting her killed.

On the night, Juniper was dressed up like half an angel, half a spy. Her outfit was all dark blues and muted greens, which would stand out less than black in partial light. It was loose, but with almost no stray fabric.

She had bought me a matching robe, so we'd have team colors. I was wearing it.

Her visor was close up against her face, a sleek glass pane across her eyes. The prism technology and coating on the visor made it anti-reflective, obscured the AugR display from the outside, and disrupted face-detecting software. There were cameras on the front and back, so I had a full 360-degree view of the world around her head. (She had buzzed her long black hair off to avoid obscuring the camera's view.)

She had a few more gadgets, as well:

- Two nearly silent camera drones smaller than her fist, which can hover in place for about two hours, or fly around for half an hour,
- A car key fob that was repurposed to transmit passwords wirelessly (Kay's informants had gotten some of the less secure passcodes off of sympathetic or apathetic employees, which was how we discovered that many of the Hale Center's passcodes were still left on their factory defaults),
- Print-obscuring fingertip sheaths, climbing gloves, sneakers, and
- A pair of slippers with about an inch of foam in them to muffle sound.

My kit included a massive tablet monitor angled toward my lap, a schematic screen with my annotations above it to the left, a web browser independent of the system to the right (for urgent new research, disconnected from the AugR so it could be linked to the internet without compromising us), a central monitor to show me whatever displays I wanted moment to moment, and side monitors for window management. I had a stylus, two keyboards, and two mice, and it had taken me a long time to get the hang of using the right controls for the right functions.

I used my motorized wheelchair, which would normally have a cell network link and a tablet screen, but those had been stripped out for security reasons. My crutches were always nearby, but the chair seemed like a better decision that night because I didn't want to over-exert myself on anything other than focusing on the mission. Our cell phones were turned off and securely deposited in the mini fridge.

The Hale Center had been turned on in October, and by the day we went in, November 8, it was just about furnished. The grand opening was a few days out. This would be our best and only shot.

Plus, we had postered, and it was going to rain.

One of Kay's colleagues had used a combination of glues and solvents to build a kind of poster that could look like a regular ad when it was posted, but once it was rained on, the poster would slough off and it would leave behind the white linework that was worked into the adhesive. Huge advertising posters all around town were set up to turn into murals that said "Help occupy the Hale" and "Come to Hale Homeless Shelter" the following morning, all with an artistic rendering of the Hale Center that featured key alterations and a link to BostonHearthProject.org.

So we'd never get a second shot if we weren't ready to defend the Hale against the police in the morning.

Juniper kissed the top of my head and left the hotel room at 4 a.m. At 4:06 she was behind the Hale Center.

She went in through a sixth story window because the first five stories had a different kind of window that wouldn't open wide enough. She used the key fob and all the windows 15 feet around her slowly glided open. She rolled in, using her weight to pressure the screen partway out of its frame, bending it enough that she could slip through but not so much that it disconnected on any emergency-system-triggering points.

Juniper ditched her climbing gear and switched from sneakers to slippers, then left the conference room she'd landed in and headed for the northeast stairwell. There, she went from the sixth floor to the third, over railings in a few leaps that made me a little dizzy (it was unnecessary but she's kind of a showoff), then back into the building proper. The northeast stairwell was primarily a fire escape, and so only led out to ground level; basement access was a little more secured.

The third floor was the top level of the atrium, so past a couple hallways she was looking out over the entryway—this was the only place in the building containing a security guard. He was distracted by his phone.

Juniper took out one of the mini drones, unfurled its wings and, crouching, slipped close enough to the railing to drop it before sliding back into the safe space out of sight. Once it was out of her hand I turned it on, and it was flying after about a three-foot drop.

The atrium was lit like moonlight—gentle, dim blues tinted everything, with only the rare lights of cars passing by providing the color and relief that would distinguish Juniper from a piece of furniture or a pattern on the wall.

It was beautiful, but we could do a little better. I added a filter to Juniper's display that amplified certain color bands so she'd see the detail the guard wouldn't.

I put the drone's camera display into Juniper's field of view, on the lower left, then I moved the drone down carefully until I could tuck it just under the second floor walkway.

Other subtle cameras glinted around the first floor lobby, and I marked them in the schematic with generous estimations of their field of view, rendering as translucent red cones on Juniper's AugR.

With the drone trained on the guard, I set the camera to detect motion, with an alert threshold of 10 percent for me, 30 percent for Juniper. Then I pulled the direct display out of her face.

"Ready?" I said, which the AugR relayed to her using bone vibration, projecting no sound into the air.

"I'm ready," she responded, in an utterly silent whisper that the AugR picked up and vocalized on my end. (It catches her pace, intonation, and mouth movements, and renders it in a computer tone, like somebody made a text-to-speech app with her accent. It's weird, but cute. We still use it instead of phone conversations sometimes.)

I dropped a countdown into her field of view.

3 . . . 2 . . . 1.

She went over the railing and back under it onto the second floor in a motion I didn't even really understand.

The guard moved; 25 percent. I put a "QUIET" notification on Juniper's display, a bright yellow word that took over the point of her eyes' focus for a split second then faded and moved to the side. She flattened herself into the corner of the floor and the wall, waiting for my signal.

I had the "QUIET" notification set up to trigger a stopwatch on one of the side displays, so I know that I left it there for 41.899 seconds, and I know that the guard had returned to below 2 percent movement by 10.

After I stopped the notification, I highlighted the railing in yellow, for caution, indicating that she should look. She did; the guard was still distracted. I made a judgment call that still makes me nervous to think about.

She could have gone around to the west side of the atrium and dropped pretty much perfectly into place, but if she did, she'd be landing on tile. She's quiet, but not so quiet that a 10-foot drop onto tile is silent. The alternative was to aim for the carpet, which would muffle the sound, but she'd be landing directly in the guard's line of sight and have to tumble into position behind the other side of his desk.

I breathed in, shut my eyes, opened them, and dropped a target on the carpet.

Juniper sailed over the railing like she could fly. She hit the mark perfectly, and followed it up with a beautiful roll.

I think. I slammed my eyes shut again for that part.

But when I opened them she was behind the desk and the guard was still as a statue. (The motion detector was flaring, because Juniper had rolled through the frame. I killed that process immediately, and dropped a quick "Sorry" into her display for the false alarm.)

"No worries," she said silently.

The next target was the open threshold into the hallway that contains the staircase to the basement. I threw up some quick graphics that showed Juniper in splashes of red and yellow that there was no path to the threshold that avoided both the camera's eye and the possible range of view of the guard from his chair. Juniper opted for the guard's view, and it paid off. She got behind the threshold—I told her to freeze, and dropped a "QUIET" notification.

The guard had stood up.

He walked past the edge of his desk, into the range of space where he could have spotted Juniper, if he knew to look for her.

He glanced about and seemed to decide he'd been hearing things. He returned to his post.

Juniper was exceptionally silent on the way down the hall.

The door at the end on the left that she needed to open was locked, though. When she placed her fob against it, the door beeped loudly and clattered as she turned the handle. She stepped through and held the door open, standing still, awaiting my word.

The guard had moved his head, but he had not put his phone back down. I wrote "Shut door quietly" and Juniper slowly, gingerly let the door move back into place in the frame while holding the inside handle down, and once it settled she slowly lifted her hand to let the bolt slide back into place.

Then she started walking down the stairs.

"Could you reassure me about the guard?" she said, and I put the video feed from the drone back on her screen for a bit. The guard's face was deeply focused on whatever he was doing on his phone, which was held sideways.

"My guess," I said, "is that he really doesn't want there to be someone here because that means he has to do stuff apart from play Polybius."

Two floors down, it was reasonable to assume that the guard wouldn't hear the door, so Juniper used the fob and opened it casually.

The basement was a laboratory as much as it was anything, containing massive tanks that worked as water filters and oxygen scrubbers, growing carefully-controlled masses of algae, and glass-walled cells with keycard readers that provided access to the tanks.

If this system were shut down, the building would be physically uninhabitable within a week, and unrecoverable a week after that. The energy output and air management that came out of this system was the key to our long-term control plan so we needed to retain its full functionality but disconnect it from possible remote control.

I had spent half my free time for a month reading everything I could about this system, and everything I could about systems so much as mentioned by the scientists and architects that collaborated on the system. I didn't know where they were, but I knew there would be two redundancy boxes—one that contained a computer, and one that contained a physical cable.

Juniper found the one with the physical cable first, so she opened up the box and then left it behind, because that one came last. She moved on to find the computer. She and I searched separately—I used the second drone—and it took about 10 minutes to find.

Once we found it, Juniper rested her fingers on the keyboard and awaited my instructions.

The AugR can't give me physical control over Juniper's body, but we practiced this technique for hours every day since we decided to break into the Hale Center, and Juniper got it down better than Conrad had ever been able to.

As I typed on the keyboard in front of me, the keys in their relative positions flashed in front of Juniper's field of vision. She read that input and channeled it through her body onto the keyboard. It's like psychically controlling Juniper's fingertips. She's incredible.

The computer connected the system to the building's intranet, which was how we needed to control the system, so we had to reassign a whole bunch of server addresses. It was a pain in the ass but it worked for the moment. In the morning occupation, we'd be installing wireless boosters like we used to connect Juniper and me through the building without using cellphone networks, so we wouldn't be relying on externally-accessible connections.

The last thing to go after that was the physical failsafe connection: Juniper positioned herself at it, wrapped her hand around the cable, and awaited my signal.

After this, it's a speed run. Into the stairwell to the seventh floor to change the passwords throughout the building, disable the cameras, and override safety mechanisms to weaponize the entryways. Then down to the lobby to kick the guard out and let the people in.

I dropped a countdown. 3 . . . 2 . . . 1.

Juniper pulled the plug, dropped it on the ground, and stomped on the prongs.

As soon as someone noticed, it'd be about eighteen minutes until we expected cops to arrive. In the meantime, they'd try to lock the building down (we just locked them out of that) and try to jam the wireless (we had our own network they wouldn't find in time). Noticing could take anywhere from a few seconds to until morning. But Kay would see it happen in real time, and would already be mobilizing people to march on the building.

Juniper went back to the stairwell and sprinted.

I checked in on the guard cam. It looked like he might have heard something, but it mattered less now. He wouldn't find her if he searched, and he'd probably just call the police, which changes basically nothing.

I checked back on Juniper. Floor 3, 4, 5, 6—

She burst onto the seventh floor, where an AugR map was waiting for her—a dotted line that led straight to the control room. She got there, used the fob to get in, went to the closest terminal, typed in the password (manufacturer default, again) and started mirroring my finger movements with an adrenaline-charged speed and focus that probably broke a record. Lots of "Are you sure?" notifications. Lots of administrator permission confirmations. Lots of screens. Safeties overridden. Passwords changed. Cameras off.

That took about seven and a half minutes, and once she was done Juniper bolted out of the room toward the stairs.

The guard definitely heard her this time. And, because she likes showing off, she left the stairwell at the second floor and headed for the atrium, vaulting over the railing and landing in a clean tumble to a still position on one knee. The guard saw her, pulled out his Taser, pointed it, and fired.

It missed completely. He looked a little bit like there was a chance he'd cry.

"Put it down," she said. He did. "Walk to the door." She stood up. He walked to the door, with his hands up. "Go out." He passed through the first bulletproof reinforced glass doorway, then the second, with Juniper behind him.

"This building is ours now. Get as far away as you can."

He looked to his left and right, and threads of lines of people were converging on the building. He ran away.

Kay had a fob to get in that was set up with the new passwords we had prepped. She had activists bring in groups of folks coming in for refuge and coordinate the 200-odd people in small clusters.

She had three friends ready to pick me up with my equipment, and we were in the Hale Center's parking garage before the first team of cops in riot gear showed up.

The garages had massive triple gates that could slam the building utterly shut, so it could manage its climate internally in extreme weather. After we got in, the lowest entrances got locked down. We took the elevator to the front hall where people were still filing in.

The air in the Hale Center is different than the city outside it. It smells like being outdoors, somewhere other than Boston. There's no smell of cars and mud and construction. There's no recycled-air-and-cleaning-products smell. There's a breeze, and it carries the varied and pleasant scents of the building's miniature biomes.

It was overcast outside, starting to rain, but in the building the sun was rising: lights like windows turned on and filled the big, open spaces with engineers' daylight.

The building was our weapon as well as our hostage. We let riot cops crowd into the first doorways and set the heat to 115. Then a subset of brave volunteers would wait until they were just about boiled and let them in the building. Maybe 10 or so got in at a time, and if they hadn't already stripped off their armor, they had heatstroke. We took everything and sent them back out in T-shirts and underwear. We disassembled their weapons, smashed important pieces with heavy objects, and rained down gun parts onto the tops of cop cars.

We held the building against an active siege for 49 days while a larger and larger body of volunteers came out to the city to join the cause. (We had a great social media team, without whom we'd never have gotten to keep the building. They made this a P.R. nightmare and rallied enough public empathy to make negotiations viable.) Stalemates led to agreements in which we brought in supplies and more people.

The building became an art project, too: Artists rappelled down from the roof to paint the façade in luminescent yellows and oranges that beautifully annihilate the sleek gray-blue hypermodern aesthetic the architects had tried to carve into the city.

The Boston Hearth Homeless Shelter is now formally recognized, and New York and Portland have both turned over building projects to activists for fear of facing another hostile takeover. It's understaffed and underfunded, there are people who volunteer to do more work than they do in their full-time paying jobs, but having a building that's designed to turtle against the outside world makes an immense difference, and we're saving a lot of lives. There was a 92 percent drop in deaths by exposure in Boston this winter.

But anyone proven to be connected with the takeover is still being prosecuted. Kay got a plea bargain for house arrest until 2025; she hasn't physically been in the Hearth at all this year. And the cops are actively searching for whoever broke into the building that night and scared off the night guard.

Teamwork was the central skill of the Hearth Project at every stage: in planning, in execution, in follow-up, and in protecting each other from the state. This work deepened my understanding of and appreciation for collective action. It's hard, and it has costs, and it demands immense trust and intimacy.

I'm excited to come to X.S.U. to join in efforts to change the world that I don't have to keep so quiet.

Speechless Love

Yilun Fan, translated by S. Qiouyi Lu

For all the children abroad whose taste buds have been numbed.

§

Morning, April 6, 2279. As I dump eggshells into the Earth-bound trash, my hovership's screen beeps and displays a neat line of black text:

"Hello! May I introduce myself?"

The corner of the screen shows that we're 25 meters apart, with a vertical distance of 111 meters.

Another stratospherian. . . . I pick a dried grain of rice off the table and summon a professional air as I say:

"Hello. Why not speak directly?"

The text vanishes. Thirty seconds later, another line of text appears, this time in sky blue.

"My audio communication systems are down."

A stratospherian who's bad at operating machines, I think. This is the third stratospherian I've encountered in four months who's having issues with their hovership.

Two hundred years ago, climate change on Earth rendered the surface uninhabitable. Tsunamis and earthquakes were common; every two years, a massive El Niño episode would occur. World leaders struggled to pacify the masses. The financial burden of colonizing space, plus bickering between nations, stopped off-planet efforts in their tracks.

Around this time, a German named Serik Lange invented the first self-sufficient hovership. Compared to traditional spaceships, the hoverships cost less and were far easier to manufacture. So atmosphere colonization replaced space colonization: Humanity had no choice but to leave Earth and drift through the atmosphere.

Initially, three billion people lived together in a utopia free of government. My grandparents' generation was the last to have a sense of nationality based on surface boundaries; I have only a vague recollection of my parents telling me that we came from a place called China.

But as time passed, conflicts began to arise among hoverships: fraud, theft, gang violence. . . . A hundred years ago, a huge war broke out and descendants of the former elite created the Hover Alliance to be the governing force of the sky. They stratified the atmosphere and delegated the troposphere to skilled workers, the stratosphere to intellectuals, and the thermosphere to criminals. Although this action brought order to the atmosphere, many decried it as the poison of the elite.

As a typical systems engineer, I'll never be banished to the thermosphere, but I also have no desire to move to the perfection of the stratosphere, either—compared to the clouds, rain, snow, and hail of the troposphere, the stratosphere is boring. Plus, no one there knows how to work machines.

"Do you need help?" I blow on the tea in my blue porcelain cup. A few leaves of biluochun sink and rise, reminding me of a phrase from a poem my late father once taught me: *A breath ripples a pool of spring water.*

"No, thank you. It's been down for a long time already. Actually, I'm used to it."

I almost spit out my sip of tea—how does this stratospherian communicate with the outside world? Do they always use text? I smile. What a strange person.

"Then . . . do you need something from me?"

After about five minutes, another line of sky-blue text appears on the screen:

"I saw your profile. You said you like to drink congee. Are you also from China?"

My parents told me that my ancestors were from Jiangsu province, "the land of fish and rice." Supposedly, erudite scholars gathered there a thousand years ago. The women were as gentle as water. Oars sounded against a backdrop of lantern-light; smoke rose within the fog. At bedtime, I flip through my father's copies of *Three Hundred Tang Poems* and *The Complete Song Dynasty Poems*. Who knows how many legends of scholars and courtesans originated there?

Drinking congee is another thing I like to do. Now that the Earth is humanity's garbage dump, the heavy metal content in its soil is enough to kill any plant. The food we eat is artificially created. My ancestors, longing for home, brought some soil aboard during the initial embarkation period. They brought tea leaves and rice seeds, too. Through the efforts of generations, they purified the dirt enough to support crops again. I have a two-square-meter patch of garden in my own hovership; I just harvested my modest rice crop this morning, their stalks plump and lustrous like expectant mothers. But because their output is limited, my harvest is only ever enough to make one bowl of plain congee a day. In this age, that's a luxury.

The head of every ship—whether individual, to sustain just one person, or symbiotic, for families—has to fill out a public profile with fields for occupation, interests, and other topics, mimicking the online social networks we had on Earth. Filling out the profile was a requirement the Hover Alliance imposed, their attempt at curbing "hover hermitism." In this individualistic Hover Era, anything can become an identity. I became the average of my parents: my father, a fan of Classical Chinese poetry, and my mother, obsessed with technology, produced me, a systems engineer for whom tea and congee are hobbies. So in the "interests" field I simply entered the words "drinking congee." To me, a world containing one person, one bowl of congee, one cup of tea, and one book is more than enough.

While "nationality" no longer has any real meaning, meeting another Chinese person in this vast atmosphere is still something of a rarity. I clear my throat and say stiffly,

"Yes. It's nice to meet you."

A response appears immediately in sky blue text: "It's nice to meet you, too."

After a pause, more words appear. "A long time ago, I had a bowl of congee made with rice from Jiangnan. I'll never forget that clean, fragrant aroma. I had a tea egg, too."

I glance at the eggshells in the trash. A strange feeling steals over my heart.

"What is your name?"

"Su Haoshuang."

This time, the characters are in black boldface, blinking on the screen as if they're a pair of pupils. I feel light-headed; I read the name aloud and can't help but sit down. After a long moment, I write one sentence on the touchscreen:

"Did your name come from *'lu bian ren si yue, hao wan ning shuang xue*[1]?*"
A sheen of sweat covers my palm as I finish writing.

"Yes, I also like Wei Zhuang's poems."

§

That's the story of how I met Shuangshuang. My friends, few as they are,

---

[1] Graceful as moonlight, a girl sells rice wine, her wrists frost-white.

make fun of me and call me an old lecher who's met a lovesick young woman. But I know that Shuangshuang and I were destined to meet.

Shuangshuang's ancestors are from Zhejiang: "The heavens are above, with Suhang beneath them." The water and earth there were once as nurturing as those of Jiangsu. In ancient times, the two places were called Jiangnan. Shuangshuang's parents have long since passed away, so she was raised by her grandfather, an educated old man who left her a trove of antique books when he died. Like me, Shuangshuang grew up reading poetry. I've eaten xiaolongbao once; she's tasted a Korean mud snail. My favorite tea is biluochun; hers is Xihu longjing, but we both use heirloom purple clay teapots.

Perhaps because she prefers books to technology, Shuangshuang has a fine appreciation for poetry, almost an instinct for it. Maybe that's why her audio communications system broke: because she never used it. I often joke with her and tell her that I can fix it, but she never takes me up on my offer.

We go from silent strangers to kindred spirits. She grew up in the stratosphere, so she's never seen real clouds, rain, hail, or snow. I gather my courage and write a poem, "Four Seasons," to express my feelings to her. When I send it, my palms start to sweat again, but then Shuangshuang gives me her response:

As a clear blue sky waits for rain, so too shall I wait for you.

§

Today is our wedding day. Nowadays, so long as two people want to get married, they just have to fill out an application with the Hover Alliance and take part in a ceremony with the marriage committee to join their hoverships together. It's a symbolic ceremony, one that also marks the christening of a new symbiotic hovership out of two individual hoverships.

The Hover Alliance encourages marriage and family planning. A married couple may only have one child—supposedly, this policy was inspired by China's—to reduce the density of the hoverships in the atmosphere. People in the stratosphere and troposphere typically don't intermarry, as stratospherians would have to move to the troposphere. Shuangshuang says she doesn't mind moving, though.

Hard as it is to believe, I still haven't seen what she looks like. I haven't even heard her voice. All our communication has been via text, or as she calls it, "carrier pigeon." But I believe that she must be beautiful, that kind of vivacious, gentle beauty, just like her name: "bright frost."

The marriage committee's official announcement of symbiosis finally sounds in the hold: "We hereby congratulate Ye Chengke, husband, and Su Haoshuang, wife, on their marriage in the 198th year of the Hover Era. May your union last until death do you part."

But I'm not paying attention to those clichéd words. Nervous and impatient, I'm standing before the cabin door, my hands wrapped tightly around my safety belt as I count down in my mind.

4, 3, 2, 1 . . . I close my eyes.

A violent lurch unites our ships. After the humming dies down, an indescribable fragrance fills the cabin. Unable to wait any longer, I open my eyes and say, "Shuangshuang, is that you?"

No response.

I've fantasized a thousand times about the moment I see Shuangshuang, but the room before me is empty. "Shuangshuang, where are you?" She must be shy.

I enter Shuangshuang's hovership—no, *our* hovership. The sight before me stops me in my tracks.

Bookcases line every wall of this modest hovership, each shelf packed full of antique tomes. Just a glance tells me that these books are from the Surface Era. Although they're old, each one is spotless. Now I understand where that curious perfume came from.

I think of a Song Dynasty saying: *Beautiful women are found within books.* In that moment, I swear I see a graceful silhouette walking toward me. As giddiness overtakes me, the hovership screen suddenly beeps. Line after line of text cascade into being, all in that beautiful, sky-blue script:

My darling Chengke,
You must already be in our home if you're reading this letter.
I'm so sorry for deceiving you. In truth, I'm not Su Haoshuang; I'm a program that Shuangshuang wrote. The real Su Haoshuang passed away twenty years ago. As you know, the Hover Alliance requires that the hovership of the deceased must be destroyed. If Shuangshuang's death were known, all the books that Grandpa left for her would have been incinerated in the thermosphere.
You probably don't know this, but Shuangshuang was the last disciple of Tianyi[2] of Ninbo. Two hundred years ago, during the chaos of atmosphere colonization, her ancestors went to great lengths to move all these precious books to this ship. Shuangshuang was cataloguing and digitizing them, but her health had deteriorated badly

---

[2] Tianyi Pavilian is located in the city of Ningbo in Zhejiang province. It is the oldest private library in China.

because of all her hard work; she needed to find a successor to ensure that these books wouldn't be destroyed. So she used the last of her energy, the last of her willpower, to create me.

Over the past twenty years, I've successfully hidden in this ship despite multiple inspections. I kept looking for her successor—until that day I saw that you'd entered "drinking congee" as one of your interests. Shuangshuang's favorite food was plain congee. She said once that in this drifting, anchorless age, someone whose taste buds long for their ancestor's food surely would not have forgotten their roots. And in my conversations with you, I found that you and Shuangshuang had so much in common. I figured that you must be the person that Shuangshuang was looking for all along.

I came to love you. Or perhaps what I mean to say is, if Shuangshuang were still alive, she would have loved you too.

Perhaps I have been selfish. I can only ask for your forgiveness; my selfishness comes from a family's reverence for their ancestors' culture and history. This is the mission of children: selfless, regretless.

I believe you'll like these books too. I hope you'll live up to Shuangshuang's final wishes and keep passing them down forever and ever.

Love,
Shuangshuang

I fall to the floor. I can practically see Shuangshuang's spirit shuttling between all those books. Frozen in the aura of that delicate fragrance, I suddenly recall a ballad that my father had played for me. The name of the song was "Speechless Love"[3]:

> *Hovering in your future*
> *Hovering in my future*
> *Hovering in water, in fire, in soup*
> *Facing the steam, waiting*
> *Waiting for*
> *A finer person to come*
> *Waiting for*
> *A better person to come. . . .*

---

[3] Zhou Yunpeng, "Speechless Love," https://www.youtube.com/watch?v=wdf4CTKcyVU

Strandbeest Dreams

Lisa M. Bradley and José M. Jimenez

after Theo Jansen's Strandbeests

When the Strandbeest started dreaming
it assumed sensor error.
Why else would it feel wavelets
braceleting its PVC ankles
where seconds before there was only

SAND SAND SAND SAND SAND SAND SAND SAND SAND SAND SAND SAND SAND

Step step stop	*the rhythm of the waves*
Scoop	*the rhythm of your work*
Sift sift sift	*it's no surprise you fell asleep*
Dump	*only that you dreamed*
Step step stop	*not a bad idea—a random false positive*
Scoop	*to keep you on point*
Sift sift sift	*but I didn't program you for nightmares*
Dump	*wrote no subroutines to soothe you*
Step step stop	*half so well as the sibilance of the shifting*

SAND SAND SAND SAND SAND SAND SAND SAND SAND SAND SAND SAND SAND

The Strandbeest dashed from danger
ripple of hollow legs pumping
with the stored overflow from gusted sails.
Zebra mussel shells rattled in its hopper
until it stopped and anchored,
its sensors reading DRY again.

The 'beest consulted GPS,
verified its position in relation
to Lake Michigan,
compared its earlier trajectory
and found no fault
no reason for a warning
no record of it in searchable memory

not even corroborating raindrops in its sails.
The 'beest suspended its beach-cleaning mission,
spiraling instead into endless diagnostics.

Oh, 'beest, trust The Hands.
Therein lies madness—
I have a note from my doctor
telling me so.
How many questions can you ask?
How many times?
We may settle on an "answer"
but we'll never know Why.

When the Strandbeest didn't come home
The Hands assumed an obstacle—
hooligans or beach trash
a tourniquet of fishing line
or simply a driftwood stumble—
left the 'beest pawing air.
So she herded the rest
of the wind walkers into
the warehouse and limped
to her dune buggy,
bouncing off into the winter

NIGHT NIGHT NIGHT NIGHT NIGHT NIGHT NIGHT NIGHT NIGHT NIGHT NIGHT

Step step step
  Bump
  Turn
Step step step

          Step
          Bump
          Turn
  Bump   Step
  Turn
  Bump
  Turn   Step step step step
          step step
          Bump

My lullaby:

sweet 'beests pacing polished concrete
ping-ponging like particles
at the mercy of Maxwell's Demon,
until they dispel sufficient energy
to achieve standby mode

so like my ricochet from doctor to
doctor,
my buggy bouncing over dunes
in the middle of the

NIGHT NIGHT NIGHT NIGHT NIGHT NIGHT NIGHT NIGHT NIGHT NIGHT NIGHT

33

The buggy's headlamps dawned
over the prodigal 'beest
stranded amid frost-flecked dunes
but upright, unencumbered by
anything but its own calculations.
Its scoop of tightly woven
plastic zip ties still hovered
halfway to the hopper,
like a soup spoon paused
en route to mouth,
full of gull bones and
mussel shards.

Star-lit, lupus-bit
The Hands reviewed the last few
screens of diagnostics, wondered at
the widening gyre of introspection
that paralyzed but

So sorry, 'beest.

cold-scoured, stiff-fingered
she simply hit REBOOT.

I hurt
in parts you don't have,
ache in ways
you can't comprehend.
All I wanted was to go home,
don an analgesic patch, and collapse,
agony not silenced,
but mercifully muted.

When the Strandbeest started dreaming
The Hands kept it home for observation,
programmed it to patrol the quarter-mile
in front of HQ.
Once the clan dispersed, each
to its own zone of eco-rehab,

The Hands conducted

TESTS TESTS TESTS TESTS TESTS TESTS TESTS TESTS TESTS TESTS TESTS TESTS TESTS

So easy to slip into clinical narrative
to recite the litany of symptoms
rehearsing, revising, repeating the story of
my sickness to P.A, RN, MD, Ph.D.,
back and forth like waves. . .

HAVE YOU OR A FAMILY MEMBER
EVER BEEN DIAGNOSED WITH. . .

ON A SCALE OF 1 TO 10, WITH 1
BEING 'NO PAIN AT ALL' AND 10
BEING. . .

In my mother's tongue,
one cannot suffer in solitude.
"Me duele" implies an invisible [it]
that inflicts: My legs don't hurt,
*"Me duelen las piernas." **They** hurt **me**.*
The wave is not the water.
The pain, within, divides me.

PLEASE CIRCLE THE SYMPTOMS YOU
HAVE EXPERIENCED IN THE LAST
WEEK

WE SHOULD KNOW MORE ONCE
WE GET BACK THE RESULTS OF
YOUR. . .

TESTS TESTS TESTS TESTS TESTS TESTS TESTS TESTS TESTS TESTS TESTS TESTS TESTS

The Hands should have known:
There's no room for a bug to hide
in this 'beest built from the bones of
forebears. The inherited pipes
may not glow like the stark white stilts
of younger iterations—
like the polyethylene-coated canvas,
they've been tanned
bone-yellow by the elements—
but they meet the stress tests.
The computer brain, though recycled,
gives all the right answers
when plugged into the test harness.
Only when assembled
does aberrant behavior arise.

The wave is not the water.
The wave moves through the water.

The Hands considers
memory leaks and "junk" DNA
how a confluence of ancestral ghosts

piggybacks on successful features
and may exert micronewtons of influence
until silent predispositions erupt,
chronic as consciousness

To sleep, perchance to dream.
There's a ghost in your machine.

and, dysfunctional or ingenious,
that syncretism is too secret
to be seen,
impossible to excise
without consequence.

In this confusion we are kin.
Like the doctors, I can't fix
what no one understands.

When the Strandbeest started dreaming
it needed an escape hatch.
So The Hands wrote a

PATCH PATCH PATCH PATCH PATCH PATCH PATCH PATCH PATCH PATCH PATCH

```
DEFINE REALITY_CHECK
BEGIN
   IF warning THEN mark and consult sensors to confirm
   IF confirmed THEN initiate FLEE
   IF not confirmed THEN
      LABEL marked warning "anomaly"
      WHILE iterations < MAX_LOOPS
         run diagnostics
         consult sensors to confirm
         IF confirmed THEN initiate FLEE and EXIT WHILE
      end
      IF not confirmed THEN RENAME "anomaly" "dream"
      SAVE "dream" to log
      CLEAR warning
      RETURN to MAIN_LOOP
END
```

The dream is

set aside,

not refuted.

The pain,

not silenced,

only muted.

END END END END END END END END END END END END END END END END END

Facing the Sun

Bogi Takács

Sunvault

Teratology

C. Samuel Rees

> *And I, and Silence, some strange Race,*
> *Wrecked, solitary, here—*
> *—Emily Dickinson*

"There always resides a monster," Winter said, behind the toolshed, by the gutting tub, in early autumn. She gripped the brook trout beneath its fins. Twin flicking barbs cast fast-sublimating droplets against her face. Winter frowned and dug her thumbs into roiling gill slits, working with a familiarity gleaned from repetition, pulping and loosening inner workings, transfiguring the trout into a flurry of gasps.

Summer had been long in leaving and ambient heat still smeared our afternoons. But sheltered beneath corrugated tin and plywood, the sun sloping behind sweet birch bordering the farm's northern fields, the late day teemed with an aberrant chill.

"Inside, outside, doesn't quite matter. Unnatural is the only sort of nature we have these days. Where the abnormality manifests isn't important. That's not why we walk the streams and fields."

The fish flailed, weakened, then draped dully in her hands. She hefted the limp mottled-green form, still twitching with the recent memory of suffocation, and studied its jaw.

"We're composed of mutations, whether they're submersed in flesh, hidden in genetic warrens, in molecular configuration, or in the lay of organs and subcutaneous tissue."

"So we're unquantifiable? Defying category and classification?"

Our exchange was redundant. Each afternoon we worked side-by-side and Winter made a point of running me through the project's tenets, what she called "constants," as we examined the specimens Maia hauled in from the lines. Winter always said, "Splice recollection with toil and what you get is a true breed of proficiency."

Any first-year psych student would crow to call it "conditioning," but I had come to think of it as "accelerated evolution." I posed questions, prodded for fallacies and tears in her hypothesis as an acknowledgment of a previous way of being: shared scientific certitude that life was, at its core, a blank chart waiting to be filled in.

Winter tapped her forearm where a hollow, translucent burl of flesh nestled among scar tissue tributaries crisscrossing veins from the heel of her hand to her elbow. Under my skin my own subdermal, barely the size of a leatherwing beetle, fed on a steady flow of biometric data.

"The Human Genome Project, CERN, the Large Hadron Collider, didn't work to map our bodies, minds, and environment; they simply reassured us that no matter how fucked things seem, no matter how deep in the woods humanity was, we would adapt, reorient, maybe even conquer."

"*Terra incognita* then."

The human body was on constant display these days. Unfelt biorhythms dressed in polymer and circuitry. What was once allowed to ripple in patterns and cycles long familiar to muscle, blood, organ, bone, now babbled data-streams into encrypted clouds mined for R&D and universal health care.

Meat, logged and downloadable; the explorable self. From soft tissue to wetware in barely twenty years.

"More base than that. You're still framing it with institutional thinking."

I handed her the buck knife, pinching the blade, offering it to her handle forward. Collecting live specimens was our duty on the farm. Winter did the judging and gutting. I was expected to remain a creature of pure osmosis until she said otherwise: listen, adopt, adapt, abide.

She slid the knife into soft meat, slipped it up from anus to gills, hooked a finger in the jaw and pulled a loop of purple-grey viscera free in a single arch.

All that useless data.

"Superstition had something to it. Not verifiable truth. All of it was bullshit, misconception, ignorance, or all three in unison. But the *way* of thinking, its base supposition that all we experience is inherently beyond us, the work of something unseen, now that's worth reexamining."

She passed the knife back. Grey guts and dull blood clung along the blade like goose flesh. Grease stippled water in the washtub like lesions on skin.

"Like marking leviathans on a sea chart."

"Bingo. *Here Be Dragons.* Except the serpents we have to watch out for swim in our genetic drink, deeper than blood. Inseparable from the very framework of human makeup."

She waved the trout at me. I grabbed it with both hands. Scales pulled at my palms. I no longer wore the neoprene work gloves Cade had given me on my first day at the farm. Gloves mute knowing a fish; bare skin allows you to anticipate how one will thrash and cut.

"Nine months into this I at least have that constant down. Give me some credit here," I said.

Winter sat on an overturned steel tub and rubbed her forearm where her subdermal once rooted. She often did this in moments when our tasks lulled and she took to elaborating on the themes and theories of our undertaking. A habit caught without its tool, like reaching to clean a pair of glasses after you've had your vision corrected or seeking to fidget with a ring on a phantom limb.

We all had them, the skin pills, the subdermals. At the age of thirteen we received two small incisions and walked away with two plastic pills left behind in the wrist and neck. Thus ran the slope of the modern age: in vitro corrections, biometric databases, patient-tailored vaccination regimes, hormone recalibration. The booster shots of the 20th century were simple dreams.

A kid catches a cold and his doctor knows before the first sniffle. Sees the deep unseen reactions of flesh and blood like some sort of data-stream soothsayer.

Without her subdermal Winter was an unknown continent. We could not decide if she purposefully avoided driving fifteen miles to Metro-General for the ten-minute procedure. Or if she believed it obsolete.

She squinted at the slouching sun.

"It's easy to believe that we finally have an eye on our interiors. Some might think that it's a necessary delusion to ascribe names to monsters waiting in our flesh. But humans are still wildernesses. I know this, you know this, and despite that it's still my task to drive the fact home each session. When you get to gutting and collecting solo we need you to have more than just rote skill to rely on. A philosophy can do wonders for your work ethic."

I squatted in the balding grass beside the tub. Winter was wearing thin and showed it. Maia caught her sleeping in the specimen hangar on a folding chair nightly, a bevy of dull-eyed brook trout appraising her from their tank. Winter rarely joined us for communal supper after our twilight duties. She'd haunt the lines and snares, a red LED headlamp strapped to her brow like a sleepless eye. Her weekly calls to the Fish and Game Commission, State Parks and Wildlife, the chairs of at least five separate university biology departments up and down the coast had devolved from cordial conversation to tense murmuring to near shouting matches over the last four months. Luce somehow convinced Winter to let her play proxy with the powers that be, relaying pertinent data, taking down notes, screening information, and passing it on.

Beneath the awning of the shed, the perpetual autumn's light took on a still-life quality: suspended, clear. We could have been subjects in a Dutch master's portrait exhausted from work and waiting for the sun to kill the golden hour and release us. The light illuminated the deep coves of her eye sockets. Crow's feet scrabbled at their corners; fissures worried her brow.

"How about we swap roles then?"

Winter was like a moth-eaten sweater, light shining through in all the wrong places, so many tears already that anticipating another was no longer guesswork, but weary certainty. She shrugged.

"There is no such thing as pristine. That's the biggest lie we live, thinking forests and fish and stones were ever untouched. By its very nature, Nature has always functioned on the principle of change through destruction. Schismogenesis. There's fracture at the very core of being."

More rote recitation. Winter had become almost indistinguishable from her routine: collect specimens, catalogue them, secure them in the hangar for observation, transfigure blood samples, observations, and measurements into quantities, hard evidence, data.

I pulled the plastic specimen bucket toward me: three mutated males in the water.

In the dirt five gutted females waited to be put on ice.

Untainted rainbow, brown, and brook trout, crappy, steelhead, rock bass, sauger, saugeye, and the rare pike ended on Winter's knife and in Luce's pan. We ate our rejects, all perfectly developed females.

The long term effects from ingesting contaminated species were yet to be decisively proven. There were similarities to other cases, namely the effects of DDT on eggshell density among bald eagles. DDT was banned a little over sixty years ago and in that margin of time the watershed was bombarded by God knows how many nameless contaminants. Pile on top of that the continual blurring of seasons and you had an Anthropocene slipping, year-by-year, into slow motion catastrophe.

The males of ten genuses of fish, two varieties of foxes, muskrats, three of the six types of weasel, and in one case a juvenile black bear Maia shot by the north end creek all displaying visible malformations and a significant decrease in fertility. Abnormalities ran the gamut from bone malformations to cryptorchidism to full-blown sterility.

Not enough data for academic vetting, but promising. More than.

I reached into our catch bucket. Cold streamed along the trout's flanks, wavered in thin steaming gusts as it mouthed for water. I worked my hands as I'd seen Winter's work. Grabbing firmly beneath the fins, examining the jaw and skull.

"No visible signs of malformation."

I lifted the buck knife from the wooden ledge above the gutting station while the trout whipped me. Pectoral fins dug into the meat of my palm.

The knife had dulled some since the first fish, but cut clean enough.

I examined the discarded heart, intestines, the arch and ridges of gore flecked gills on the ground between us. Organs once vital, rife with information, transformed into a coiled, abstract mess against yellowing newspaper.

"This one's female. All the organs appear to be properly developed."

"Double-check."

I looked at Winter, meaning to give her a bruised sigh. Her eyes were closed, face turned up to the last vestiges of ragged light caught along the corrugated steel awning. Her breathing was shallow, her eyes like pits where mountains had been sheared, her cheeks scooped out by a lack of rest and an excess of work. She looked as if she had fallen asleep.

I moved to drop the trout in the gutting tub.

"Double-check."

She leveled a bloodshot eye at me; grey iris nested in red webwork.

I poked through organs with the tip of the buck knife.

"She's clean."

We kept our monsters alive, all male, and crossed fingers for anomalies, working to prove Winter's dismal supposition. Her entire program hinged on verifying that the mutation generated in male reproductive tissue. With that much we could offer up a root, if not a reason, to secure further funding, maybe another two or three years' worth. Dig in deep, maybe leave a lasting mark.

It was a joke between Cade, Luce, Maia, and I that Winter recruited female candidates to symbolically reflect her hypothesis. These days I frequently suspected she really did believe that like follows like. That if she stocked her farm and lab with women, perhaps only the males of certain species would turn-up genetically twisted. That by virtue of our sex, we might bless the program with some sort of preternatural immunity against the blight spreading from watershed to watershed like kudzu across a berm. I came to think of it as Winter's superstitious foolproofing. When you find yourself beyond understanding, wouldn't it seem rational to adopt an irrational fallback philosophy?

As above, so below. There are more things in heaven and earth. That sort of stuff.

I felt blindly through water until I grasped the final fish, a white perch, and took up the knife.

"Grab the specimen bucket," she said.

"It's clean. Perch don't demonstrate the malformation. They can't. You said so."

Winter stood, kicking back the tub she sat on, and snatched the fish from me. She stood motionless, examining the perch as it pummeled her wrist. Her forearm's striated scar tissue shimmered and flexed as she twisted the perch side-to-side, inspecting it closely.

She'd been slit from elbow to bicep by a hibernating pike last summer.

It had gone from sluggish to berserk seconds after she snatched it from the stasis pail. Fins and tail-barbs still ghosted by frost left an archipelago of lacerations halfway up her arm. Haloed in blood and greasy water, Winter's subdermal looked like a slick, featureless pill brimming with enigmas and promise. Polymer and circuitry encasing the secrets of meat settled at the bottom of the bucket and blood obscured it from view. I couldn't help but wonder what the last shred of data it had gathered was, or if it really mattered at all.

She bled off and on for three hours. A person could die pretty quick from a bleed like that. Our isolation made us worry all the more. The farm is three miles from the town road. Six miles' walk over pasture or down the intestinal coil of old back lanes to historic Burnt Tree and its crossroads, bar, inn, and corner store. Cade wanted to call the emergency technicians from the Burnt Tree Fire Department or at least drive her to the horse doctor on Brindle Road, but Winter had been vehement, almost volatile. Luce patched her with gauze and ice to slow the bleeding and we waited for it to clot.

She was down for three days. When she woke she was furious to learn that Cade had called the horse doctor anyway.

"Here we are," Winter said. She shook the fish at me. "The bucket."

She was excited to the point of agitation. Her eyes were wide, and she gnawed her lower lip with her canines.

"It's a perch, they're protogynous. They can't develop the mutation."

"We thought so. All females, to start at least. Some sort of natural avoidance strategy: slipping from female to male as the population demands. An immunity. But this is tangible proof that that theory's fucked."

She let the perch slip into the specimen bucket. At the addition of the interloping fish, brook trout seethed and slapped the surface with their bodies.

Winter stood staring through water and lengthening shadows at the perch. In the gloaming her eyes seemed to shine. She trembled all over and clasped and unclasped her hands rapidly. What I had taken for excitement in the last shreds of day now looked more animal, more instinctual, in the incoming dusk. Fear.

We each kept to our patterns. Luce was maybe in the hangar nursery, kitchen, garage, or house. Napping or taking measurements of our fresh-spawned fingerlings.

Maia was out trawling our nexus of creeks and tributaries, checking the lines and seine nets. Cade was most likely walking the stonewalls along the northern corn plot where we lined the property with snares and cage traps. They studied the contingent species—heron, eagle, mink, muskrat, coyote, grey and red foxes—and chased off the occasional line poacher with warning shots, obtained names, addresses, and blood samples.

The others had been on the plot longer than I had. Winter for four years, Maia and Luce thirty-one months, Cade nineteen.

By now there was at least the semblance of an understanding between us and the residents of Burnt Tree's outlying farms and cul-de-sacs. To them property lines, regardless of who owned them, were as physical as a ditch between road and dogwoods. Most residents gave our farm wide berth, driven by an instinctual response: heuristic, stewed in genetic memory.

The others were trespassers. Cade distinguished them by their inverted response to warning signs: transgress and therefore adapt.

"Better to shoot them," Winter told us. We took it as a joke. We had to. "They poach enough trout, dine on them weekly, and in a generation—two at most—they'll all be infertile."

Winter said we were making more work for ourselves in the long run: constant perimeter checks, walking the seines and line traps, the fliers and warnings posted at the library, church, bar, and town hall which we later found pulped along the county road or stuffed into trash cans.

We didn't even own the property; we leased it from a university dean once enamored with Winter's project. These days there wasn't much word from him, only the rent notices we received at the end of each month. Six more until the grant money dried up. Until we had to face a reckoning ravenous for tangible results. For a solution or the groundwork for one. We each felt the crush. It didn't matter how many months or years we had sown in Winter's project.

So we kept our patterns constant. Did our tasks. Gathered our data. We were creatures of diligence. Creatures, at this point, and our work was our habitat. Fear of the repercussions of our work, or the cessation of it, our driving imperative.

Winter crouched over the bucket.

"Mouth like a shovel," Winter said.

"Shoveling mud," I said.

An old mnemonic device Winter had concocted. What you could repeat you could recall; what you could recall could save you from choosing or not choosing the wrong fish.

She pointed at the perch with a shaking finger.

"The signs are faint. He can't have reached sexual maturity until very recently. You can see it most in the mandibles, ribs, and dorsal fin."

"Thickened, bones more pronounced, more brutal," I said.

Winter nodded. Something in the gene pool drove the development of heavier bone structure, giving the males of the species a shovel-like jaw. Regardless of genus, they began to settle predominantly on the bottom of river or creek beds, in silt and the fool's maps of flood detritus.

It wasn't fish kill. Perhaps an adaptation to decreasing algae, insects, and prey species. Instead of offering death, Nature offered an alternative: a new class of bottom feeders fed on a steady influx of industrial contaminants.

Then mammals fed on them.

Foxes, muskrats, bears, weasels, birds manifested the mutation in a more subtle way. Infertility proved to be the most minor effect. The absence or overabundance of features, unformed organs, uniform cryptorchidism, cloacae and fistulas, each species kept to its own teratogenic misfire. Each bloodline killed off slowly, birth by birth.

Winter hefted the specimen bucket and set off across the lawn. I paused, cleaned her buck knife with a rag, slipped it into my pocket.

The cast-off wetware of perch and trout went into a lidded cylinder for Maia and Cade to lay out as bait along the creeks and fields.

Gutted females glistened in their bucket, disrupted systems, products of a biome bred on fallout and runoff.

I pressed my thumb against the subdermal biometer in my forearm, rubbed its twin implant nestled between tendons and veins where my clavicle met my shoulder. It was as if we all harbored parasitic twins beneath our skin, kept alive by the steady influx of blood pressure, pulse, body temperature.

I wondered what hope or fear or intention meant to our subdermals. Or what my body looked like as a data stream.

Blood seen through a skein of flesh is blue. A fish meets oxygen, it chokes to death. What is inescapable forces reaction, adaptation, or destruction. Necessity breeds emergence. It's the same with all of us.

§

I left our gutted fish by the kitchen door, rapped on the oak frame, in case Luce was in the farmhouse, and headed for the corrugated hangar by the east woods.

Winter had ducked out of sight, anomalies in hand.

As I climbed the grassy swale between farmhouse and fields, a blue heron unfolded from the south-plot creeks, a limp shadow pinned in its beak.

The heron arched, adjusted to the flow of air currents, and set off north following the path of water below. With Maia creekside its plummet was inevitable and out-paced the report of her 30.06. Rhododendron and pine swallowed the baffled coil of feather and bone. Tainted, more than likely. Compromised.

Trajectory was a tricky thing a mile off but we'd collect it in the end. I mentally mapped where it could have fallen, in case Maia lost track of it. Made a note of a few locations it might have fallen to.

Winter squatted by the last specimen tank. The scarce illumination in the hangar came from eerie fluorescents strained through water and the brutish shadows of fish. It was the only empty tank in a line of eleven. She had written *PERCH* in black marker on a strip of masking tape. The label stared like a blind eye.

She dragged her bandana across her arms and hands.

"You can never get the smell off you."

Even in here the tainted watershed spread its tributaries; the hangar was half-mired in the ever-cloying odor of standing water and blood. Each shelf, bottle, bucket, test tube brimmed with silt-smell, dusk, and inescapable creeks.

The perch took to the bottom like an insult to an ear.

"Unnatural," I said.

"Renatured," Winter said. She looked down the line of tanks.

She dug in her pocket and pulled out a dead bird, a fresh-killed blue jay.

As it sunk she traced its fall with her forefinger. The body's urge to reduce succinctly displayed by simple descent.

Small cupolas of ribs and skulls, half-furled in feather, flesh, and algae blooms, dotted the mud tangled tank bottom. The feeding perch, another ghost to populate our aftermath. All the proof we needed to know we knew exactly nothing.

I wiped creek water from my palms onto my jeans, wondering if superstition could infect.

Another gunshot took flight from the north.

"Heron or poacher?" I said.

Winter tapped the glass and shrugged. The perch regarded her with alien eyes. I tried to unearth shared ancestry in its look. There was none. We had adapted, they stayed put.

"Does it matter?" I said.

Winter walked down the row of tanks.

"Does any of this matter? If this is a numbers game, we're losing. We're not working to solve anything are we? Only looking to prove that in the long run we're screwed."

She stopped at the door.

"Lock up when you leave," she said.

Winter studied the verge where asphalt morphed into dirt. I zipped my coat and joined her. Behind us the dull gazes of our specimens tangled the dark hangar like flood debris.

I locked them away.

Winter's hooked scars shone with slanting sunlight. Her folded buck knife worried my thigh. I'd keep it for now, for my tasks, those assigned and those I'd keep secret. Winter could bear to lose her knife for a few days.

I pressed my thumb into the subdermal in my forearm. How would resignation read in biometrics? I tried to imagine Winter as it would. As an electric mass reacting to and shrugging away from the world, reading everything through a sheath of membrane. Not at all Winter and fundamentally her.

The world didn't feel unutterably different. The sun had disappeared and autumn settled in for the night. Tomorrow would be unseasonable and hot, or it wouldn't, the next season blurring the borders as seamlessly as a hand disrupting a stream's surface.

A third shot took to our ears like a derelict to open water. The horizon bristled with its intractable presence, with pines and hybrid chestnuts and all the creeks we couldn't see from here.

Eight Cities

Iona Sharma

They've done some rough arithmetic, some ABCs and ka-kha-ga. Then Kim's Game—given a tray of objects and one minute to look, how many could they write down and remember—and now the children are dropping things over the edge of the boat.

"Which falls faster?" Nagin asks, her bare feet stirring the water. "The big stone, or the small one?"

"The big one," says the nearest child, puffed up with its own cleverness. Nagin never learns their names, but they love hers, calling, *Nagin, Nagin,* when they see a snake slide through the murk.

"No," Nagin says, gentle. "Look. *Look.*"

The two pebbles leave her cupped hands and hit the water at exactly the same time. The impacts shatter her reflection, each scattered droplet carrying its own load of sunlight. Nagin is breathless, broadsided by the beauty of it, her ears ringing, the hair on the back of her neck prickling despite the noonday sun. The child mutters to a friend; the friend mutters knowingly back.

Nagin waits for it to pass and says, "You see. You don't need to guess, or believe. You only have to look."

They all look at her, caught between understanding and doubt. One of them picks two more pebbles out of the bucket provided and drops them in the water. Nagin smiles.

And then another child—who might have been there before and might not; to Nagin the children are indistinguishable, but inevitable as the weather—is bouncing along from boat to boat, making them all rock gently in their ropes, the floating lanterns slipping in and out of line. "Naginji! Raonaid-auntie is here!"

It's delighted to be the bearer of good news. Nagin turns, ready to tell the child that it must be mistaken, that Raonaid left two months ago and can't be back so soon, and then remembers her own advice and looks up.

"They told me you've run mad," Raonaid says, disapproving. Rather than wade, she has come out to the raat-bazaar in a small courier boat, the pole creeping silently through the water.

"I have not run mad," Nagin says. "And that's not what they told you."

"She keeps crying all the time," pipes up the herald-child. Nagin sighs and throws another pebble into the water, listening for the splash.

"Is that so," Raonaid murmurs. She still sounds disapproving, the light washing her skin through to harsh bones. Nagin wonders what is going undelivered because of Raonaid's precipitate return; how many people are watching the horizon, waiting for news. Raonaid was once a diplomatic messenger, carrying the great messages of state. These days she carries the state itself.

"What did they tell you really?" Nagin asks, wishing for a moment that she had never spoken of it to anyone, and then she's just happy, again, joy like pain cracking open her bones.

"That you've found God," Raonaid says, worry and disbelief in her voice, and Nagin doesn't doubt that she heard and dropped everything, because she thought Nagin needed her.

§

Dilli-raat-bazaar-ki, Delhi of the night markets. They climb out of the courier boat as the water becomes too shallow for it, and Nagin considers if she and this city she was born in are undergoing transformation together. When she was born, it was the most populous metropolitan conurbation in the world, frenetic, smoky, desert-dry. As Raonaid leads the way through quiet streets, cheery with sun-faded paint, Nagin feels the great stillness of a place she never knew in youth.

"Well?" Raonaid says, at last. "Have you really ... found religion, Nagin?"

Nagin hesitates over her answer, her attention caught elsewhere. A boy is taking his bath by the pump, a striped plastic mug in hand. He ought to move swiftly in the crisp, luminous chill, but he reaches into a gulmohar tree for the pleasure of touching its leaves. The branch springs away from his grip, and he lets the water splash on his head, gleaming on polished skin. Nagin's father taught her of Brahman, the unknowable creator, of atman, the imperishable within all life, and after all these years she is stilled by it, the tenable divine.

"Yes," she says, her voice cracking. Raonaid gives her an exasperated look. "I'm fine."

"Nagin," Raonaid says, and spits at the gutter in annoyance at the name. "I wish you wouldn't let them call you that. It's insulting."

It's not meant as insult, Nagin is sure; cobras are quick and clever. The raat-bazaar-wallas give her the name for the striped hood she often wears, and her eyes, the irises nearly black. "I like it."

"You would," Raonaid says. "Nagin, for God's sake, do you never come home?"

They claimed this space after the city was drained of people. There are bare lightbulbs wired across the ceiling, thick blankets on the jhula hanging over the verandah. But in these days of Raonaid's absence and her own becoming, Nagin has preferred the rock of the boats beneath her feet, and the dust here is thick. She says nothing, unwilling to attract further ire. Raonaid moves to wipe down the jhula and sets it in vicious motion instead, the ropes twisting above. She hooks it out of the way and tips the contents of her canvas bag on the floor. Nagin looks without comment at Raonaid's talismans and shibboleths. An old two-anna coin amid the shrapnel of more recent currency. A ration book. A bound volume of the last Government of India Act. A gazette in scrappy printing with a modern seal. All the things she carries to the remote places, the villages which have not seen a stranger in her lifetime.

At the bottom of the bag is the hand-crank radio. Raonaid winds it with a sound like a mosquito whining and flicks the switch.

"One, two, three, four," says a voice distorted by static. Something quickens in Nagin's heart at the sound. *"One, two, three, four."*

"It'll be on longwave soon," Raonaid says. "And I ought to be out there above the plains, telling people so. Instead I'm here, chasing after you."

Nagin lets that pass, sitting cross-legged on the floor, listening to the test signal. One, two, three, four. She lets it run several more times before she asks, "Why are you so angry with me?"

"I need you to be what you are," Raonaid says, fretful.

"What's that?"

"A scientist," Raonaid says. "Especially now, Nagin. This," she gestures at the radio, "will change everything."

"Some things," Nagin says. It won't reverse the inundation. She may live a thousand lives, or just this one. The uncertainty doesn't concern her. But however the hereafter, she won't ever forget the weight of water, the snowmelt overwhelming the banks of the Jamuna. "It will change us, perhaps."

"Yes!" Raonaid looks like she wants to spit again. "And I thought I could rely on you. I go out there and tell people there's nothing to be afraid of! What happened wasn't a judgement on us."

"There is nothing to be afraid of," Nagin says. "We had our faiths before the flood. We were more than—"

Ash and dust, she thinks, remembering the God of Raonaid's upbringing, who brought hellfire and vengeance. Nagin thinks she might cry again, waiting for that overwhelmed feeling, but it doesn't come. She's steady and calm, aware of what transcends the mundane in herself and in Raonaid; in the city of Delhi; in all other living things.

"More than what we can see," Nagin says.

"It's superstitious nonsense!" Raonaid says. "Wish-fulfilment for those who need to believe it."

"I see," Nagin murmurs, delicately. "Like your pahari."

It's a calculated remark. Pahari, hill-folk, an old-fashioned pejorative— but Raonaid came from such people, a lifetime and half a world away. Nagin walks out after that, clambering down the crumbling stones beneath the neem trees, back to the bazaar.

§

Some people are concerned by the new lights at the top of the hill, visible for miles around. Nagin sits at the edge of a boat where by day they sell spices, breathing in dal-chinni, elaichi, and hing, and points up towards the high ground. She has taken the children up there to see the radio transmitter up close. Some were fearful of it; others wanted to climb to the top and find out how far they could see. She had hoped they might carry their new knowledge home to their parents, but none really understood its purpose.

"Invisible waves," Nagin says, again, pointing upwards, but the children who attend the night classes are unimpressed. Until today, they had never heard a recording of a human voice.

"They don't believe in what they can't see," Raonaid says, softly, jumping from the nearest boat. She's carrying chameli from the far edge markets, the scent luscious in the saturated air. Around them, the raat-bazaar bustles with laughter, music, people calling their wares. The long lines of floating lanterns clank together, clank apart.

"It's not my area of specialism," Nagin says, the academic's phrasing rising complete from the depths of her mind. It's true: Nagin's post-doctoral research concerned the chemistry of the noble gases.

"I suppose not," Raonaid says, tentative. Nagin has been dozing afloat, rather than going home. Until now, she was unsure if Raonaid had set out for the north again. "But you're trying."

"I will find a way of explaining it to them."

"Yes, you will," Raonaid says. Nagin wonders if it's an apology, and then Raonaid hands her the armful of flowers, and she knows it is.

"Rachel," she says, and Raonaid looks at her sharply. She keeps her name in her own tongue, disliking it in English. But Nagin values the old language, and in particular its impersonal consonants, permissive of distance from what is spoken of.

"This is something new," she says, meaning whatever it is that's happening inside her, this coming of faith or consciousness of the ineffable, or merely a recognition, in the twilight of a frantic life, that she has come to where she ought to be. "And so are the longwave transmissions. But you're right. There's nothing to be afraid of."

Raonaid nods, slowly. "They'll be calling you panditji," she says, not as though this is a thing to be welcomed.

"They called my father that," Nagin says, lightly, as Raonaid puts a flower in her hair. "All right, my children. Once more."

She hits the switch on the radio. Around her, the children start at the sound. *One, two, three, four*—and they begin again.

Panditji means scholar, as well as priest. If it comes to pass, it will do.

§

"You could come with me," Raonaid says, the morning she leaves, the long road stretching ahead beneath the open sky.

"I will," Nagin says. "Some day."

Perhaps some day they won't have to go on foot. Perhaps they will in any case, step by step, across the soil of this land that's still theirs. On her way back across the water, Nagin rows past a cobra in a neon sign, curled snugly around the loop of an R. Like her, it's content to be where it is. Nagin doesn't disturb.

Sunvault

Radio Silence

Carlin Reynolds

Sunvault

The Sailor-Boys

Brandon O'Brien

We is some rebels, yes.
We does still sneak out the window
close to midnight with we sailboards
under we arms, scaling the outer
island walls to ride the winds.

Up here, we ibis-free, the bellies
of we boards scarlet, or yellow
like kingbirds, cutting the gale
like skipped stones could split water.
We is some *aves*, yes,

watching cormorants stain in the
blackwater beyond the beaches
where rigged exploitations did catch fire
but couldn't have enough water to douse it.
We is some blessed ones, yes.

My mother did say we was once like
the black(-gold)-and-white(-collar) world of the developed,
all of their bigger pictures with no solutions,
but we let all our colors fly. Like
us boys doing now before sunrise,

we is some fresh starts, yes.
We does soar over sighing tragedy,
the heaving high tide of Mama Dlo short of breath,
and laugh, cheer the wind on as we float.
We is some rebels, yes.

Dust

Daniel José Older

Very late at night, when the buzz of drill dozers has died out, I can hear her breathing. I know that sounds crazy. I don't care.

Tonight, I have to concentrate extra hard because there's a man lying beside me; he's snoring with the contented abandon of the well-fucked and all that panting has heavied up the air in my quarters. Still, I can hear her, hear her like she's right behind my ear or curled up inside my heart. She's not of course. If anything, I'm curled up in hers.

But then again, her dust covers everything, all of us. It coats the inner walls of this station even though it's airtight. It coats my inner walls. It's reddish and probably lethal, but who knows? We've never seen anything like it before.

The man beside me is Arkex. He is just another dustfucker amongst many; he mans the drill. Today I'm a man too—very much so it turns out—and I was surprised because I'd always taken Arkex for straight. I don't bother hiding my stares when his muscles gleam in the foul glare of our excavation lights. He never looked back, though, not on my man days, not on my woman days, and I gave up noticing. But tonight he showed up, appeared at my door without a word, just a smile softer than any I'd seen him wear before. Before, his only smiles fought off the impossible monotony of the 'stroid mines or spilled sloppily out at bad jokes over Vanguard at the Rustvine. This one comes from deeper in him: comely, it requests permission to be held.

I considered for a few moments, took my time. In these thick seconds, he maybe thought back on the times he'd snickered with the others. The jokes about me I'm sure I'd rather not know, the ones I can see from across the bar in sidewise glances, suppressed laughs. On the days I wake up a woman, Arkex's sneer thickens. We're all hidden beneath layers of protective gear out there in the caves, just thick genderless grunts, hard at work and always on the brink of death. Still, word gets out what body I've woken to, idiocy ensues.

Tonight, his shoulders hunched, his eyes ask forgiveness. I scowled, took the fullness of him: a tight shirt, once white, now dust red, and those big yellow shield pants, all laden with pouches and rope. Skin red like mine. I stepped to the side and motioned him in with my chin.

It's not like he's the first. Usually, I turn them away. They are curious, hungry for a story to yap out at Rustvine, and suddenly meek. The handful I've let in, their vulnerability radiated past the layers of dust and couldn't be faked.

It doesn't matter to me: their soft smiles and whispered promises in the thick of the heat. They always fall asleep and then I lie there, tuning out their snores so I can hear her breath; trying to match mine with hers. Silently, impossible like love, I feel it inside me. And tonight, tonight, for no reason I can discern and for just a few perfect, rockstar seconds, I catch hold and we do breathe as one, the asteroid and I, taking in the immensity of space. In the moment between, when the air lingers inside, I ask it to shift course. I don't ask, I plead. Because time is running out. *Swerve*, goes my prayer. One word: *swerve*. Because a full turn just seems like too much to ask. A U-turn? Come now: these are celestial bodies, not space ships. So, *swerve*, I whisper silently. And when we exhale, together, we release that tiny prayer and mountains and mountains of dust.

§

A few hours later, I'm bleary eyed and raw at the Rustvine. I'd passed out to the lullaby of the asteroid's susurrations and woke up with wet pebbles in my head. Too much Vanguard. Still, something had happened. It's nothing I could explain to anyone, not without getting thrown in the brig and losing my hard-earned Chief Engineer position. But I know it was real.

Slid my hand beneath the sheets between my own legs and I'd switched again; soft folds where last night was a full throbbing dick, put to good use, too. It's happening more and more these days. I linger. A few tasty ghosts of last night at my fingertips: Arkex beneath me, behind me, his hands on my shoulders, mine on his. I wondered if he'd grasp my womanbody with the same savage tenderness. Would he be too gentle? Not interested at all? I leaned over him, my fingers still rolling circles between my legs, but then the gnawing sense of somewhere to be surfaced, overtook everything. The Triumvirate. Their star glider was probably already docked in the hangar, their irritating little envoy slinking his way along our dust-covered corridors to the Rustvine.

I disentangled from the sheets. All my shield pants and dress shirts lay crumpled in the bin. All that was left was this stupid skirt that I only have for stupid parties I show up to uninvited. Absurd. But I threw it on, laced up my caving boots beneath it and pulled on an old Sour Kings t-shirt. Glanced in the mirror, ignored the feeling that it wasn't quite me looking back and then nudged Arkex with a steel-tipped toe.

"Ay. Got places to be. Find your way out, eh."

Arkex had mumbled a curse, not even registering I was now a woman, maybe not caring, and turned over. The sheets slipped from his body; the redness even tinged his chest. I poured the dregs of yesterday's coffee into a stained paper cup and shambled down the corridors.

§

At the far end of the Rustvine, the more ornery dustfuckers trade grimaces and slurp down Vanguard shots. A whispered debate rages, you can see it play out in those tiny face flinches. Everyone knows impact is only a matter of hours now; everyone knows the galaxy may be about to witness the most colossal suicide mission of all time. Discontent catches slow fire, thickens every day.

Arkex is among them now, having risen from his satisfied stupor, and so is Zan, one of the few female squad leaders. From their scowls and studious refusal to even glance my way, I know some foul fuckery is afoot.

They say the best cure for Vanguard pebble brain is Vanguard, so I order my second shot and turn back to the awkward little man sitting across from me.

"Jax," Dravish says, glaring at me. "Are you even paying attention?"

"His Holiness the Hierophant," I say, "Minister of the Noble Triumvirate, who you represent most humbly, wants an update on our trajectory, delicately reminds the crew of asteroid Post 7Quad9 that the destruction of the asteroid and the post along with it is on the pulldown menu of possibilities if Earth remains at risk."

Dravish nods, trying to affect a meaningful glare but only getting a half-smirk peeking out from somewhere beneath his handlebar mustache. "All eyes are on you, Jax. The universe is watching."

"Even though," I add unnecessarily, "no one lives on Earth any more. Are you enjoying your stay at our lovely facility?"

He's a small man with alarmingly long fingers and a tendency to call attention to them by rubbing his hands together like a plotting marsupial. "I don't like being without my jag pistons. The Barons have spies everywhere."

I shrug. There's enough firepower and political intrigue focused on this one hurling rock to destroy several galaxies, so I instituted a strict no firearms policy from the get-go. Anyway, it makes bar fights more fun. "It just means you have to be more creative when you kill people, Dravish. I'm sure you'll think of something."

Dravish taps his steel cane on the tiled floor and snorts.

I have more important things to consider than the Hierophant and his passive aggressive secretaries. The dustfuckers have stopped consorting and spread out across the room; more trouble. Beyond all that, I still carry the memory of that perfect clicking into place earlier, when our breathing became one.

"There's something else, Jax." Annoyed that I'm not looking at him, Dravish fiddles his fingers faster against themselves. A murmur ripples through the Rustvine; someone unusual has just entered and the denizens accumulate to catch a glimpse.

My shot arrives. "What?" I throw it back.

"The Hierophant sent his daughter along with me."

I spit the shot back into the glass. "Maya?"

"He has only one."

The crowd opens and a figure in a long black robe strides out. The ornate silver machinery of the Triumvirate halos her; beneath it, a gilded faceguard catches the ill orange glow of the Rustvine's security lights. Elaborate leather belts crisscross her chest and another wraps around her waist. Still, she moves like a leaf pushed in on a gale of wind. Real wind, I mean, not the endless monotony of exhaust fans. She is a thing alive, glistening even, and completely out of place in this underground trashhole of dustfuckers and the taste of disaster.

Moving effortlessly, she sits. I put a handrolled Garafuna in my mouth, light it. Dravish mumbles something and finds somewhere else to be. The faceguard emits a mechanical sigh, lifts, and there's Maya, smiling like a jerk. "Smoking is bad for the environment."

I exhale a ringlette and take in her face. It hasn't changed much since the academy days. Maya has three moles reaching like Orion's belt from the edge of her mouth to her right eye. That's the eye that's always squinting, just a little bit, like she doesn't quite believe you. It's the gap between her two front teeth that gets you, though. You can't miss 'em, those big ol' teeth, and whenever she lets that grin loose, the gap reaches out to you and says hi. She has pudgy cheeks, too, like a brown girl version of those horrible little dolls the Chemical Barons distribute to make us all forget how they flooded Earth. Except the dolls are heinous and Maya, Maya is stunning.

"You know what else is bad for the environment?" I take another drag. Exhale. "Blowing up people's asteroid homes."

She scrunches her face. "It's not your home, it's your job."

"It's a busy season; I keep having to sleep at the office."

"Is that why I haven't seen you in two years?"

I shrug, tear my eyes away from her face. "I'm not hard to find."

The Rustvine has settled back into its regular banter: filthy, dust-covered men mutter their dust-covered prayers to each other, sip Vanguard till everything tastes like oblivion, which is slightly less bitter than disaster. Directly across from me, Arkex hunches over the bar. A few seats away, Zan mutters to one of her men.

"As an opening gambit, I'd say you've softened some since our Ac days."

I look back at Maya, scowl, look away. "You want a drink?"

"Really, Jax?"

"People change. You could be a regular heathen like the rest of us now. I don't make assumptions. A simple 'no, thank you' would do."

"But why pass up a chance to annoy you?"

Finally, I allow a smile out. She's been demanding one since she sat down and I've never been able to say no to her.

She sits back, releases the gap-tooth grin. "See now! There it is."

"Shut up, Maya."

A few tables away, Dravish eyes the bar. He sees it too—the small ways that men move when their bodies teeter on the brink of violence, the stiff backs and forced stillness. Dravish's long fingers caress the empty air above his holsters.

"Anyway, you were telling me what you'd discovered," Maya says.

I laugh, swig from the bottle of Vanguard that just arrived. "Hardly."

"Hardly discovered anything or you were hardly telling me?"

"Both. Neither."

"Jax."

I peel my eyes from goings on at the bar and meet hers. "Maya."

"How much time is left?"

"Before impact?"

She nods.

I'm familiar with this wide-eyed face of hers. It is used for pleading. "Depends."

The wide eyes narrow. This is when Maya doesn't get what face #1 had quietly demanded. She used to make this one a lot in close combat class. It's not a bluff; Maya was the only student to make it through the academy without a single point being scored off her and she hospitalized a few of the biggest grunts along the way.

"Hours," I say. "Less than a dozen. Assuming Earth doesn't suddenly jump out of its regular orbit. And assuming 7Quad9 doesn't change course by itself."

Maya eases out of her attack face, raises one eyebrow. "Is that even possible?"

"Literally, at this moment, and I'm not being coy with you at all, anything is possible." This is a test. I raise my eyebrows when I'm done. Maya's face can do so many things right now, and each will be a message.

She hunches her shoulders and leans across the table, a conspiratorial smile across her face. The ever-squinting eye squints tighter. "Go on."

"I think I can get it to swerve." I say it very, very quietly.

Now both eyes squint; the smile fades. "Oh?"

"I . . . I know I can." I hadn't meant for that to come out; that information is a surprise even to me. The Vanguard may have taken the wheel at this point.

"How? You're rigging up an engine of some kind? You don't give updates, Jax! This shit matters."

I shake my head. "No engine."

A whole new kind of understanding dawns on Maya's face; it is wide open.

"There is no precedent for what this is. The dust matches nothing we've seen. The corner of space it comes from is a star graveyard: there is nothing there. But something about it is . . . familiar. I think maybe. . . ." My voice trails off as I feel the haze of Vanguard settle in a little deeper. "Maybe."

"Well, look, the Triumvirate wants to study it too, but you're talking about a matter of hours."

"Study until it's a threat and then destroy, huh? That's the name of the game."

"Jax, if the Barons get ahold of. . . ."

"Shh," I whisper.

"Wha. . . ."

"Shh!"

My eyes are closed, purple and green blobs dance across the darkness. I block out Maya's gnawing impatience, concentrate on whatever it was in the air that just caught my attention. It's quiet. That's what it is: it's quiet. The Rustvine is never quiet. My hands close around the metal legs of my chair, I open my eyes as I stand, swinging the chair over my head. I only catch a momentary glimpse of the dustfucker throng advancing before I hurl the chair with all my strength at Zan. It catches her full in the face, topples her. I grab the bottle of Vanguard and brain the next closest one.

Maya dives forward, out of the fray and out of my sightline, and then they close around me, a throbbing mass of yells and pumping fists. Someone's chain club finds my cheek and a few more get their hits in as I stumble to the side. They're easily stumped, though; my fall makes them sloppy with such a quick victory. I catch one with a steel-tipped boot to the 'nads, and then slip on spilled Vanguard. I roll out of the fray, topple a table, and rise just in time to see three dustfuckers collapse beneath a vicious swatting from Dravish's metal cane. Each hit is precise and the aging Triumvirate secretary moves easily out of the way from dustfuckers' haphazard flailing.

I'm tensing to launch into the throng when Dravish stops moving. His cane clatters to the ground and a rusty metal shaft pokes out of his chest.

Zan's face appears behind Dravish. She's bleeding from where she caught the chair with her face. "Kill the faggot middling and his Triumvirate bitch friend," she says into the sudden silence. "And then we take the 'stroid."

Dravish sputters, blood speckles his elegant mustache, then he drops. The dustfuckers turn to me. I have the Vanguard in my hand still, and my stupid skirt on. And I'm tipsy. I smash the bottle on the floor and hold up the business end. Two of the bigger guys come swinging forward and then for a millisecond everything goes bright white. A bang so loud I can feel it inside my brain shatters the air around me. I'm ducking when the second one erupts. Zan and another dustfucker lay hemorrhaging in front of me; the others have all scattered for cover.

"C'mon," Maya says. Smoke rises from the jag piston in her hand. She doesn't even look fazed.

"You. . . ." I stutter.

"Come. The fuck. On."

I've never stopped loving this woman.

§

When we first carved our way onto this asteroid with drill-headed subterranean tanks and dynamite, we didn't know there were actual canals reaching through the thing. It'd be rock rock rock and then nothing, and the nothing was deep enough to crash a few of our best drillteams. Maybe two dozen dustfuckers got crushed or incinerated before we figured out we could build the outpost along the natural corridors instead of going against them. Now, reinforced steel lines the canal walls and wraps above them, creating wild, windy corridors that dip and circle through the asteroidal bowels. Red dust stains every surface, a mottled, ever-growing paint job that no one knows how to keep at bay.

"You have a jag piston," I say. We're both panting, working a quick, careful path through the tunnels. The overheads cast grim specters of light, divided by darkness.

"I saved your life."

"I know, I wasn't complaining. I'm sorry about Dravish."

The corridor winds around a sharp curve, becomes dim. We stop and breathe. Maya shakes her head, one arm leaning up against the wall. "Dravish died doing what he loves the most."

A clamor of boots and angry voices echoes down the corridor. "My room," I say. "I have a codex. We can get a message out to your people."

Maya doesn't follow me, gazes instead down the hallway behind us. "The Chemical Barons have someone down here. They've infiltrated the dustfuckers."

"Wouldn't be surprised. They've gotten so irritable from so much of the same. Makes 'em easy to rile up. And that fight was more coordinated than I've ever seen them."

"That and the imminent collision with Earth. You could see how they might have a pretty decent gripe. Anyway, Zan was probably in on it, but there's someone else, too, from what we can tell."

She's right. My mind begins cycling through faces, but part of me already knows.

"If the Barons take control of the 'stroid, they can weaponize it. And then . . . well, game over, so to speak."

I just shake my head. "It wasn't enough fucking up Earth? They gotta ruin everything else too?"

Down the corridor, someone screams. "Get him down," a voice yells. "Get him." There's more yelling, another scream, and then the sound of boots stomping gets louder. I imagine Arkex is with them.

Maya pulls the shiny cylinder from her robes, holds it ready.

"How many shots you got in that thing?"

"Not enough."

We climb a slope, wind around another corner and then I tap a code into a keypad and a section of the wall groans and gives way into darkness. Maya eyes me, then ducks in.

The floor is littered with rumpled clothes and, yes, a few bottles. An ashtray—not spilled, though. Not spilled. There's a desk somewhere beneath all those paper stacks and books.

"Doesn't this even bother you on the days you wake up as a woman?" Maya says.

I sneer. "Your simplistic ass. I'm even messier on my woman days. Anyway, look." Wires snake out of a brand new hole in the wall. "He took my codex and the damn mount I charged it with."

"Who?"

"Arkex. The Chemical Baron's man underground."

"How'd he. . . ."

By way of an answer, I look at the ruffled sheets on my cot.

Maya shakes her head. "Oh, Jax."

"Occasionally, I make very reckless decisions."

"But. . . ."

"We don't have time for you to browbeat me at this moment. They're sure gonna head straight for my den."

Maya's mouth wrestles with a retort but she stays quiet.

"If we go out into the corridor, we're done."

"Where then?"

"Up."

§

For a few minutes, the only sound is our knees and elbows clanging along the corrugated metal air duct and me panting and wheezing. Then we stop, and when I catch my breath, I light a Garafuna. Maya just rolls her eyes.

"I know," I say. "And I'm not interested."

"You don't think they'll smell it? They're already probably crawling through these pipes trying to get to us."

I shake my head, take a drag in a nonchalant kind of way that I'm sure drives Maya up the wall. "They don't know I have an entranceway through my room. They're scouring the corridors, and there's plenty for them to scour."

"Well, then, what now?"

I point down. "The hangar's right below us. They're going to check it. Then we put you on your ship and send you on your way."

"You're not. . . ."

Far away, someone yells. A metal clanging echoes its way through the vast open space beneath us. We wait. Nothing happens. We wait.

§

"Do they care here?" We have our backs against opposite sides of the duct; our bent knees form an M shape in the middle of the passageway.

I give her a look. I know what she means but I want her to say it.

"About . . . you know. . . ."

"Of course." I relent. I don't have it in me to play games with people's discomfort after all. "They're quieter about it than they were at the Academy, of course, but only because I'm in charge here. And they don't try to study me here like they did there, no more pee samples and blood draws. Here they just glare and mutter. I shut things down quick with a few nasty scuffles at the Rustvine and everyone got into place."

"You always were quick to clobber a fool that stepped out of line."

I shrug, look away. "Survival."

Maya stares at me. I feel that glare burning into my cheek like laser beams and I think maybe, maybe, she kind of understands. So I look at her. Those eyes have gone wide again; they want something. Her lips are slightly parted, those round cheeks illuminated by the dim light strips along the duct. Framed by her robes and the Triumvirate crown, Maya's face looks like the moon. I realize how long it's been since I've breathed fresh air, felt the embrace of the night instead of the air conditioners and vent systems.

"More than a year," I say.

"What?"

"Been on this thing."

"Ah."

"Your face."

"What about it?"

"Reminds me of the moon."

I've never said anything like that to Maya. I don't say things like that. I think them. Sometimes, on nights drenched in Vanguard and the loneliness of the life on an asteroid, I write them on sprawling messages on my codex, put her communique address in the To field and let my finger hover over the Send button. Then I delete them and troll whatever porn the dustfuckers are posting till I pass out.

Maya doesn't smile, doesn't even move, and my stomach clenches. I don't look away though, a tiny victory over my usual chickenshittedness. She doesn't look away either. Is there a move I'm supposed to make? It's easy with the others; they come to me. I turn them away or I don't. With Maya, all my move-making information always seems to get lost between my two bodies: out of reach. For all our intimacy, she never reveals what she has a taste for. Maybe nothing. I've forgotten, for a moment, what I woke up as today. In the chaos it ceased to matter, or maybe it's being with Maya that has rendered it irrelevant. Maybe, but no: then it comes crashing back down and I'm neither-nor and woefully not enough and anyway.

And anyway, I feel filthy. Filthy from the dust of a year of asteroid life. Filthy from Arkex and Delmond, Catinflax and Sastra. Filthy from all these cheap nights with heartless fucks I barely bothered staying awake for and then gleefully booted before dawn. Looking back, they become a blur: some were men, some the rare female dustfucker. Sometimes I was a man, sometimes a woman. I topped and bottomed, sighed, grunted, cursed, came. And still I am empty.

Maya reaches out her hand, palm out. I put mine against it. According to Jax's third rule of booty-getting, if I close my fingers, the culminating momentum will peak and the sudden burst of energy will propel us both forward into a tangled embrace, layers will slide off easily, like all along our bodies had been begging to be naked together, and together we will float slightly above the corrugated steel as our belts and boots dance through the air away from us. My fingers will find their way inside her, and hers inside me and I will hear the asteroid breathing like it does when it's very quiet, late at night.

I don't close my fingers, though; I close my eyes. I hear her long breaths, they let me know she's in this moment, too: her heart beats through her palm. Beneath that I hear something else: the asteroid breathing like it does when it's very quiet, late at night.

And then, just like that, Maya's breathing falls away and there is only the asteroid, and our breath is one. I keep my eyes closed, because if I think too hard, if I allow the rest of the world in, everything will shatter. Our breath is one, and I let the tiny prayer erupt from me, *swerve,* but this time, instead of another breath, there is a tremor.

Somewhere far, far away, Maya says, "What was that?"

Swerve.

The world trembles, a lover on the brink. *Swerve.* Not pleading this time, a command. Another shiver erupts. Maya yells but me, I'm smiling. I exhale, the asteroid exhales with me. Because inside me, there is dust, it coats my lungs, my heart, it heeds me, and inside the asteroid, there is me, tiny, complex, and alive with desire. We breathe as one.

"Jax." Maya's eyes don't ask for anything now. They're wide, yes, but not with pleading. Her jag piston glares out at me from her robes.

I cock my head to the side, frown. "You never came to negotiate."

"No."

"The sitdown was a ruse."

"Well, I did want to speak to you."

One of my eyebrows goes up; the skeptical one. I can't help it.

"But I knew you wouldn't listen."

"The Triumvirate has given up on the asteroid."

"Long ago. I'm the only thing keeping them from blowing it, and you're the only thing keeping me from keeping them from blowing it."

"I'll be that."

"Jax, you're coming off this thing with me. And we're sending a transport for the dustfuckers. If the Chemical Barons get a hold of it. . . ."

"They won't."

"They were a bar fight away from doing it just now. And if you can't divert the thing before it hits earth."

"Come."

"Jax. What just happened?"

"Come with me, I'll show you."

Maya doesn't lower the gun but ever so slightly her face relaxes. Tears slide down the round cheeks, her jawline, her neck. Instead of kissing them away, I stand, smile, help her up.

I'm sure I'm glowing. Or maybe it's the dust that covers my body, the dust that marks places on Maya's body I have touched.

§

She removes the paneling and climbs down a ladder into the hangar. More yelling erupts from somewhere, not far away; I can't tell if it's celebration or anger. I don't care. The hangar dwarfs everything; we are two tiny specks crossing beneath its cavernous void, darting between the landing gear of dust-covered transporters and armored drilldozer wheels to the Triumvirate's sleek star glider. It's already slightly reddened from its brief stay here. In the small cockpit, she turns to me and is about to speak when a codex crackles to life right beside us. *"Triumvirate Station Seven-five to Harpsbringer, copy."*

Maya's jag piston is already out and directed at the cockpit storage closet when the door swings slowly open.

I roll my eyes. "Don't shoot him."

Arkex is crying, cradling the codex, hemmed in by tubes and wires like some pathetic saint in a box. "I . . . I. . . . Last night wasn't just about this," he gurgles. "I'm sorry."

"What did they give you?" I ask.

"They promised they'd get me offa here. Said we'd crash into Earth if I didn't."

"Triumvirate Station Seven-five to Harpsbringer, do you copy?" the codex crackles. *"We have an urgent message. Do you copy Harpsbringer?"*

I put out my hand and Arkex gives me the codex.

"This is Harpsbringer."

"Be advised, your course has changed, Harpsbringer. Repeat, your course has changed. New coordinates take you outside of the Earth's gravitational pull." In the background, I hear celebrating. Cheers go up around the ship. Arkex has tears streaming down his face.

Maya just shakes her head. I give Arkex the fuck-off look and he stumbles off the ship in a hurry. I'll deal with what needs to be dealt with later. "So," Maya says.

"So."

"Don't look so pleased with yourself. Whatever you did, the Barons are still gonna be throwing whatever they got at this thing to get it on their side."

"Good thing I have friends in powerful places with lots of spaceships and fancy guns."

"We'll see about that."

Then we pause, and the moment becomes thick between us. I breathe deep, the asteroid breathes with me, and I let the moment slide away, because there will be another, better one in the not too distant future. Right now, though, right now the galaxy around us has just let out an enormous cheer all at the same time, like a breath released in perfect synchronicity, as one.

The Death of Pax

Santiago Belluco

I leave the planet in a ship sculpted out of my dead friend's bones and stitched with his elastic skin. The ship is but a token of Gendo technology, an improvisation built with cast-off parts and borrowed labor. Still it's greater than anything I will find back on Earth. The outlines of Pax's corpse are clear below as I ascend: his fifty-kilometer long shell eerily still, the familiar plains and crags of his back refusing to blend into the surrounding geography. Even from low orbit I see the telltale signs of design in his form, the combined effort of the myriad symbionts on his shell and flesh, a culmination of thousands of years of meticulous work and study. Maybe Alina is down there, looking for me again, and in many ways I will miss her.

I can see the other eleven Gendoji on Naginata's surface crawling towards Pax to show their final respects, the world redrawn in their wake. Soon even the single Gendoji living in orbit will join the others by gently reentering the atmosphere, an expenditure of energy dwarfing the combined power output of all human history several times over. Not for the first time I regret having to leave the sprawling depth of the Gendo civilization for our feeble struggles in the Sol system. *Our* struggles, not *theirs*. I need to get used to belonging to humanity again. As if to punctuate my expulsion, my ship passes the small orbital research station I used to call home. It looks so frail and insignificant compared to the Gendoji below, a little tin can rusting away in space.

§

My last day with Pax was inefficient, but all I had left was my chosen duty. I grabbed each of the many shoulder-high hairs jutting out of the ground and gently pulled up with both my hands, the thick, silky bundle brushing against my legs, chest, and face. The mites lodged onto the hair's cuticle clawed out at the disturbance and spread across the field to help clear off the slowly accumulating dust. Pax was beyond such preening, which is probably why the mites needed rousing in the first place, but I continued the minor task nonetheless. It felt like the proper thing to do.

The ground shifted as Pax groaned, the cracks in his claws exhaling steam in the distance. Claws that once broke open mountains and slashed the sky to drink clouds now swayed in agony and smelled of spreading rot. I was reminded of my mother surrounded by the pale cloth of a hospital gown, her dark skin dulled, as if the prim Japanese nurses packed away the offending color together with her clothes, just to get it out of the way.

I straightened up so I could be seen over the swaying hairs and waved at Alina. She was too loud in her environmental suit, its tubes and rough edges improperly crashing through the red brush.

"How are you feeling, Sanjit?" she asked, her voice warped by ill-tuned speakers.

The suit broke my ability to feel her in the way that I felt the mites sulking at the hair and the claw-sharpening birds flying above, occasionally even some of Pax himself. She was an absence, a tear at something meant to be whole.

That was the Handy Worm speaking, of course, so I asked the small symbiont nestled inside my chest to be quiet for a while. It took the Worm a moment, but she eventually drifted into a restful lull. My Worm-sense dulled as Handy Worm restricted herself to the core functions that kept me alive in Naginata's atmosphere.

I looked up at Alina again. I couldn't feel the air currents warping along the sky or the depths of biological complexity unfurling beneath my feet. Left behind were my shallow human senses, and the first thing they saw were Alina's sharp green eyes, bright even behind her visor.

To be the first human to engage in symbiotic contract with a Gendoji was a great source of pride to me during my early days on Pax, a desperate grasp for meaning after I was expelled from the station and cut off from the scientific community, left adrift from any chance of scientific immortality. Much of that ambition fell away in my time with the Gendo, all except for my need to impress Alina. The life we once shared still pulled at me, even after so much had changed.

"I'm well enough," I replied, "given the circumstances."

She waited, expecting more, whether out of genuine worry or professional concern, I couldn't tell. I thought back to her sitting on my room's tatami at the station, perfect posture and a lithe beauty I couldn't bear to look away from. Some of it was her own charm, I'm sure, but in retrospect, much of the appeal was probably due to the aesthetic modifications. Not her fault, of course, just an inheritance passed down in her genetic code, a minor genetic alteration her Martian great-grandparents bought before even such trifling modifications were made illegal.

"Your Worm-pulse is getting erratic," she said.

"I know."

"You might not survive when Handy Worm fails." She must have been serious, she hated using the nickname I idly gave my Worm when I first took her on, unaware of what having a symbiont really meant and trying to mask my ignorance with humor.

"I know."

"We're worried about you."

We. The orbital station monitoring staff, the field of Gendo-system research, the suit. Not Alina, not really. I wished she would not come during the day, when the mucosal membrane clinging to my naked body was so thick and bright.

"Is this why you came down again? These daily visits are probably getting expensive."

Alina paused and straightened up, turned on the mic, then off, then on again, eyes looking away.

"No, it's not. Did you get the chance to ask Pax for a sample?"

I suspected this was why she kept coming, but I was still disappointed. Even after all these years off-station and after all I became under Pax, she still had this much sway over me. Such a feeble dependence, a weakness even more pathetic than losing my career in the vain attempt to get her back. Around her I wasn't a scientist, a man, or even a Pax symbiont, I was refuse cast aside. I swore never to be so stupid during the countless nights my mother stayed up weeping for the man who left us for the nostalgia of India and a new wife. Another promise broken to the lonely child growing up in one of the many gaijin run-ups packing the outskirts of Osaka.

"Pax hasn't spoken to me since he fell," I confessed, with more shame than I cared to admit. "He has billions of symbionts to directly care for. Trillions, maybe. A third-panther of my level barely hears directly from him once a week, even at a feeding lull."

"You're not a third-panther." Alina couldn't know how much the rank meant to me, how hard I struggled to earn the position within Pax's ecosystem. And she clearly didn't care how much her glib dismissal stung.

Gendo symbionts are crafted well before conception, but each symbiont must develop the skill to modify themselves beyond their original designs to earn a rank worthy of the higher needs of a Gendoji. That a human could work as a sensorial panther at all was damn near impossible. My rising as high as a third felt better than any of the academic trivialities that consumed me before I joined Pax. Alina never fully understood that, never saw past the mucus and the Worm in my chest.

"I may not be a proper panther, but I'm also not quite human anymore either. And Pax is dying."

Alina's brow furrowed, and she looked at me, past me. I knew this look. She was steeling herself to do what needed to be done, itching for a hint that would lead to the replication of Gendo bio-fusion, the most tempting technology available to the Gendoji. I still don't know what it is, what morsel of Pax provided the seemingly limitless energy that can fuel something as massive as a Gendoji. The promise of such a power source is the only reason the orbital station gets any funding these days.

"I know you've gotten close to Pax over the years, but you need to step up. Too much is at stake, and you are the only one who took to its parasite. Stop sulking, go up to the damn thing, and do your fucking job."

"Stop it." I can see now what she was doing, but at the time I just got angry and walked up to her, refusing to feel small even as she towered over me. "You do not get to talk about him like this, not here!"

My chest was shaking with anger, Handy Worm shivering, warping my sight with leaking Worm-sense. Alina looked down at me, eyes soft with pity. I tried to push her away, but the suit was too solid, and I only managed to throw myself back, tripping over a cuticle's ridge and stumbling across Pax's outer skin. As I collapsed in an awkward tangle of long-hair and disturbed mites, I realized it wasn't pity that I saw in her eyes. It was disgust.

Handy Worm went tight, and my heart clenched. My vision blurred as my senses, human and Worm, melted together with a dull ache. Handy Worm curled up at a pocket between my heart and left lung, releasing her grip on my body cavity. I tried to calm her down, but she retreated even further, forgetting to purify the noxious air entering my lungs. The yellow serum she continually released from my skin to protect against the air turned sour and thin. My eyes burned as my tears became inadequately buffered. I vaguely remember crying out for my mother as I gasped for air. The pain quickly grew too intense, and I passed out.

I woke up to a haze of green sky streaked with too many pale orange clouds. I lifted my head and saw Alina a few meters away, kneeling on the ground between two fifth-raptors. Against the haze of confusion I remembered our argument, that Pax was no longer moving, that he was about to die. That I was about to die. Alina had a patch of my yellow ichor on her suit where I had tried to push her away, streaked and blurred by a failed attempt to wipe it off with the back of her gloves.

I struggled to get up but was pushed back down by a soft paw covered in golden fur. I looked to the side and saw a first-panther looking down at me, her sensory tendrils forming a thick aura around a vaguely equine face. Oquail, come to help again.

"Remain still a while longer, Sanjit," the panther spoke, whispering through Handy Worm. "Your symbiont Worm is still recovering from the strain."

I lifted a hand to rub an itch on my face, but it was covered by a sticky ooze connected to a small hole in the first-panther's otherwise immaculate flank. I once saw a white tiger at the Uedo zoo and was struck by its quiet grace and implicit power. I felt that same awe every time I saw Oquail. "How long have I been out?"

Oquail took my hand in her paw and put it to the side, away from the mask keeping me alive. "Half a day. I'm glad I was within assist range, any further delay in treatment and you could have suffered real organ damage. Pax wants to see you now. I will bring you to him when you are stable."

I noticed my pulse rise and Handy Worm stir at the chance to talk to Pax before he died. The thought hit me with equal parts dread and relief. The last time I felt this way, I was opening the sliding door to my dying mother's room before heading off to the Gendoji system, still hoping that she would understand this priceless opportunity. But she just started sobbing at the idea of being left alone. I heard of her death as my flight was halfway to Naginata.

"Are you all right?" Alina asked as she started to get up, but a low growl from the raptors brought her back down.

"How dare you?" Oquail replied, a deep human voice rumbling from a raised paw. "Reckless human, you knew his symbiont was vulnerable, and you still taunted him in a foolish attempt to draw Pax's attention. A childish, ill-conceived notion. You will be quiet or you will be forcefully removed from our presence."

"Sanjit," Oquail continued through Handy Worm, "should we send her back as punishment for her willful aggression?"

"No," I muttered, "I'll ask the raptors to keep her here, we might need to talk after I speak to Pax."

"As is your right, fellow panther," Oquail replied, then retracted her supporting limbs and facemask as I slowly got up.

Without a word, Oquail lowered her flank and let me climb on. It had been a long time since she needed to carry me, but I didn't really mind meeting Pax this way. All symbionts were suffering with their Gendoji retracting, some differently than others, but we all suffered. In some small way I appreciated this. My weakness drew me closer to my fellow symbionts, bridging the impossible divide in our biology. Still, as I climbed onto Oquail I tried to hide my slow movement and hunched back from Alina.

Oquail, on the other hand, barely seemed affected by Pax's retraction, her five large eyes still sharp and clear. It's unlikely I will ever see her eyes again, and I now regret not accepting her offers to study them more often. Each of Oquail's eyes has a triple-pupil that refracts light of different wavelengths far beyond the human visible light spectrum, each wavelength band channeled into unique foveal furrows. She can see to the very edge of the planet's curvature, crisp to the resolution of a single photon. There seems to be nothing she cannot see. I can only imagine the extent to which she understands her own biology, the thought she must have put into designing such subtle detectors and robust neurocircuitry.

Maybe humanity could have been able to obtain such wonders if not for the genetic engineering bans implemented back in the Sol system. Sitting in a ship that hums with pliable sinew stronger than the densest carbon lattice and pulsing with blood richer than concentrated uranium makes such bans seem medieval and absurd. But these old fears routinely threaten the funding of the orbital monitoring station, the entire field of Gendo-systems research suffering from mistrust back on Earth and Mars. So many have been convinced that no good can come from studying creatures that so heavily modify themselves. Well, the Sol traditionalists will soon have much more to mistrust when a Gendo-designed ship lands on Earth and delivers Pax's dying gift.

I assumed at the time that Oquail would choose another Gendoji once Pax died, dreading that she might be placed in a position unsuited to her talents or that she might even be torn apart for study. I had seen it happen with samples Pax got from other Gendoji, small animals that were dissected in sterile alcoves full of prodding first-raptors under the supervision of his cruelest silphid beetles. The thought of long silphid talons touching Oquail's golden fur made Handy Worm shudder again.

"I am touched by your concern," Oquail spoke to me, calming Handy Worm with skill I didn't possess, "but I won't contract to another. I will live out my life among Pax's ruins, hunting prey for nourishment and perhaps even breeding a clutch of my own."

I was embarrassed that she could so readily detect my thoughts. Even after all this time with Handy Worm, I was barely as competent in the field of symbiont manipulation as a third-panther mewling. Thankfully this is not an important skillset for a sensorial panther, since we detect the nuances of Gendoji environmental conditions and don't really manage symbionts downstream in ranking. But to see Oquail be so competent at nearly everything was always impressive.

"You are also misinformed," she continued, "only symbionts of lesser than sixth rank are studied as you witnessed. They have limited conscious thought and contain neural patterns that are mostly instinct and reflex. The Gendoji do not use such invasive methods on one of our complexity; we must be recruited under very specific and mutually agreed upon terms."

"I apologize. I assumed when I should not have." I was careful, knowing that I was nearing a topic I was not allowed to discuss.

"None is needed. Since you have not been permitted to inquire about other Gendoji, your ignorance is understandable. This might change now."

"Really? Why?"

"It's not my place to tell you, my friend."

We arrived. I felt it as soon as we crested a steep slope. A central tower almost a hundred meters high rose up at the highest point of Pax's gently arched back. It looked like a simple bony outgrowth, almost a claw, but gnarled and twisted. Many of the higher-ranked symbionts idled about the tower's base: panthers, raptors, pterosyls, and dozens of creatures I couldn't identify. There was even a silphid, a much larger one than I saw at the dissections, all knobbed carapace and arachnid arms.

Oquail slowed down and brought me closer to a side of the tower that almost looked like it had a human face carved into it. But the pattern shifted like liquid mercury tinted with the color of bone.

"Sanjit." Pax spoke, and Handy Worm was fully functional, letting me see not only the world around Pax's body, but within my own form. The pulsing heart and firing nerves, cleansing stream of blood into liver into blood, the guttural peristalsis of the digestive system, the soft hum of shedding skin. Not much detail but a comforting totality to the mechanism of my humanity, a glimpse of the carefully constructed insight of the Gendoji and their higher symbionts. "You have taken to my Worm as well as any human could, but its design is incomplete and will not survive without my control."

"Should I then go to another Gendoji?" I did not like the idea, but must admit I was a bit curious about life on a Gendoji other than Pax.

"None have accepted you, not the eleven remaining in this planet nor any in our other fifty-six colonies. I even asked the few who keep to various orbits and those in transit between systems. There is no place for you among us."

"I see," I said, assured of my death sentence. I saw myself covered by a thin gown in the station's infirmary, my death as disjointed as my mother's. A foreigner dying in a borrowed bed. I tried to keep the bitter thought from Pax, but couldn't with Handy Worm so aroused.

"There is an alternative. A different role you may choose to take."

"What is it?" I asked, a bit too quickly.

"I assume you have wondered why I have accepted a human onto myself while the rest of the Gendo refuse to interact with your species."

"Yes, of course I have."

"There was surprise among us when we discovered humans, since we have met other space-faring species only a handful of times in our history. However, and I want there to be no confusion over this: it became apparent very quickly that you had nothing to offer us."

"I know, our technology is not as advanc—"

"Current level of technology is not the issue. I refer to human biology. It stands as a classical example of passive engagement with evolutionary forces. There is only so much your species will obtain with the same sensory organs and neural circuitry that your primate forefathers used to pick at ants from the ground. This is the reason we don't simply give you the technologies you seek; you have neither the ability to understand them nor the industrial capacity needed for their construction. Most other Gendoji are sickened by such genetic provincialism, and those who are not find it darkly comical at best. I was only allowed to accept humans onto my territory and body if I promised the others I would not enable you to contact any of their symbionts or divulge any information on them."

"So why accept me at all?"

"Several millennia ago, a fellow Gendoji assisted me when my technical skills were lacking to support my newly expanded shell. He was heavily criticized for interfering in the necessary rigors of my development and suffered a punitive loss in territory as a result. But thanks to his help, I survived. When I recently realized my techniques would be insufficient to support any more growth and thus I would begin to die, I found myself prone to a similar measure of generosity. So I contacted your species, and, when you joined my ecosystem three years ago, I began to design this."

A small sphere slid out from the surface of the tower. It was pale red, with a small creature inside, much like how Handy Worm looked when I first received her from one of Pax's seventh-raptors at the docking bay of a landed shuttlecraft. There were sixteen other volunteers receiving their own Worms back then, but I was the only one that survived swallowing mine. There have been no other volunteers since.

"Is this another symbiont Worm? But I thought you said no Gendoji would take me?"

"This is not a prototype Worm like the one you acquired before. Your current Worm allows me to extend your sensory perception well enough for you to engage in a very minimal symbiotic contract with me and provide further data on your biology. This new Worm allows you to produce a second generation of Worms."

"What?"

"This is a seeder Worm. It will produce Worms that other humans will be able to contract with, even allow survival in all the planets the Gendo have thus far colonized. They also allow some measure of self-modification, enough to make the new humans attractive to symbiotic contracts for many Gendoji. This will enable humans to keep interacting with us, but, more importantly, it will give humanity some preliminary tools with which to modify your own biology and properly accelerate your advancement."

"So this Seeder Worm will let me not only stay here but in any other Gendoji colony?"

"No. The seeder Worm itself doesn't have any of the environmental protection functions of the prototype. I know this isn't the solution you wanted, but I'm giving you a chance to further your people and spawn a new generation of humanity."

"But I can't do that!" I thought of myself with an engorged belly teeming with symbionts and remembered the sneer of Alina's disgust.

"I understand that this might be a difficult role to accept given your culture's social constructions of gender; unfortunately I could only design the seeder Worm to interface with you specifically."

"Wait. I just don't want to go back. There is so much for me here. Can't I have another Worm that will survive your passing? Maybe—"

"No. I am not interested in coddling your individual weakness, I seek to further your species as a whole. But I will not force you into a contract, of course. You may choose to ingest the seeder Worm and thus accept a new symbiont contract or not. Without the Seeder, the prototype Worm will wither and die, leaving you much like you were before. That is the choice I offer you. The Seeder will survive for a day in its receptacle. You have that long to make your decision."

I stopped, letting my anxiety subside as I looked closely at the Seeder Worm, its undulating curves and small, precise claws. I put my hand over its holding orb, and it swam up to nuzzle against my palm. I saw that my disgust was just human insecurity, a weak, frayed part of myself that seemed to melt away with the Seeder's cooing touch. How did I forget that my mother was with me at the Uedo zoo, holding my hand as I watched the white tiger? I remembered looking up to her broad smile as she saw the magnificent creature, giddy at how big and loud it was. "Now this is real beauty," she whispered, almost to herself.

I stood for a long moment with my hand over the Seeder, waiting for Pax to continue, but he remained silent as Handy Worm slowly returned to my limited control.

"I understand," I eventually responded, knowing this would be the last time I talked to Pax. "I will miss you."

"Whatever you decide, Sanjit, I wish you luck in your future endeavors. You have given me cause to hope that humanity will become more than what it is. Goodbye."

Then Pax retreated, and my world felt unbearably narrow again. The tower felt somewhat greyer now, more static. I reached out and gently touched the surface. It was warm and pulsed slightly. I had probably never been closer to the biological nexus of my Gendoji. Pax was always spread along the countless ganglia of his massive body, greater than the tower, sure, but more diluted. At that moment he was a single entity, compressed in the deathbed and tombstone to the oldest Gendoji on the planet. I imagined then I should be reminded of my absent father, that perhaps Pax replaced that role in my life, but I had no memories of him so the comparison felt awkward and incomplete. But I'm glad that I never belittled him with the comparison, never projecting the awkward structures of human authority onto him. He was never a mentor, a father, or boss. I call him a friend, glad to have the true meaning of what he was to me lost in the trite vagaries of the word. I knelt in front of the seeder Worm and picked up the sphere, the small creature inside again seeking my touch.

"What will you do?" asked Oquail behind me.

"May you please take me back to Alina? I could take a raptor, but I would rather go with you."

"Yes. I have no further contract with Pax and am thus free to do as I may."

I climbed back onto Oquail, the first-panther smoothly running back towards where we left Alina. The planet's second sun started rising, bathing Pax's humming body with gamma radiation. Many creatures changed in response to the damaging light, each with their own protective strategy. Oquail's fur matted down into a tessellating lattice, its nanocrystal fibers reflecting the radiation through a physical process I never managed to understand. My own Worm pumped out an extra thick fluid for shielding, a blunter, less elegant solution.

We arrived back, and Alina was standing again, the raptors letting her move around since they knew she couldn't outrun them. She turned sharply to us as we drew near.

"Did you get a sample?" she asked, voice straining against the microphone. "Is that what you're holding?"

"No." She stopped as I moved the sphere away from her, as if to protect the Seeder. "Not quite."

"What is it? Some other tech?"

I got off Oquail, whispering my thanks to her via Handy Worm. Alina got closer, her visor fully opaque to prevent radiation exposure. I thought not seeing her would make talking with her easier, but it didn't.

"It's a new Worm." She stopped, then took a half step back.

"Yes, it is," I replied. "This one can only produce new Worms but won't allow me to survive planetside. I'll have to go back if I take it. Well, I have to go back either way. My current Worm won't make it without Pax."

There was a short moment of heavy silence. "I see. Well, you certainly will be welcome back to the station."

"Will I have my old position back?" What a desperate, foolish question. Even before I took Handy Worm that option was lost to me.

"Of course. We have a full new wing waiting for you."

"What do you mean a new wing? As in quarantined quarters?"

Alina paused again. It had never been this hard to get her to talk. We used to be so good together. Or at least so I thought, standing there, hoping for her to reach out to me. But she diligently stayed three meters apart, the protocol distance for avoiding biological contamination.

"Only temporarily, until we determine your medical status. We don't know what the risks of exposure to Gendo modifications are, or even if our germs can harm you."

I should have expected this. After all, I looked like a Worm myself, eyes red-tinted and naked body covered in mucus. I wouldn't be a fellow scientist to them anymore, I'd be just another sample.

Before I took Handy Worm, back when I was still a researcher at the orbital station, I fabricated data in a desperate attempt to regain the faltering affection of the brilliant and beautiful Alina Hertz. But I was caught, and the committee assessment was swift and merciless. To avoid being sent back to Earth in disgrace, I volunteered to be in the first group to receive a Worm. All the other candidates were elderly or terminally ill. Each one desperate for some final miracle, just like me. When I was told the Worms worked on nobody else, I was so happy for the opportunity to remain at the periphery of Alina's life. But she was already out of my reach, had been before I ever doctored my samples.

I looked at Oquail, turning my back on the environmental suit, letting Alina have her sterile distance. Oquail could probably see right through the suit, past Alina's eyes all the way down to each of her lesser photoreceptor cells.

"Oquail, I want to build a ship, take the Seeder to Earth and pick my own candidates to bring back to the Gendo. This would also give me the chance to develop my own biology away from the reach of those who would try to contain me."

Oquail's sensory filaments flared in red and green, then she lowered her muzzle close to my face. "I would gladly help you accomplish such a thing. I have centuries to hunt and breed. This will be a fitting tribute to one of Pax's final wishes."

"It will be difficult for me to survive here with the new Worm," I replied, "I would need your help keeping me alive."

"Yes, and I offer it freely. We do not have human limitations on manufacturing or resource allocation, especially with so much of Pax's body now unused, so you will not need me for too long. I will recruit some newly released symbionts for this construction. Many have not yet decided what to do when Pax dies, and this will serve as a pleasant distraction as they consider their future contracts."

I turned to Alina again, who now looked like a sliver of awkward metal, pitiful among vast rolling plains of true technological mastery. Something from an old life better left behind.

"I will stay here, Alina. Maybe I'll contact the station later to inform them of my plans, but you will likely never see me again. Goodbye."

She tried to speak but I reached out with Handy Worm and turned off the speakers on her suit. Such an unreliable system, all it took was cutting a single wire.

Not looking back, I got on Oquail, and we rode to the distant crags at the edge of Pax's body, where naked white shell flared up into kilometer-high barbs bridged by a tight webbing of purple tissue. At the base of one of the barbs, a small cluster of creatures waited, all responding to Oquail's plea. There were dozens of builder raptors and several sensorial panthers, even a handful of second- and third-silphid engineers.

The released symbionts were expecting us, and as soon as we reached them I retreated into a small cavern a few of my fellow third-panthers had dug for me. They must have heard of the seeder Worm and imagined what I would go through to ingest it. Sitting with my back against the lukewarm wall, I pried open the Seeder's sphere and tilted the opening onto my lips. The Seeder slithered down my throat with unexpected ease. The cut it made on my esophageal lining stung and filled my mouth with blood. But that was nothing.

The real pain came when the Seeder confronted Handy Worm. For what felt like hours I tore at my chest and screamed in agony as the Seeder violently pushed aside my poor Worm. Handy Worm slowly shriveled and died as the Seeder displaced each of her connections then ate her twitching remains. She was a good symbiont and deserved better than the short, mean life she was designed for.

Later that evening I was recuperating in a protective bubble on Oquail's side, feeling so very warm and safe, when each symbiont scuttling across the incomplete spaceship paused in their work to look up. A piercing wail filled the air as the screams and howls rolled across the Gendoji's shell to herald the death of Pax and the frantic grief of his symbionts.

Even without Handy Worm I could feel the suffocating brutality of his absence, as if a cutting emptiness seeped into the air and oozed from the walls. Teeth bared and panting, Oquail lowered her head to me, and we wept and roared and clutched to each other like wounded children. "This will be a good ship," she muttered between sobs. "You will do good things with it."

§

As I sail towards Earth, I'm certain that the change I bring will be welcomed by some but resisted by many. Maybe they will come to realize the benefits of what the Gendo offer, or maybe only a few will be willing to leave behind their fossilized traditions, the Sol system fading into irrelevance as humanity carries on. I might also be shot out of the sky before even landing.

Trying not to concern myself with what happens on Earth, I drift within the tight corridors of a ship that doesn't need my control. The Seeder Worm is busy knitting a womb inside my abdomen, but often it turns aside from its work and lets me see into my own flesh with a clarity that Handy Worm never possessed. But I no longer have Oquail's guidance or Pax's gentle oversight, so I am careful with each modification I test, knowing there is nobody to help me should something go wrong. It is clear that I am no longer a Gendo symbiont much like I am not Alina's lover. Strangely, more than ever before I feel like my mother's son, my own alien motherhood an extension of hers.

I am simultaneously exhilarated and terrified, occasionally even in pain as I struggle to improve my body in concert with the Seeder's evolving needs. Sometimes I indulge in the bittersweet memories of Pax in all his boundless magnificence, but more often I wonder what my future children will create, what elegance they will bring to their flesh.

Sunvault

light sail star bound

joel nathanael

discourse could sail our
                            solar vessel
cutting light
                through astral seas

pick a star(s)
            &
                 we'll make it our own

endless permutations of
                          cosmic trade winds

photon propulsion
       would keep taut
             our copper & micron sails

we could train our hands to speak &
       untie knots of extradimensional
            language

phonemes we cannot yet articulate
       new vowels
voiced   unvoiced   dual-voiced

       we could round centauris
              alpha   beta   proxima
we could winter there
       our personal perihelion

before we leave for
                       andromeda

Synthesis: This Shining Confluence

Bogi Takács

> *"Measure yourself against infinity"*
> *—Attila József*

Tendrils snap-tied into flesh, the flood rolling
rumbling underneath, the sun ever-high
and the wind-shear biting into your cheeks
    you rise;
on the back of the Livyatan of old, riding
the runaway serpent, the planet turning
under you, your twined bodies leaving
    spark-foam in your wake;
you run hands—flippers—fins through
the seasalt, reach out to sensors bobbing
on the surface, grab their data streams in
    the sheer joy of motion;
merge—unify, as you are unified by
this shining confluence of technology
and magic, this breathless rush toward
    the city-domes in the distance;
the human-shape a singular part of
an ever-evolving whole teeming with
krill and plankton, eddies and whirls
    of crystallized secrets;
a raw historical perspective of coral and
whale fossils, your head snapping to take in
information from every direction, glory
    singing in your gasps;
survival and precise adjustment and
metastable states and gradient descent
and a careful calibration based on your
    minute handiwork;
the fundamental substrate of life is
within your reach as you swim onward,
always serving the endless light
    within and around you.

Solar Powered Giraffes

Jack Pevyhouse

The sleek machines
traverse the land
like gilded towers.

Their footsteps
enrich the soil.
Their tongues
purify the water.

Sunvault

Pan, Legs Resting

Sireesha Reddy

Sunvault

Last Chance

Tyler Young

The trip is always harder on you than it is on the children, Grace reminded herself. After nearly twenty years as a teacher, Grace was accustomed to most of the hardships imposed by the Ikehara-Baasch curriculum. But taking the children on their first above-ground visit never got any easier, even after you'd done it a hundred times.

She moved down the line, checking the 11-year-olds' exposure suits, rad sensors, and rebreather lines. They were nearly giddy with excitement, hopping from foot to foot, chattering their questions to each other and to her. She had explained to them, of course, how brutal and dangerous the surface was. She'd drilled it into them for weeks, their whole lives, really. And she had made them practice exposure-suit discipline daily for the past month. Four of the boys hadn't taken that regimen seriously enough and wouldn't be going up.

Yet the children seemed to think they were being given a great treat. They always did, and Grace couldn't really blame them. After a life inside, hemmed in, constantly surrounded by other people, they were going outside. They were finally going to see where their absent parents struggled to provide for them.

"Maybe we'll see a giraffe!" one of the girls chirped.

A soft voice corrected her. "There aren't any giraffes up there. The only ones alive are in the ark."

Grace glanced down the line at Michael, the dark-haired boy who had spoken. He noticed Grace looking and grinned. She knew she shouldn't have favorites, but it was hard not to love a boy like Michael: thoughtful, precocious, and quirky. He reminded Grace of herself at that age, more interested in talking to the teacher than her classmates.

Grace continued down the line, reassuring and chiding as necessary. When she reached Michael, she muttered under her breath, "Kingside castle." Michael grinned and then looked up at the ceiling as he considered her move. In the two years they had been playing she had never let him win, but this time he had her on the run.

Grace moved to the last girl in line. She noticed a loose fitting, tightened it, and then moved to the hatch.

"Do I have your attention?"

The children answered in a singsong voice. "Yes, Ms. Swenson."

"We will be on the surface for one hour. It is every bit as dangerous as you've learned, so follow the precautions. If I see anyone goofing around, you will not go back on the surface for years. Understood?"

"Yes, Ms. Swenson," they answered in unison.

"Good."

Grace turned and put her hands on the wheel that opened the hatch. She closed her eyes for a moment and silently repeated the mantra of academy teachers: *we must be cruel to be kind.* The heavy steel door opened with a harsh squeal, and dust came billowing into the chamber. Looking out at the blasted landscape, Grace felt a brief but powerful wave of nausea hit her, always a terrifying, claustrophobic experience when wearing an exposure helmet. She swallowed her queasiness and focused on the next hour, which would be one of the most important experiences in the kids' education.

§

Grace never spent too much energy on instruction during a surface visit, particularly the first one. The conditions were education enough. Instead, she let the kids play. The surface was so scalding hot that the children would inevitably settle down and join her in the shade of the hatch. Then she would point out the most significant features of the inclement, ruined landscape: the total absence of animal and vegetable life and the blistering temperatures (as if the children hadn't noticed).

If they had time, she might walk them over to look at a nearby pool of noxious yellow sludge that the teachers charitably called a lake. It was so polluted, she would tell them, that a single sip could kill you. The kids probably wouldn't retain anything she said during the entire surface visit, but that didn't really matter.

About half of her class was already lying prostrate in the shade when Jane raised a hand and called, "Ms. Swenson!" Grace jogged to her, wincing when the sunlight hit her. Jane's usually cheerful face was ashen.

"Are you okay, honey?"

Jane pointed down into a shallow valley. A child was lying motionless at the bottom of the depression. Grace gasped and hit her panic button. A shrill alarm sounded. Grace knew that the emergency surface team would be rushing out to guide the children back into the hatch. She had eyes only for the figure face down in the dirt. She slid down the rocky hillside and rolled the body over. Michael's face was as white as a skull, which made the blood pouring from his nose seem shockingly, gruesomely red. *Please not him,* Grace thought.

"Medical emergency!" she called. Moments later, men were next to her, lifting the boy's body, which suddenly seemed tiny and fragile, onto a stretcher. One of the corpsmen reached out and pulled his hand out of hers. Then they were gone.

It was just the heat, she told herself. It happened occasionally. The combination of heat and excitement caused a child to faint. If anything, this heightened the sense of terror and danger the children associated with the surface. And that was for the best.

Grace looked back at the hatch. There were no children in sight. They would spend several hours in decon before reentering the academy's compound. Grace pulled off her helmet. The heat was oppressive, but the fresh air cleared her nausea instantly. She savored the opportunity to drop the act for a moment. She bypassed the decon facilities, scanned her palm at an access panel, and walked through the door marked "STAFF ONLY."

§

Grace had planned to spend the morning with her class in "decontamination," but the emergency crew was handling that performance now. She found that, unexpectedly, she had nothing on her calendar until the afternoon's graduation ceremony. Although she was sick with worry about Michael, she decided to make the most of the free time by visiting the gym. She hadn't had a decent workout in days, and if she rode the bike, she could kill two birds and write an email to her husband, Forrest.

Grace was in sight of the gym when Tanya, her newest apprentice, waved and approached her.

"Do you have a minute?"

Grace suppressed her frustration and smiled. "What's up?"

"I wanted to ask about Brad, from the three-four group, you know? He's having a really hard time with the separation. He's obviously bright, but he isn't developing socially. He doesn't even play with the other kids."

"Yes, that happens. Children develop at different speeds. I've looked at his file, and although he's proceeding slowly in terms of social development, there's no indication of anything pathological. Just give him time."

Grace started to edge away, hoping that the conversation was over. But Tanya called her back.

"I know. It's just—this is my first rotation with the younger kids, you know?"

Grace nodded encouragingly. Tanya was an extremely bright and effective teacher, but the girl took forever to get to the point. *Woman,* Grace corrected herself. *When had twenty-two started to seem young?* Grace wondered.

"It's so much harder than I expected. The older kids are used to everything. But every day Brad cries for his mom, and I have to tell him that she isn't coming. I'm having a really hard time dealing with it." The last few words came out in a high, tremulous rush.

"Sit down," Grace said, pointing to a nearby cluster of couches. "Please."

"I know our method is hard, Tanya. It has to be. Remember we're doing this for the kids' own good. I would love it—believe me—if we could teach this lesson the same way we teach math. But, as you know, that's been tried before. This is the only way: the children *need to suffer.*"

Tanya nodded, a tear rolling down her cheek. Grace pulled her into a hug. "Remember, it's not forever."

Grace watched the apprentice walk away, dabbing her eyes. *She won't make it,* Grace thought sadly. Then again, few did. Only one in five finished the grueling five-year apprenticeship and became teachers. And less than half of those would join Grace as master teachers, qualified to train the next generation of apprentices.

The softhearted ones quit after a few years. Grace had seen it a thousand times. They would say that they couldn't handle the weak light, the recycled air, the food rationing, the crowding, the cruelty. They would say they couldn't stand the deception. They knew it was the right thing to do, they would say, but they just couldn't lie all day long.

Grace felt suddenly exhausted. She desperately wanted to go back to her room and take a long morning nap. Instead, she forced herself to stand up. Another wave of nausea hit her. *No,* she thought, *I can't be. How long has it been since Forrest's last visit? Six weeks?* She pushed the thought aside and headed for the gym. The doctors had told her long ago that it would never happen.

§

Grace stood outside the teachers' entrance to the auditorium, waiting for the signal. She didn't loathe the monthly graduations the way some of the other teachers did, so she ended up covering more than her fair share. All the same, leading a graduation ceremony was always an intense experience that left her feeling wrung out and battered. She closed her eyes and concentrated on slowing her breathing. When she opened her eyes, Meghan, a trim brunette, was standing in front of her wearing an uncertain look.

"Didn't you want me to cover this session for you?" Grace asked.

"I did. But I heard about Michael, and I thought—I thought you might want a break."

In fact, a break was the last thing Grace wanted. Forrest was in the field again, studying one of the native species of lizards, so she couldn't call him. And the hospital staff hadn't responded to any of her emails about Michael. The thought of returning to her empty apartment and her worries was nearly unbearable.

"That's thoughtful but, really, right now I could use the distraction."

Meghan hesitated until Grace shooed her away. "Come on, get out of here."

The transom light flashed. Grace scanned her palm and walked onto the stage. Thirty-four graduating seniors, all born during the same month sixteen years ago, watched her in expectant silence. None of them had any idea what would happen at the ceremony: the academy's graduates never returned to the dormitories.

"Congratulations," Grace intoned, "today you become full citizens in our society. But before you do, you need to understand the truth about our history."

"Millennia ago, humanity fled the smoking ruin of Earth. Your ancestors were among those select few lucky enough to find a place on those seventeen colonial ships."

Grace could feel the students' anticipation dissipating. They knew this by rote. She could see them only dimly through the harsh stage lights, but she knew they were leaning back, crossing their arms and legs, waiting for this remedial history lesson to end.

"Earth's survivors recognized the new planet they found for what it was and named it Salvation. And for a few generations, they treated the planet accordingly. But when the ruin of Earth had faded from living memory and was nothing more than a dry fact in a textbook, the colonists started to make exceptions, to take shortcuts for profit and comfort. And in the span of four hundred years, they destroyed the second Eden. *It can never happen again,* students. There are no more habitable planets within our reach. That's why our forefathers named this planet, your home, Last Chance."

Grace gestured and the floor-to-ceiling screen behind her glowed to life. It showed a red planet against the black backdrop of space. "This is the Last Chance you know."

Grace flicked her wrist and the planet was replaced by an image of people in exposure suits struggling to assemble industrial machinery in a harsh red landscape. "This is what we've prepared you for: a brutal, painful life spent trying to scratch out something better for the next generation."

Grace took a deep breath to steady her nerves.

"But that was all a lie."

Grace let the silence draw out. When the students started to mutter, she gestured again. A new image filled the screen: a green and blue planet hanging in space. The camera plummeted toward the surface. Unblemished natural landscapes rolled by: craggy mountains, grassy yellow plains, sapphire blue lakes, and endless rows of towering trees.

"This is the real Last Chance. The desert above us is only a tiny fraction of the planet. Our world is a paradise."

Grace gestured again, and the screen now showed a town square. Fit, smiling couples walked arm in arm down tree-shaded avenues. An elderly man rode a bicycle down the street, a loaf of bread and a bottle of wine in his basket. "And this is where you will be going to live: New Paris."

The screen went black. For a long moment, the room was dead silent— the students weren't even breathing. Grace waited. And then all of the students began to shout at once. She let them howl for a full minute and then blew an earsplitting note on a whistle.

"You're outraged. I know. I felt the same way when I found out. But all we've done is justified—it's necessary. You'll never forget what a blessing this world is. You will live modestly, sustainably, and you'll never even consider risking this planet—for anything."

"Your parents are waiting next door. You'll be leaving with them tonight, whenever you're ready. You'll have a month to reconnect with your families and explore New Paris. At that point, a counsellor will contact you to talk through your education and career options. I hope that some of you will have the courage to come back to the academy as apprentice teachers."

A boy scoffed loudly. Grace ignored him.

"For now, I'm here to answer any questions you might have."

She moved away from the podium and stood in the center of the stage. Within seconds, she was surrounded by students, some furious, some hurt, some plain lost. She didn't leave the auditorium for six hours.

§

The next morning, two blue lines stared up at Grace. She had taken the test twice, just to be sure. She was pregnant. She felt a strange mixture of excitement, anxiety, and a touch of irritation.

In her twenties, Grace had wanted a child desperately. She had visited the leading fertility specialists, all of whom had told her it was hopeless. It had been a terrible time; she and Forrest had fought constantly. Only in retrospect did she realize she had been testing him to find out if he wanted to leave her for someone who could give him a child.

But they stayed together, and she threw herself into her work, filling the void by nurturing other people's children. The life of an academy teacher wasn't easy, but she had a talent for it, and it was satisfying to know that she was doing the most important job in the world. And *now* she was pregnant.

She studied her reflection in the mirror. Her face was already marked by smile lines and crows' feet. What would she look like when her baby emerged from the academy? Teacher or not, she wouldn't be allowed to visit her child until after graduation. She would be in her fifties then. Her face split into a wide grin. She couldn't help it. The timing wasn't perfect, but she was going to be a mom.

§

Diana Martinez, the seventy-fourth headmistress of the Ikehara-Baasch Academy, was a plump grey-haired woman of sixty-three. Grace found her, as usual, sitting behind her desk, reading and sipping her Fukamushicha tea. Grace waited until the Headmistress put down her tablet before speaking.

"Pardon me, Headmistress."

Diana looked up over half-moon spectacles and smiled. "Hello, Grace. I was just getting ready to call you."

"Oh?"

"Yes, but you obviously have something on your mind. You go first."

For a moment, Grace didn't know how to proceed. In the end, she blurted it out: "I'm pregnant."

The older woman shoved her chair back and came around the desk to hug Grace. "I'm *so* happy for you, dear."

"Thank you, Headmistress."

"Right now it's Diana."

"Diana." Grace couldn't stop smiling.

"Have you told Forrest?"

"Not yet. I was hoping to tell him in person. I was wondering if you could—"

§

Diana raised a hand to interrupt. "It's done. No problem."

At first, the two women chatted happily about names, and baby showers, and diaper changes. Gradually they shifted to serious matters: who would cover Grace's duties during the two precious years she was allowed before her child had to enter the academy. After forty-five minutes, Grace remembered the way the conversation had started.

"I've been going on and on. You said you had something you needed to talk to me about."

Diana frowned and moved to sit behind her desk again. "Yes. I'm sorry to tell you this today, but it can't wait. The report I was reading was from the hospital. Michael has type-K lymphoblastic leukemia."

Grace felt as if a bucket of cold water had been dumped over her. She hadn't even thought about Michael since she took the test. The nausea, which was quickly becoming her constant companion, flared up again.

"Will he . . . what's his. . . ."

"A year. Maybe two if they give him the toughest treatment course, but that would be two years of misery. I've already informed his parents. They will be here tomorrow. You've been taking care of Michael for years—I'm hoping you can meet them when they arrive and help them break the news to Michael."

"Of course, Headmistress." Grace stood up to leave.

Diana took a sip of her now-cold tea and pulled a face. "I'll get Forrest out here as soon as I can."

§

Grace sat on her couch, waiting for Michael's parents. Over the past twenty-four hours she had obsessed over the best way to approach the conversation. In the end, she decided that there was no best way. She would just be as open and honest as she could.

Her door slid open silently and Heather and Thatcher McCoy stepped into the room. Grace moved forward to shake hands, but found herself pulled into a tight hug.

"I'm glad he's had you as his teacher," Heather whispered in her ear. "He's always going on about you in his letters."

Grace pulled back and looked at Michael's father, a tough, grim-looking man. Grace held out her hand and Thatcher shook it. His eyes were wet and he was blinking rapidly.

"I've been so lucky to have Michael in my class," Grace began. Before she could say more, her voice dissolved into sobs. Suddenly they were all crying, standing there in the entryway. When the tears subsided, Grace ushered them into her sitting room.

"I'm sorry for that. I should be comforting you. Not the other way around."

Thatcher, calmer now that he had cried, waved her apology away.

"Don't be sorry," Heather said. "I'm glad he's had someone who loved him nearby when we couldn't be."

Grace seized that sentiment as a natural segue. "Well, he never needs to be away from you again." She stopped and bit her cheek to keep from losing it again.

"Everything has already been approved. You can take him back to New Paris tonight so that he can spend whatever time he has in comfort. I'm happy to help you figure out the best way to explain the truth about the planet and the academy and, well, everything else. I'll tell you from experience, there's a real possibility that he'll hate the messenger, so I'm happy to tell him myself, if that's what you prefer. Just let me know how I can help."

The McCoys exchanged a look. Thatcher nodded at Heather, who said, "We appreciate your offer, Ms. Swenson. But we're not going to tell him. He's only got a year left. He doesn't need to spend that hating us and knowing what he'll be missing."

Grace started to speak, but Heather held up a hand to stop her.

"We've thought about this a lot. It would be different if he had one healthy year left. He doesn't. He's going to be weak, in and out of the hospital. We'll stay here, at the academy, for as long as he has left. We don't want him to know—ever."

Heather reached out and put her hand on Grace's knee. "I know this is hard for you to accept. You would make a different choice. But I really do hope that you will come and visit him as often as you can. He loves you very much."

Heather nodded to her husband, and they stood up to leave. Grace was speechless, her mind racing. *He has a whole year left, maybe two, and they're going to make him spend it in this metal coffin?* She knew she should respect their wishes, but the thought made her sick.

"He deserves a chance to feel the wind in his hair!"

Michael's parents stopped in the doorway. Thatcher turned and spoke for the first time. "You're right. But he has enough pain ahead of him without knowing that he spent his whole life down here for nothing."

Grace sat staring into space for hours after the McCoys left. She was startled from her reverie when her seldom-used phone rang. Forrest's worried face filled the screen. He had a five-day beard and mud smeared on his cheek.

"I got a radio message saying you needed me ASAP. What's going on?"

"I'm fine, honey. It's . . . one of my students is dying."

Talking to Forrest usually calmed her. But Grace found herself getting angrier and angrier as she recounted her conversation with the McCoys. "They're just wrong!" she shouted as she paced around the room. "He should see the ocean; he should feel the sun on his shoulders; he should ride a horse. There's still time!"

Forrest looked troubled.

"I agree. That's what I would do if it were our kid."

Grace's heart skipped a beat at those last two words. For a split-second, she almost told him about the baby then and there. But she decided it would be too cruel if it turned out to be a false alarm. She would go to her OB first thing in the morning and tell him when she knew for sure.

"I could just tell Michael," she said quietly. "If I told him the truth there would be no taking it back. Then Heather and Thatcher would have no reason to keep him down here."

Forrest recoiled as if she had struck him.

"You know you can't do that."

"Why shouldn't I?" Grace resumed her pacing. "He's terminal, so he's already been cleared to learn the truth. I wouldn't be breaking any laws. Hell, I don't think I'd be breaking any school rules. Why shouldn't I?" she repeated.

"You know why."

Grace looked away and crossed her arms.

"He's not our son. And how would Michael feel if he found out that his parents intended to keep the truth from him?"

Grace wasn't persuaded. She would make sure Michael never knew that she had ignored his parents' wishes. Sure, his parents might hate her for a while, but they would forget about that when they saw their son walking on a beach at sunset. Besides, Heather and Thatcher didn't really *know* Michael; they didn't know how curious and kind and thoughtful he was. They hadn't watched over him every day as he grew up; she had.

"Just sleep on it, okay? I'll be there as soon as I can."

§

Grace went to her doctor before sunrise the next morning. Afterward, she went straight to Michael. She knew she should slow down and think things over, but after her appointment, she found that she couldn't stay away. She loved the boy like he was her own child, and she needed to see him.

He looked exactly the same. That surprised her, until she realized that only three days had passed since his collapse. *Could that be right?* she wondered. It seemed like a lifetime.

When Michael saw her walk in, he tossed aside his tablet and sat up in bed. "Hi, Ms. Swenson," he piped, smiling.

"Hello, Michael. How are you?" She moved to sit on the edge of his bed.

"Oh fine, I guess. I feel a little dizzy when I get up, but that's all. I know it's going to get worse." He trailed off and looked down. Grace reached out and brushed a lock of hair out of his face.

"What are you reading?"

"Huck Finn. You were right—it's great! I just got to the part where Huck and Jim miss the Ohio River in the fog." He chattered happily for a while, describing his favorite parts of the story and what he would have done differently, if he were Huck.

"Well, I'm glad you're enjoying it. I can send you some other books I bet you'll like."

It's time, Grace told herself. She took a deep breath, steeling herself, but then her voice died in her throat. She had given the speech hundreds of times—she didn't even need to rehearse before graduations anymore—but now she couldn't find the words to begin. She looked down at her hands clenched in her lap.

"And we can still play chess, right, Ms. Swenson?"

Grace looked up at his face, open and hopeful, despite everything that had happened to him.

"Every day."

She pulled him into a hug. "Call me Grace," she whispered.

§

Forrest was waiting for her when she returned to the apartment. They hugged, and then she flopped down in her favorite overstuffed chair. She felt completely drained.

"Did you tell him?"

"No. I didn't."

Forrest nodded. "Why not?"

"I realized I was only thinking about myself—what I wanted. That's the kind of selfish thinking I've spent my whole life fighting."

Forrest furrowed his brow. "You knew that yesterday. What changed your mind?"

"I guess you persuaded me."

He laughed. "Yeah, that would be a first. Come on, tell me."

Grace sighed. One of the things she loved about Forrest was that he would never say *I told you so*. One of the things she hated about him was that he wanted an explanation for everything. She knew he wouldn't stop digging until he got the truth or something close to it.

"It wasn't a logical process. I just realized that when you love someone and you know something that will hurt them and telling them won't change anything—"

She choked back a sob as she put her hand on her stomach—her stomach that would never swell with new life—and then forced her voice back under control.

"—you protect them, because you love them. It's the right thing to do, even if it means lying to them."

Forrest knelt down in front of Grace and put his arms around her. She allowed herself a moment to imagine that the doctor had told her something else. She pictured Forrest's disbelief, followed by his wild, barking laugh, and the gleeful calls to their parents. Then she took a deep shuddering breath and closed a door in her heart.

I'll never tell him, she decided. It would be her gift to him to carry this hurt alone. She knew she could do it; she was no stranger to secrecy or to pain. Besides, she didn't have time to grieve. She had work to do, the most important work in the world.

The Desert, Blooming

Lev Mirov

The first time I heard rain, it sluiced down the sides of the Dome door like the wet spray of a root mister, if a root mister could pummel you flat. The sound was nothing like a drumbeat. Oh, it was repetitive, but not the kind of repetition you could build a melody on top of—erratic, windblown, and dripping like a faulty pipe letting out too much water in the botanical garden.

Over the sound of the rain, my parent laughed. "What do you think, Luyn?" Ibra called to me, stepping into one of the bright saffron suits that would protect us all from the acidic elements outside. "Ready to feel rain for the first time?"

I had read about rain, watched recordings of my professors and mentors suit up in their emerald suits to prepare for the onslaught that made the flight to the Burned City possible. At nineteen, I wasn't sure I was ready. But I *was* tall enough to fit into a suit, big enough to wear a helmet, heavy enough not to be blown over by the torrential winds. I had trained my whole life to leave someday. Ibra thought I was ready to put trees down, and I wanted to live up to my parent's expert estimation.

I was used to water. The City of Lotuses is one of the wettest places in the world. Its endless maze of channels and waterways and time-perfected ecosystem grow enough food to provide for the other Dome Cities of Tumry. The wind and sand, the poisonous particulates in the rain, and the threat of the sun vapors worried me.

Ibra had been born under the sun and the trees in the east where the Desert had become grassland full of trees and oases built over hundreds of years so the trees slowed the endless wind and the rain formed pools and the air was cleansed. I had never seen the grasslands and the orchards of Ibra's home, except in images or the calls from Ibra's parents. They always asked if Ibra was ever coming home, if I would make religious pilgrimage to the ancient city Ibra had come from.

So far, since coming to the Dome, Ibra had only left for these missions to plant trees in the rain. I had never been out at all.

Katharos, black hair plaited in tight rows to keep the helmet snug, was suiting up in the emerald green survival suit of archeologists for the trip down into the Burned City. I was too proud to admit fear in front of both my parents so I only shrugged at Ibra, as if to say, *rain's rain,* though it spooked me even more than the occasional sound of dust storms sweeping against the enviro-skin of the Dome.

"Check that crate again," Katharos said to my lucky older classmate Maryim, who was going down with the archeologists. "If the skiff isn't loaded just right we'll topple over in the first strong gust and waste precious time reloading."

Part of me wished I was going into the Burned City to take samples of the ruins; Katharos had a crew of the best students to unearth a trash pit and dig for seeds and other samples of biomatter remains. I dreamed of seeing the remnants of the shrines, especially the preservations of the Shrine of the Cup-bearer, the face of God who had given us medicine, my particular interest and my sworn patron.

But they were all years ahead of me in their studies. I had only just begun the practicals for archaeological work. I was going with Ibra to put trees in the ground, while the soil was wet and the trees would take root. I had never seen Ibra at work outside, only in the laboratories, grafting tree stock and hybridizing fruits and seeding the wild grasses grown in the labs from the things Katharos found in waste pits to see how they would take in field conditions. Unlike me, the students were going for credit. Katharos took things out of the ground, Ibra put things in. I wondered, sometimes, how two such opposed disciplines had met and made a life—made me, carefully cradled for the gestational months in a tube not so different from the one that Ibra sprouted fruit trees and shrubs in, save for size.

"Come on, Luyn, check your helmet," Ibra said to me cheerfully. Ibra's voice was louder in the helmet earpiece than in the enormous hangar. The Dome would open, rain would wet these grounds, soft underfoot with mosses that could tolerate the irregular conditions of loading and unloading and purify the air and rain that came in. The best pilot in the Dome of Lotuses would fly us out the gate and drop the archeologists off underneath the sheltered, smaller dome of the Burned City, then turn to the Green Belt.

The enormous ship slowly filled up with trees and seed beds and archaeological equipment. The air inside was breathable, but accidents happened.

When I was still a small child, a pilot lost control of the ship in the wind. For days Katharos and I had mourned, inconsolable as Dawith ran scenario after scenario trying to convince the Dome pilots to send someone out to look for possible survivors, or, at the worst, recover some of the precious trees that had been Ibra and Dawith's shared labor in the laboratory. Only Ibra reappeared on the far edge of the Burned Dome when the ship finally launched. Only Ibra had suited up early and worn a helmet during the crash, and still the suit had not protected Ibra's hand from permanent damage after exposure to the elements.

Sometimes at night I heard Ibra scream from the other bedroom in piercing agony. I had always known what that was about. There were new rules, now. We all were fully suited inside the carriers. The new rules had never stopped the screaming.

The Sunborn are not like the Domeborn, Katharos had said, when Ibra returned and sought medical treatment, just as when Ibra did something not done in the Dome or was being recalcitrant. But I knew what Katharos had meant: *I would not have survived it.*

My parents loved each other, and perhaps because the Sunborn have a resilience Dome-families have lost, they chose to make me in Ibra's image, using that genetic stock as the root to graft me onto, a hybrid. The choice had been controversial at the time. Nobody called it controversial now.

"Are you sure your kid can really help us with planting?" Professor Dawith from outside the Dome asked, looking at me with a familiar sneer as I fastened my suit up all the way and secured the helmet in place, double-checking the gloves to leave nothing exposed to the gritty sand or the ferocious water. I felt my stomach plummet. This again. I was too young, everyone said.

"That kid," Ibra said, prickly with authority that came whenever challenged, "is strong enough to lift trees and knows more about the landscape and what grows here than they ever taught *you* in school at the same age, Dawith. Do you want your trees planted on time or not?"

I squared my shoulders. "If you don't like it," I said, trying to sound as tough as I could, "you could always try lifting the trees yourself instead of flirting with the pilot while the rest of us are working. I understand, of course, senior professors aren't expected to do heavy labor, but with the harvest coming in, it's down to every strong hand, and I have two."

That wasn't going to endear me to Dawith, who had been Ibra's rival and professional colleague a long time, when they'd both come to the Dome as outsiders. But Dawith had never really liked me, and I had never liked Dawith (*intruding on important work,* Dawith once said, not knowing I was in earshot).

Dawith only shot me a surly look and said no more. I was accustomed to Dawith being surly until someone had pulled out a bottle of liquor, when Dawith's friendlier side emerged, and I got to hear about what they did in the south where the other green belt was being pushed forward by Dawith's relatives.

"Stop, the skiff's unbalanced," Katharos shouted. The student landed the skiff just feet from the enormous transport ship. "Do it wrong, do it twice," Katharos snapped, clearly grumpy. "We're not putting that thing in there until there's *no* chance of tipping. Get it right this time. Use your pads to calculate weights if you have to. They're integrated into your helmets. Use *every* part of the suit."

I went to help with the reloading of the skiff. My parents were talking with their microphones off, side by side arguing about something: maybe the correct way to load skiffs into the transport ship or something else that would make or break the flight. It was reassuring to see them their normal, decisive, argumentative selves. Ibra's gloved hand was laced tightly around Katharos' dark green one, as if pressure could sink through the thick protective suits and give them physical contact again.

The other students didn't hide annoyance when I calculated the ideal weight distribution of the skiff, but they listened. Everyone thought I was there because of who my parents were, but I would prove them wrong and pull my own weight.

Once we had settled questions of weight and loading, we all strapped into the transport ship. Through the air purifier in my helmet I could smell the green of the date palms and the grasses we would root into the limans Ibra's team had constructed on some previous journey. The ground was ready for desalinification, for filtration through planting, to turn the Desert into a blooming place that herds might travel from oasis to oasis.

I knew Ibra's fevered descriptions of the project by heart. Someday the Green Belt to the south and our Green Belt would meet. We could drive the Desert back until the sand-winds no longer ravaged the coastline and the great river could sustain farming life again. Someday we would abandon Domes entirely, Ibra said, except as places of sanctuary in emergency conditions. I didn't really believe it was possible, but the modest proposal of windbreaks Ibra had come to work on now promised far more, once joined to Katharos' expertise on the ancient plants that had grown here once and Dawith's work with hybridization and rootstocks that would survive the wind and rain alike.

"Check your helmet," Ibra said again. It was strange to see that familiar mouth moving and yet hear nothing except through the earpiece settled awkwardly just beside my ear in the helmet.

I checked my helmet. I checked everything else, too. The scanner on the helmet read me off the data on the gloves, the collar my helmet fit into, the air purification pump. The systems display on the screen of my helmet was our only advanced warning of a sudden weather shift that could end the mission. I was determined to know it well.

The doors of the Dome opened. Water blew in sheets; I could see just enough out the window to see it splatter across the pane and keep rolling.

I suppressed a visceral shudder, a sudden fear of being beaten to death under the downpour. The transport shift lifted, engines humming. Suddenly we were off the ground, sailing out into that torrential wind and rain. My stomach dropped as the ship pitched sideways, throwing us against the belts, and then righted itself. I could see weather-beaten trees below us; they had looked so different in the laboratories, or the test fields. Flash-flood rivers ran into collection pools. It was only a flight of ten minutes between the Dome and the Burned City, and I gripped the edge of my seat nervously. Inside the Burned City, a dome would protect Katharos and the students from the elements. I would have no shelter from the bruising rain and buffeting winds.

"What do you think?" Ibra asked me on a private channel, leaning over as if I would hear beyond the helmet instead of through it. "Someday Katharos will walk this path instead of flying it and go to the Burned City whenever desire arises."

"No I won't," Katharos replied, "do you know how heavy my equipment is? We'll be flying skiffs, thank you."

We all laughed, and that felt almost normal, as the ship tilted and swayed in the wind. If the ship was struggling against the wind, how would any of us make headway? Maybe Dawith was right and I was too young for tree planting after all.

Ten minutes we struggled in the wind and sheeting rain until the heavy transport slid underneath the shelter of the Dome of the Burned City. I peered through the water-streaked windows, desperate to see anything. There was next to nothing to look at; the city had been burned thousands of years ago and nobody landed heavy ships on top of valuable ruins. I saw only grasses growing wild, blown every direction by the rotating engines, as Katharos and the archeology students prepared to drive the skiff off and disembark.

As Katharos stood up next to me, I reached out to catch Katharos' hand. "I love you," I said, not caring that everyone could hear us on the public channel. Once the transport ship pulled out of the dome, the wind would make interference a problem with communication. My parents vanished every time dust turned to rain. I was used to nothing but silence for days or sometimes weeks, alone with all the reports the datapads could stream back whenever a connection could be established.

"It'll only be a few days," Katharos said, less of a promise than a hope. It could be less than twenty-four hours, if the weather didn't hold, and there was no way to get the archeologists home if the ships couldn't fly. "Soon you'll be doing a different kind of digging."

I watched my parents embrace, sensible enough to say their goodbyes on a private channel. There was the possibility—however faint—that my parents might be saying goodbye for the last time. I could scarcely begin to count the things that had the potential to go wrong; I had counted them up as a kid, every time they left me in the hands of a friend from the archeology department who did not go out on expeditions. A suit failure. A sudden dust storm. A flash flood. A dome failure in the Burned City. A ship crashing. We all could die at any moment on such expeditions. I comforted myself with the reminder that sudden death was just as possible among the Lotus-canals and waterways—falling in and drowning, an environmental accident, the dreaded Dome failure.

I checked my gloves again. The screen in my helmet said they were in perfect condition and helpfully listed every single person who had ever worn them before me, none of whom I had heard of. I thought of Ibra's broken hand, held together with synthetic bone and skin, hidden beneath the glove, and wondered what the sensor would say about that hand.

As Katharos piloted the skiff off the transport ship and steered it clear of the doors, I tried not to worry. Meanwhile, we rebalanced the ship for the strong winds outside. Dawith and Ibra argued about a plan that was the exact same plan until Dawith could take credit for it. Another twenty minutes by flight would reach the far edge of the Green Belt, where Ibra had prepared the ground for these trees on a previous journey, cut short by a weather change.

My primary job was to watch the weather; we could not rely on satellites and without someone watching every horizon, the weather analysis would not reliably run on its own. The rain might last days or hours, and the satellites wouldn't tell us which with any reliability, depending on how fast a dust storm brewed.

I watched out the rain-streaked windows, looking at Ibra's life work, shared with Katharos and Dawith. The artificial dunes broke up the Desert; the windbreak between the Dome and the Desert, the rain soaked grasses, the trees and the pools supporting them. Two or three temporary shelters shimmered bright electric blue against the landscape; encampments of Sunborn goatherds and shepherds who drifted from oasis to oasis to feed and water their flocks, picked the fruit Dawith and Ibra had spent years experimenting into sustainable crop. Ibra's voice echoed in memory: *It is the nature of the Sunborn to live under the sky, even when the wind blows dark. We must give them lives, too.* I had never asked what had driven Ibra to leave the homeland, to live in the Dome and never see a real sun or the stars. But I didn't have to ask. We had left the answer behind us in the Burned City.

§

The transport ship came down in wet sand with a crunch. As the crew drove the diggers and other equipment out into the sand, I checked my suit one last time. The first rain falling on me felt almost as strange as the sand underfoot; the readings on air quality flooded the visual interface of my helmet at once. The air was breathable, just hot, and like the rain, full of contaminants I had only a few hours to take in without damaging myself. The water hit me. Heavy, strange pellets of sensation rolled off my suit and made an erratic tapping noise against my helmet. I engaged the heaviest weight of my boots and dragged myself through the sand towards the windbreak Ibra had made some journey ago. Water was pooling there, waiting for us to come and plant.

Dawith and Ibra were arguing, which was normal. Dawith could not come into our house without arguing with somebody; I thought maybe it was a hobby. I listened with half an ear: where to put the trees, how to make the grass take to the wet soil, as the two marked up the map that overlaid my vision seamlessly with where to put things and in what order.

A minute or two after watching dots moving on the map, I decided to do the one thing I had trained to do my entire life. I knelt by the water, feeling the wet sand crunch under my knees through the skin-tight suit, and prayed. I whispered the words, not wanting to interrupt the public argument. There was no escaping except by turning off the public channel.

I shut my eyes to avoid distraction and prayed the words Ibra had taught me, the religion of the homeland I had never seen; to the Face of God who lived in the water, in the rain, in the Desert itself, in the trees we were about to plant and the grasses we were about to lay down.

Other students knelt by me, repeating the prayers of the Domeborn, Katharos' prayers. I joined those, too. I knew all the prayers. I loved the sound of them and had learned many over the years; the prayers of the homeland, the prayers of my home, even prayers to Faces of God no one remembered in the Dome anymore.

Over the sound of Dawith shouting grumpily about the correct way to plant a date palm, we prayed. Trees were about to root into the earth, about to become part of the Desert, about to whisper underground to each other in the divine language of trees. Birds would flock in the trees. Animals would come to eat. Strangers would pitch their tents alongside the water. The students and I consecrated the holy ground, to the Faces of God that would come in all these forms, and others unknown to us.

Dawith and Ibra finally stopped arguing. They came to the water that rippled with wind and rain, to pray with us.

"We'll be planting the trees first and then laying out the grasses," Dawith said, as if it was not the idea Ibra had suggested from the beginning. "Luyn, make yourself useful, mark the places the trees will go so the digger can make space to root them in."

I walked along the track the visual display of my helmet laid out for me, stomping large circles in the places where the digging machine would have to go into the wet ground. In the shelter of the liman, the wind was not so strong as it had been in the air. I was almost accustomed to being buffed around, gently bending my knees and swaying when a particularly strong gust came from an unexpected direction, and the spray of water that followed.

The digging machine drove out of the transport ship to follow after my footsteps. Some students set up an emergency shelter. Others slowly moved the trees out of the transport ship, singing the hymn of planting to the trees. At last they would progress from root balls to things in the ground, interconnected with all other living things.

I wondered if the archeologists sang hymns in the holy places of our ancestors.

After marking out the digging places with my boots, I disengaged the heaviest setting of my boots and skidded across the wet sand up onto the artificial dune my parent had built. I scanned the horizon, ignoring all the visual commands and instructions flashing past me as I focused on the weather in all four directions. The edge of the rain was farther than my human eyes could see, but the scanner knew things I didn't, and my whole job was to make sure we would know how long this rainstorm among the cycling storms might last. "We have six hours before the storm breaks!" I called through the communal frequency, watching every other direction. Six hours for us, a few more for Katharos, safe in the shelter of the dome that protected the Burned City. The satellites showed multiple storms, coming in waves. There would be another chance to plant the grass down.

I slid back down the liman and tried to figure out what would be the most help. I decided to focus on the emergency tent. A dust-storm following after such heavy rain was *unlikely*, but not impossible. Even if you survived being smothered by the dust, the contamination in the dust clouds would poison you slowly. I had read about that excruciating death hundreds of times. I had read about everything that could kill you. The terrible diseases that followed exposure to the sun or the rain, I knew well. The old wars had left the Desert a wasteland and the waters poisoned. Only trees and the sophisticated filtration from Ibra's homeland could slowly reclaim them.

The students and I set up the tent, and I scanned over and over that it was safe. Every opening was secure and closed correctly, airtight. The emergency rations were up to standard, every part of the medical pack was present. The air inside was purified, and I could have taken my helmet off, but I was getting used to it, and the constant stream of information of what everyone was doing and where they were was comforting, if overwhelming.

"You don't have to be so paranoid," our medic Layladin said wryly. After the disaster of Ibra's ship, and the Lost Eight, there were always contingencies. Always. "Everything was checked before we got here."

"I like knowing," I said, shrugging a little. I left Layladin and went back out to take in the weather, sliding my way back up the liman. It was easier now that the wind had died down. A good number of trees had already gone in, and the grass was rolling out on schedule for a six-hour timetable. The chatter of labor was just soothing noise in my ear as I watched the weather. I could see the edge of the stormhead, now, and the sunlight beyond it. It was the first time I had ever seen the real sun. I stopped short, watching the light shine behind the cloudhead. I had seen the artificial sun rise and set so many times I had expected the real sun to look the same. It didn't, though; it was a ruddy pollution red behind the gray stormhead, strange and surreal, beautiful and menacing at once.

"Look up," I said. Some of the Domeborn laughed—confused, delighted, a little afraid—and I heard Ibra laughing too. It was hard to believe the surreal sunlight could wound us, but I knew it wouldn't take long. I paid attention again to the weather readings. "Timeline's shortened. We have a half-hour before sunlight hits."

Sunlight, as beautiful as it was in a distant shimmer, meant no more work. It was too dangerous, with the sun heating the poisonous vapors in the air and the way it would sear flesh on even brief contact. Even the Sunborn herders wouldn't move their flocks by day; daylight was for the protection of the tents. But the rain didn't always fall at night, and once the rain stopped falling, we would have to wait until nightfall and hope the ground was still wet enough for planting, or wait for another storm to roll in some hours from now. These trees had been growing for years to be planted in this season's rains.

I slid back down into the wet sand, and hurried my way to help with the planting. Trying to speed the process wasn't easy. I poured fertilizer and shouted tree health readings as thick young trees went into the Desert sand, packed down and the wet sand covered. The trees were hard to move and too important to be left in the hands of a machine that would damage the branches or scratch the tree trunks. We had been working in teams of four; now we were down to two or three per tree, to get everything in the ground fast enough.

As Dawith and I worked side by side on one of the last two trees, the rain slowed to a drizzle, and then it stopped. "We have minutes!" Dawith shouted, hands steadying a tree trunk as I desperately shoveled sand over top of it. The professor's gloves flashed in front of my helmet, the display screen reading out messages.

Damaged, the screen warned in sun-red as Dawith darted off to the next of the tree trunks. The diagnostic ran almost faster than I could read it. *Exterior lining cracked.*

"Professor!" I shouted. Dawith ignored me as I ran behind, leaving the tree only half packed in, the student who had been working the ground on the other side bellowing in confusion, trying to finish what we'd left unfinished. "Professor!" I repeated as Dawith tried to get the last tree properly planted, hands grasping the round acacia trunk. "Your gloves!"

"Not now!" Dawith shouted. "The clouds are about to break!" To the student struggling to stomp the ground around the tree, Dawith shouted, "Get inside, Akila, I'll finish it!"

I shoved my way in front of the professor, stomping hard on the bright orange boots while engaging the heaviest gravity setting. The jolt of pain got some attention at last. "Your gloves," I repeated, almost screaming, "are cracked! They won't protect you from the sun!"

The clouds were beginning to part overhead. "Everyone inside!" Ibra shouted. "Dawith, leave it. You heard Luyn. Leave it!" The work was unfinished; not every tree had been covered properly. I grabbed the protective sheeting from Dawith's hands. "I'll finish." Our voices over the communal channel were a confusing cacophony of instructions, last directives, how to keep the trees from withering, frantic attempts to cover the ground, footsteps in the wet sand making chaotic trails. I kept stomping the earth into place, watching the clouds slowly stretch out into a thin film between us and the bright light beyond.

My helmet wouldn't stop counting the seconds to direct sunlight contact. As the heavy sheeting to protect the vulnerable tree roots was self-anchoring, I only needed to spread it across the wet earth around the tree and it would hold itself in place. I threw the sheeting down, heard the weights engage. Everyone else was already running. They moved so slow, their boots set to stomp the earth down with weight. "Change your boot settings!" I shouted, and I let my boots lift me along as I raced to join them. Ibra stood at the door of the shelter, determined to be the last.

The sun broke from behind the clouds, dazzling me with its intensity. The light blinded me as it caught against the pool of water, illuminating into a giant ruddy mirror just as I skidded into the tent. The last sign of it I saw was orange-red light glaring bright off all the wet sand, Ibra's wet helmet glowing like fire in the sudden flush of light as the door shut. The pneumatic seal sucked in tight and left us with familiar artificial yellow-white lighting.

In the tent, Layladin had stripped the gloves off Dawith's hands. "Soaked," the medic scolded, running a scanner across the professor's hands. "How didn't you notice? Didn't you check your suit before you put it on?"

"I thought the wetness inside was sweat," Dawith said, hands ruddy and swollen out of the gloves. I had never seen chemical burns before and tried not to stare. Indomitable Dawith was apologizing. I had not seen Dawith so distressed since Ibra's disappearance, and that had been so long ago sometimes I felt I had imagined it. "With the shortened timetable, there was no room for delays. I thought—"

Layladin cut Dawith off. "We've caught it just in time. A course of medication and rest and your hands should recover from the pollutants in the rain. You can't go out in those gloves again. They're worse than rubbish. Completely contaminated. You're lucky. You'll have to consult the rest of this run; if I catch you lifting anything. . . ."

"This work is too important," Dawith replied, some of the old bluster back, as if the suggestion offended. "I'll stay inside and run diagnostics. I didn't leave my family and green trees for the work to be interrupted before it's finished."

Exhausted, I sat down by the door. Everyone else was decontaminating their suits and stripping down, but even those motions were too much for me. I could only think of all the disasters we had barely averted.

Carefully, Ibra removed the bright orange helmet, still wet, and crouched down next to me. "You okay?"

"Just tired," I lied. "When the next storm rolls in we'll have to go back out there and plant the grasses. This is just one site, and you have three more to visit. How do you do this all the time?"

Ibra smiled. "Wait till we go check the levels at some of the older sites.

You'll see then. It's worth it, to see the Desert bloom. Are you sure you want to be an archeologist like Katharos? You're pretty good at this. You probably saved Dawith's hands. Dawith would have stayed until it was finished. Dawith is always last."

I could see tension lines around those familiar brown eyes as Ibra watched me, as if the smile wouldn't quite stick. How strange it would have been for the Desert to burn the hands of both architects of the Green Belt. I felt chilled, and suddenly wanted to pray, but didn't know what Face of God I wanted to call to, Ibra's or Dawith's or some other.

I smiled at Ibra, trying to reassure myself. "We'll see if I change my mind when I've seen the finished product."

"The work is never finished," Ibra replied solemnly, reaching for my hand. Our contaminated-glove fingers met, but I felt the familiar tight squeeze through the glove just the same as it had been since childhood, the fingers that were not quite like everyone else's. "But at least it is begun. Come on, let's get you unsuited and put some food in you, you look like you've seen a ghost."

As the students ate and Dawith watched the weather radar with rain-swollen hands, Ibra and I sat together in quiet, content to wait as sunlight made the Desert bloom outside.

The Seven Species

Aleksei Valentín

Skeletal, fruitless trees litter the world
with fallow fields, nothing left for widows and orphans to glean.
But I was given a sacred task:
a hopeless one, it seemed,
when the desert blew across gentle green places
we had carved from her edges and made fruitful,
as if demanding back the space we had only ever borrowed.
Of everyone, I was chosen, my name the ordained sign:

עֲרָבָה, Arava, willow and desert,
among the plants of Sukkot, chosen for beauty,
gathered with prayers for water, filled with secrets,
the miracle of living exposed and vulnerable yet unharmed.

It took years for the rains to come again, for the crisis to pass,
and for people to return to the land, bearing tools ready for farming,
newly developed and prepared to sway with the unsteady world.
The desert has stepped back, and at last I have come forward.
I have held the crimson box of holy treasure
for longer than any lifetime,
long generations bound in exile,
this land nothing but a dream for many, but my dreams were different.
Given the years and merits of the Patriarchs,
I alone remember the shade of ancient trees.

We are a people of memory
so I have carried the kernels of what sustains us,
seven precious seeds:
wheat, barley, grape, fig, pomegranate, olive, and date.

I carry them in a sacred box, like the Aron haBrit,
but this covenant is with the land of our ancestors,
with our people and all we once knew.
The land must be made green again, not with new crops,
but with these crops, what grows to feed the soul of Israel.

Wheat, to feed and nourish the human soul and body.
Barley, to feed our animals and our animal instincts that bind us to the earth.
Grape, to make wine and make joy,
to bring color and revelation to the world.
Fig, to hold us together as a people and know the world,
to put our souls to the task of life.
Pomegranate, to be filled with deeds of goodness and to rejoice in beauty.
Olive, to struggle with God, and when pressed, yield liquid gold of faith.
Date, to remind us it takes time to blossom,
but we will come forth in our hour of peace.

I have carried this box of holiness and wisdom,
sometimes light as air, sometimes heavy as guilt,
as everyone I know passes away
and my people become beloved strangers to me.
Still I remain, chosen to remember what cannot be forgotten.

As the desert blooms again, as my people dig the earth,
I know the box was never mine to keep, only to tend,
to give away, ancient as the oldest date palm.
Let my words be sweet, let us bend to become fruitful,
let Israel be sustained by her blessed gifts of spirit into body
bringing holy light to soil so that even this dry dust becomes a sacred thing.

When the crops flourish from the seed,
when sanctity and memory ripen on the trees,
I know my charge is lifted. I have been the priestess of green memory,
serving the spirit of God as She hovered over us in our fear and hunger,
and held us safe until it turned to us once more
to make Israel a green land, faith and wisdom planted on the same tree
holy earth fed by irrigation systems,
and watched with technology I am too tired to understand.

I am the oldest now, and I am ready.
I am ready to take my turn beneath the soil,
to rest beneath the Mount of Olives,
and leave my holy task to bloom above me, splendor once again.

The Trees Between

Karyn L. Stecyk

The initial jerk from the primary wave had been stronger than anticipated and sent Miraiha careening into a sapling for support. The shock made her heart skip a beat, but feeling the force in this world was a promising sign.

"Did it work?" Miraiha wondered aloud.

"Felt like it," Trent said inside her head.

She jumped at his voice. Miraiha didn't realize she had sent her thoughts through the grove's communications channel. A communion of people and link-trees, she had relayed her feelings to everything. She scolded herself. A leader voicing doubts in a time of crisis was never good. She wrung her hands and suddenly realized how cold her fingers were.

"Rosela," Miraiha said, willing authority back into her tone. "Check the outer ring for seismic recordings."

"On it."

"Leaves still online?" Miraiha sent the query through New Gaia, the artificial reality that absorbed the seismic energy, and to the others in the grove's network. This was the first true field test of seismic disaster mitigation, and she wasn't sure how well the auxiliary systems would hold.

She crossed her fingers. Seismologists had forecast the superquake for decades. The last event flattened sixty percent of the city and took two hundred thousand lives, and yet the city did nothing more than implement stricter building codes. She imagined the quake's tendrils thrusting through water and soil, uprooting everything, bent on destroying their homes once and for all. Thinking about failure wrung her gut like a wet cloth.

Status reports from each of the seven hundred ash trees linked to their individual hosts trickled into *Yggdrasil,* Miraiha's vessel, and therefore into her consciousness. All canopies continued recycling run-off gases from the city and nearby farms and pumping sulfur into the atmosphere. Although an important system, its simplicity contrasted with the technological complexities of the grove's primary functions: to absorb and redirect seismic energy into an alternate reality.

Trent opened a private channel between him and Miraiha. "Listen, Miraiha, don't worry so much. If Cradle's canopies can survive the typhoons we've been getting, they can survive this."

"Quakes can do damage where you least expect it."

Trent sighed. "Yes, we understand that. That day never fades." Miraiha didn't want to remember. "That's why I'm here. We're not risking our lives blindly. We fought alongside you for years. We believe in this. And we believe in you. You need to, too."

Miraiha considered his words. The three of them together, she, Trent, and Rosela, had realized they could never prevent a fault from slipping but could always be more prepared. The government had been skeptical, but multi-functionality was the key to securing land and funding: atmospheric treatments via leaves, combined with a sprawling root system, a lattice that hindered liquefaction and held both soil and solid rock together. She had spearheaded the sowing of Sisters' Cradle, the first grove, just north of the reclaimed island peninsula and encapsulating the city. When they had engineered the link-trees, she didn't doubt their effectiveness. Why did she now?

"You're right," Miraiha sighed. "I need to refocus. *Yggdrasil*—Cradle— depends on me. Thanks for the reminder."

"We all depend on you, but don't forget this relationship is mutual." His voice was an early sunrise, light and promising. Miraiha could picture his gentle smile. "I'm always here to pass tea if you need me, Mirai."

Miraiha chuckled. During their endless nights in study rooms as students, they'd pass around a pot of tea—but only when someone hit a mental wall or looked about to fall asleep. She recalled one exhausting night when Trent had kept passing to her as a joke, and their fingers lingered on the handle longer than usual.

"Great news," Rosela announced, voice teeming with elation. Miraiha's pensiveness fell away and she thanked Trent for his support. "No seismic activity registered at any points beyond the grove. Complete mitigation."

"Excellent," Miraiha said with a smile. "We might just pull this off."

"Roger that."

With the communication channels quieted, Miraiha relaxed.

Deep in meditation within *Yggdrasil*'s pod, she re-centered herself. Sisters' Cradle had been successful in redirecting the ground's innate power into New Gaia. This time, the seismic waves had met resistance, a resistance led by the sacred union of Miraiha and her link-tree. The waves reared back in disgust before being sucked away into other channels where damage was minimized. Despite being weakened from drought, the grove was proving its worth, proving that meaningful bonds within and between worlds could still be formed.

No longer would roadways fall atop one another, crushing civilians stuck in the wrong place at the wrong time. The ground wouldn't swallow buildings or topple them like dominos. This time, her family would be safe—everyone's families would be safe. The city would breathe easy, not gasp for air laden with dust and embers and tears.

Miraiha looked out over the sun-kissed hills that rolled into grasslands and verdurous mountains, which parted just enough to flash the shimmering sea beyond, and walked down to the damp sand trimming the stream. The landscape she had spent months programming, all the while aware of its imminent destruction. Once the seismic energy was absorbed by the link-trees, her code's functions would transform it to pass through the channels connecting to New Gaia. There, the energy would be released. A tinge of guilt crawled through her insides. She questioned why she would destroy the one world she could explore free of hoverchairs or robotic appendages that made her skin itch. A world untouched by pollution with a horizon unbroken by cityscapes. New Gaia was as much Cradle's world as it was hers, and it was soon to be ravaged by the natural disasters her primary world could no longer endure. She hoped the grove understood and that their bond of trust wouldn't waver.

Yet nature denied direct dissolution of its wild forces, and there was no other choice but to channel the raw seismic energy into New Gaia. Energy required space to run free as nature intended; New Gaia could provide.

Stream water lapped at Miraiha's toes. The cool sensation was one she could only feel here. She caught herself and shunted the emotions aside to brace her body and mind for the secondary and subsequent surface waves. She willed her comrades to do the same. Seismology studies taught her that the most violent and destructive components of the quake had yet to come.

The secondary seismic wave sheared the rock, twisted the grove's roots, strained them. The shaking threatened to tear Miraiha from her trance, but she sank deeper into *Yggdrasil* and fought back the dread rumbling in her core. Her focus was imperative to transferring the energy to New Gaia. If she faltered, the connection could break. And she wasn't certain the others could keep the alternate world spinning without her. She had designed it, had a flawless synchronicity with it that her companions envied.

The surface waves swung the planet's crust side-to-side. Miraiha was thrown off balance and a full step into the stream. Cold water splashed up her thighs. Pebbles jittered across the ground as it moaned, cracked, and ruptured before her eyes. The image was replaced with memories of splitting cement and screeching metal. Memories of being pinned beneath fallen ceiling and unable to reach—

She supported herself against a boulder protruding from the bank and tried to regain a crystalline state of being. The spiritual, physical, and emotional draw made her veins magma. The same sensation consumed

Cradle's root system.

Within the vastness of her consciousness, a connection severed—a tree snapped, its host crushed by the shearing forces. Despite being only one of hundreds, the loss was a knee to the gut. The network in that region flickered, but Rosela and Trent bridged the gap.

"How did—" Miraiha started, impressed at their reflexes. "Never mind. Is the connection stable?"

"Trying to keep it that way," said Trent. Each word was a standalone pulse.

"Could use an extra link in kyu-twelve fourteen-eff," Rosela said, voice strained.

Amid the continuous tremors, trees both north and south of the endangered quadrant offered their support. In the primary world, roots shot toward each other, coiling into thick braids and spinning nets to catch the propagating waves. Miraiha would have stretched *Yggdrasil* as well, but being the heart of the grove mandated her focus remain where it was.

Brief moments of stillness allowed the link-trees and their partners to catch their breath and reconnect. Rolling waves threw ground both horizontal and vertical. Yet despite their intensity, the grove met them with a peaceful calm. Rather than stifle it, Sisters' Cradle acknowledged and channeled the planet's stress and anger. It was a practice in acceptance long overdue.

As the final currents subsided, Miraiha sat on the grass in a semi-circle of violet flowers. She reached out to both worlds. Her lips parted in exultation. She offered understanding and oneness.

"Peace, harmony, serenity, I pledge," the words came in ceremonial drumbeats, a mantra. "With all my being, everything I was, am, and will be, I swear to do whatever necessary to reverse the damage wreaked by my ancestors. Again together, we will thrive. A single harmonious spirit."

Her energy graced New Gaia's clouds and soothed its open wounds. It oozed from *Yggdrasil*'s roots and canopy, seeped into soil and air far beyond. She could feel the grove's collective soul beat within her. Others were with her, shared her promise. She repeated the words over and over.

"Peace, harmony, serenity, I pledge. . . ."

§

Something twitched at the edge of Miraiha's mind. A slight tapping. She recognized the movement as outside New Gaia, but let it float by, labeling it inconsequential. While awaiting the aftershocks, she wondered whether their efforts had been enough to keep their city and people alive. The tapping continued, exploding into a loud knocking she could no longer ignore.

Sitting in the pod in the center of her link-tree, Miraiha's eyes shot open. The purple blossoms, whispering stream, luscious mountains, and broken ground—vanished. They were replaced by fibrous walls coated in sleek link-conductivity film. The xylem and phloem carrying nutrients for the tree's biological components wrapped around the pod like arteries circling a heart. They tangled with thick electrical cables. An array of orange holo-images spanned before her, showing data from the grove and the seismic recordings from all stations and drones in the region that Rosela had forwarded to her.

Another thud sounded behind her. Drenched in sweat that curled her dark hair and stung her eyes, she turned toward the sound. *Yggdrasil* didn't like visitors. Communion with a link-tree was sacred; one tree, one person. Balance was key. She twisted a fleshy growth on the floor and the hatch unlocked.

"This had better be important," Miraiha growled, but fatigue tainted the command of her voice.

"Fire," Miraiha's aunt, Nell, said. Exasperation cross-hatched her face. "There's a fire encroaching. Couldn't reach you on normal channels. Came as fast as I could. Evacuation's been issued for the whole area. You can't stay here."

"A fire? Did we fail?"

"Against the quake? No. The city stands strong as ever. For now." She wiped at her brow. "Fire's coming from the hills."

Miraiha shook her head. "I can't abandon Sisters' Cradle. There'll be aftershocks. We must mitigate them."

"The whole grove will burn down."

Miraiha met her aunt's gaze. Distress glazed her eyes. She knew what she was thinking, what she was remembering. Miraiha wet her lips. "This fire, did the quake start it? Did a remote power line break?"

"We don't know what sparked it, could have been anything in this drought—but it doesn't matter. We have to evacuate."

"I can't do that," Miraiha said, returning her attention to the data in front of her. "This is my place. I won't let *Yggdrasil* burn. I can't let the city fall. You said yourself that it still stands. How do you expect us to just pack up and leave now? The grove cannot stand on its own."

"How much more do you want to lose, Mirai?"

Her heart lodged between her ribs. Flashes of her sister's lifeless body being pulled from rubble burned into her head. She could hear her father's panicked shouts for everyone to take cover. The phantom limb pain she thought she had long since overcome returned. She looked down at where her legs should be.

Nell swallowed. "You're all I have left."

The ground trembled. Miraiha separated a sliver of her consciousness from her whole and let it seep into the tree. A minor tremor for now, but that didn't mean larger ones weren't on the way.

"This grove is all we have left," Miraiha said, her voice a sharp breeze. "Sisters' Cradle is our key to salvation. We ravaged too much. Without making amends, we will be wiped away. A mass cleansing we've already witnessed the beginnings of. The Red Ring eruptions, the Tallis islands being swallowed by the boiling sea. If we prove Cradle's worth here, we can plant groves across the globe."

"Do you still think we can reverse all this?"

"Have to try."

"If the fire doesn't change course—"

"Then it doesn't change course," Miraiha said.

"But—"

"Please, leave now while you can. I will be fine."

"How can you say that? These trees will burn, just like all the others."

"That remains to be seen." Miraiha sighed. "Please, Aunt, go. The grove calls me. I must concentrate."

"Mirai, please."

Miraiha lifted a hand and started to settle herself back into the grove. She could already see New Gaia's mountains forming inside her mind.

"I don't want to drag you out of here."

"Then don't. I'm needed here."

Nell's hand gripped Miraiha's shoulder. The physical contact turned the mountains to haze and brought her back to the pod just as Nell started to haul her up under her armpits.

"Let go—" Anger erupted from Miraiha. She flailed, cursing and baring her teeth. Her livid rage cared little of her aunt's good intentions.

"Mirai, please."

But Miraiha's heart was too choked by Nell's imposition to hear the plea. Too overwhelmed with indignation to want to hear it.

Yggdrasil called to her, alarmed at her unannounced disconnection and sensing her pain. The tree's serenity seeped into her, reminded her where she was, what she had left to do. It promised her roots and reach beyond her physical body.

Miraiha ceased her struggle and fused her consciousness back into the tree. She pulled a cord from the pod's wall, molding it into an extension of her will. At Miraiha's command, the cord took Nell by the ankle and yanked hard. Nell released Miraiha, and threw her arms out to catch herself. She blinked, mouth agape. A second cable removed itself from the wall and joined the first in dragging the woman out of the pod. Nell's face contorted, she mouthed something, but Miraiha wasn't listening.

"I'll meet you at the dome." Miraiha sealed the hatch.

§

"Everything all right over there?" As soon as Miraiha's feet touched grass again, Rosela's voice encompassed her.

"We have a problem," Miraiha broadcast to the entire grove. She assessed the network's stability following the roaring of another aftershock. New Gaia bellowed as it swallowed.

"Severity?"

Miraiha filled them in to the threat.

There was no swearing or angry muttering, only silent acceptance. They had gambled once with testing Sisters' Cradle against a superquake, and now she asked them to do it again. Holding the planet's crust together was what the trees had been designed for, not playing with fire.

Miraiha stared out over the splintered landscape. The ground was warped like crumpled paper, but aside from some uprooted trees, the world was still beautiful. It was transformed, fissured, but still the world she had generated. The low sun dipped the sky in pink and red; it was a sunset that no longer existed in the primary reality. This was the type of world they fought to restore.

Miraiha traveled through Cradle's surface-level roots in search of the fire. Even for sensors that didn't have such perception in their original design, she could feel the radiating heat. The fire was still far to the east, but in this drought, fire spread fast. She established a link to satellite imagery and ran ETA calculations.

"Priority remains on nullifying aftershocks," Miraiha said. "I'm sending the fire's estimated time of arrival and projected path. Data will be updated as I receive it."

Trent materialized on a mound of soil before her. His narrow face and cool eyes regarded her.

"This is my private place, Trent." Miraiha forced down a flash of irritation. "We agreed to respect each other's abodes."

"And I do," he said. "I wanted to speak with you."

"The grove connects us as well as we can ever be."

He looked guilty. "Guess I'm still sometimes a sucker for seeing is believing."

"Fine," Miraiha sighed, trying to hide the beginnings of a smile. "But I'm speaking to everyone."

Trent sat and ran his fingers through the grass. She was pretty certain he was taller here than he was in primary reality. He had never peeked into her space before, but it didn't bother her as much as she expected it to. Classmates for years before becoming colleagues, he understood her better than anyone. If his intuition told him to manifest here, she trusted it was for good reason.

"Preliminary assessment—combined with information from an outside source—indicates that our efforts against the quake were successful." Miraiha paced as she spoke into the air, as if the clouds carried her voice to the others positioned in their own sanctuaries. "But we must remain vigilant. If this fire indeed threatens Cradle, we will meet it just as we did this quake."

Concern came from a distant link-tree. "But Cradle was not designed—"

"We will adapt," Miraiha said with resolution, despite still grasping for a tangible plan. "If we are firm in our intention, we can prevail."

Another voice tried to argue but Miraiha cut it short as well. There was no time to entertain doubt.

"Everyone, look around you," Miraiha said. "We just transferred a quake from one world to another. How many lives did we save? How many hundreds of thousands—if not millions—more will we save with future iterations of this project? Right now, we have two goals: to protect our city and to keep Cradle safe."

"Safe against a wildfire?" The skepticism came from many.

"Yes, I understand the concern," Miraiha said, crossing her arms. "But if the fire-fighting forces could not contain and redirect it, we're the city's last defense. It is not a matter of trying but of doing." She took a steadying breath and collected her thoughts. A solution began to emerge. "Everyone, stretch roots toward the surface and calibrate pores to ex-seventeen-point-five-five-nine. We'll see if we can attack hotspots. And reprogram solar drains to absorb the fire's heat, but seal all moisture pores. In this drought, we can't afford to lose any water."

"And of course the new irrigation system isn't online until next week," Rosela said. Her voice creaked with nerves.

"Poor timing, yes. But there's nothing we can do about it now. We must use what we have. If we simultaneously pull from the roots and solar drains, our focus should be sufficient to channel the fire's energy into New Gaia. Just like we did with the quake."

Trent nodded to himself. "Perhaps you are right. Energy is energy."

"This year is the driest in recorded history. This fire would not threaten us had we not set the stage. We must share in the responsibility."

The grove agreed. It wasn't a subject of debate.

"Remember, we are all one," she said. "As one, we pledged to save this planet. If we abandon our promise now, we leave Cradle and our city to burn to ash. We shielded our city from disaster once; there is no reason we cannot do it again. Cradle is strong. New Gaia is strong. We are strong. As one, we can do this."

Murmurs of agreement rippled through the grove.

Miraiha addressed Trent alone. "Now's not quite the time for words, Trent, but if you have them, speak quick."

"You answered my main question." He crossed his legs and cupped his hands in his lap. "Not that I'm complaining, but does it not bother you to destroy this world just to save our immediate one?"

"I thought it would," Miraiha said, sitting next to him. "But I realize these natural events only add texture to the landscape. It's a part of nature. Perhaps when the collective becomes one with nature again, we can embrace these changes for what they are without fearing extinction. Perhaps more groves like Cradle will help us realize this."

"It would be unnatural for us to live indefinitely."

"It would," she said as she rolled a blade of grass between her fingers. "But perhaps we can live in harmony until that time."

"I hope we will be around to see it," Trent said.

"Further motivation to push for change."

A mild tremor shook the ground.

"Guess that's our cue," Trent said, pressing his palms to the dirt and splaying his fingers. He smiled at Miraiha. "Tea in Blay Gardens once this is all done?"

He disappeared before she could respond, but not before color flushed her cheeks. Amid chaos, he thought of tea. A warm cup did sound nice. And Blay Gardens had a reputation of steeping to perfection. For a second, she wondered whether he intended them to share a pot, then settled into concentration. The air smelled like sweet chamomile, and it pulled a smile from her lips.

§

The next aftershock was aggressive. The planet was a wild beast, shaking to rid itself of the people on its back. Miraiha remained seated to avoid losing her balance, had to keep at bay the inkling fear of another tree snapping free. Knowing what to feel for, she found strain in three quadrants. Fatigue was beginning to settle in.

She sent private commands to the neighboring trees, urged them to offer whatever assistance they could. The ground continued to roar, but Sisters' Cradle stood tall in defiance. The stress in the quadrants dissipated, and Miraiha breathed easy. The subsequent aftershocks disturbed little more than sand.

Another hour passed before flames frisked the first leaves. Regardless of the time they had to prepare for the encounter, the fire snatched and devoured the first line of trees. It was too quick. They fought with desperate vigor, but the fire and its intense heat brought flickers of doubt as it encroached. Doubt that bled into the link-trees and their hosts like poison, evoking fear from the core of ego. Many succumbed to terror and despair. All burned with their vessels. The rest of the grove felt their panic, their dying thoughts, heard unbridled screams of pain. Their strength hadn't been enough. Urgent requests for reassessment rang out through New Gaia, which, despite multiple spikes in surface temperature, saw no fire of its own. Grief conspired with the thought of having condemned the entire grove and the city it swore to protect to their deaths, sending Miraiha's heart and stomach into turmoil. She choked trying to swallow rising bile.

Miraiha couldn't understand what had gone wrong. They had done well against the quake. They knew exactly when, and where, to focus on the fire. She ran through the possibility that it came down to mechanical design: the fact that trees burned. She asked *Yggdrasil* for insight, but it had none to offer. Its branches drooped in apology.

"Miraiha." Rosela and Trent's voices hung in the air.

"I know," Miraiha said. "I'm thinking."

"Synchronicity was too low," Trent said. "They were distracted—eight nearly disconnected. Should we reallocate resources to the front?"

Miraiha ran the rough calculations. "Yes, let's try that."

"Sending protocol then."

Those who weren't on the front line allocated sixty-five percent of their resources to those who were. Miraiha commandeered the system. Flames shivered in protest. New Gaia saw sparks. Temperature climbed, then crashed as the hosts jerked in response to the ignition of leaves and branches. The wind tossed embers high into canopies, raining fire from above. Without the hosts' dedication, the support from the rest of the grove failed. Trees, and all within them, roasted, burst open like chestnuts.

Miraiha slipped into the space of one of the endangered hosts. She couldn't help him, but she could gain insight into what was going wrong. His pod was a chamber of smoke and body odor that brought tears to her eyes. From here, she could feel beyond the tree's exterior. What she saw choked her. The sheer audacity of fire taller than the trees themselves, and the knowledge that trees fell to flame, broke the hosts. The image coaxed thoughts of mortality. Screamed for them.

She returned to the stream in New Gaia. Unless substantially weakened, it would take them all. She dipped her hands into the water, relished in its coolness, as she searched for solutions. They needed an army of water or sand bombers. Barriers to keep the fire from eating the trees before they could transfer its energy. She splashed the stream water into her face, settled her attention to follow each path of water that drained down her chin. They dripped into her hands and pooled.

She smiled at the small ocean in her hands as its water soaked into her skin. The water was as much energy as everything. New Gaia would still save them.

§

It was a curious sight from outside. Flames bent backwards, twisting away from the very matter they craved. Torrents of water rushed from invisible pores, beat back the flames and soaked the ground. Oxygen voids shrunk the tallest of flames back below the canopies. Everything moved in concert.

Miraiha stood on a cliff overlooking the ocean. Before her, the visual of churning water helped her focus. Behind her, grasslands spontaneously combusted. The heat at her back was reassurance she no longer needed. Cradle's collective felt all. Controlled all activity.

Canopy leaves were reprogrammed to suck oxygen into New Gaia; moisture pores were reopened and New Gaia's oceans fell like sweat from the trees; and the excess water pounding into the soil was reabsorbed and cycled back up to drench the flames again. The drained fire could now be harnessed and pulled toward New Gaia's empty terrain.

Miraiha's legs wobbled where she stood. Redirecting bursts of seismic energy had been a challenge. Moving seas was another. Her exhaustion from the primary reality manifesting here as well was not a good sign.

But as oxygen fell in one world and grew in the other, the fire learned where it could survive and began to escort itself to New Gaia. Trent alerted her to the shift, herself too preoccupied to notice. That was one burden alleviated. Her legs ceased shaking, but she still dropped to the ground. For the remainder of the exercise, she sat cross-legged, sea foam spraying in her face and hair, cast high by swirling tides.

The threat to the grove was extinguished. Cries of rejoicing rang through New Gaia's sky like bird songs.

"Of course Cradle and New Gaia's connection is omnidirectional," Miraiha mumbled to herself. "Everything is . . . so delusional to have not thought of it sooner."

"Don't be so harsh on yourself," Rosela said.

Miraiha cursed. Had she broadcast her thoughts again?

"At least you realized it. We were all distracted and too focused on removing, not adding."

"We can't get everything right the first time," Trent said.

Miraiha sighed and nodded.

While others retired for well-deserved rest, Miraiha lingered. New Gaia's land blazed lavishing reds and oranges, painting the sky with smoke that twisted the final moments of sunset somehow more beautiful. Here, only land was ravaged. She wondered what would have befallen the city had Sisters' Cradle not existed. But it wasn't something she wanted to imagine. There was no point to such musings anyway, not when they had succeeded.

This was the first step to restoring harmony. The next—she smiled— was tea.

Boltzmann Brain

Kristine Ong Muslim

We hope you are out there, and you are reading this message. We are broadcasting from 78°14'09"N 15°29'29"E, the Svalbard Global Seed Vault. On this day 70 years ago, the planet's last polar bear, Arturo, died, his body freed at last, after 22 years of slowly going insane from the sweltering heat and unremitting stress of captivity inside a concrete pit at Argentina's Mendoza Zoological Park. On this day 85 years ago, collared, chained, drugged, and used as a mascot for the torch ceremony of the second to the last Olympic Games, one of the last remaining jaguars in the world was gunned down when it attempted to escape from the clutches of people wanting to take selfies with it. On this day 92 years ago, the last remaining species of *Ceratotherium simum cottoni,* the magnificent northern white rhinoceros, was killed by a poacher who bribed one of the guards in a nature reserve in Sudan. And on this day 150 years ago, we were like you in many ways—either well-dressed in one of the corporate offices in one of the world's megacities or hunched in capitalist enclaves toiling to earn our hourly wage—kidding ourselves again and again that the human race was worthy of celebration.

We are now preparing the deployment of a robotic feeler to the nature park of Phrumsengla in Bhutan. Thick smoke has been spotted by an aerial go by courtesy of newly repaired Hover-567. The smoke may be from a human encampment. We hope that this mission will yield something, someone. Numerous bees and butterflies are sighted in and around Phrumsengla. Pollination activity is proceeding as expected for a protracted summer.

Meanwhile, one of the lateral heat-sensing screens shows a walrus and its calves two miles from here. They seem to be frolicking in the snow. They can laze all they want in this infinity of cool reflective whiteness. Nobody will ever hurt them again.

It is still relatively dark outside the vault. It is always relatively dark.

§

We hope you are out there, and you are reading this message. We are broadcasting from 78°14'09"N 15°29'29"E, the Svalbard Global Seed Vault.

On this day 61 years ago, the Amazon carbon sink had failed. It failed permanently. The primeval rainforest, which once drew atmospheric carbon for storage in its soil or trees, was emitting more greenhouse gases than it could take in. On this day 102 years ago, it had been discovered too late that all the plastic wastes dumped into what was formerly known as the United Kingdom were washed into the Arctic region within two years. Autopsy results showed that all marine animals collected in that region for the next one hundred years hence had plastic inside of them. And on this day 98 years ago, the melting of the permafrost in Siberia was finally kicked off by years and years of massive deforestation. Subterranean craters were revealed once the trees that insulated the frozen ground for millions of years were removed. With these craters came the release of methane into the atmosphere, effectively accelerating global warming.

Then the eventual megaslump, the precession of the Earth's axis from the melting of Antarctic and Greenland ice sheets, the dominos that mark all possible paths to extinction quietly falling in place. Then came the isolated tribe in Peru, driven from their native land by a four-day wildfire. Four days in the city square, and they succumbed to various illnesses as they had not developed immunity nor have been vaccinated against even the most ordinary of diseases. One even contracted common cold and ended up coughing up lung tissues, throat swollen and bloodied, until he died. All in all, 16 out of the 89 members of the Peruvian indigenous tribe survived.

Remember how it all started in the once frozen north. Remember the thawing of the permafrost that bared all—the anthrax outbreak in Russia and then the mutation and subsequent spread of the once dormant 50,000-year-old *Mollivirus sibericum* virus, first discovered close to Chukotka, in East Siberia, the subsequent deaths of women. Patient Zero was Dr. Emilia Gattskill of the State of the Global Climate Research Center. Survivors of the deadly disease, who were mostly men, were ultimately felled by extreme weather disturbances and the drought from the eternal summer in the few yet-to-be submerged habitable parts of the world.

Right now, we look inside the twentieth floor of an apartment building submerged from 18 stories down. Inside a living room, there's a framed poster of a wind turbine whose nacelle and rotor blade are on fire. Atop the turbine are two men, their sole exit blocked by the roaring fire. They are embracing, waiting for the flames to engulf them. Black mold has taken over the living room, the bedroom, everything.

Days like these, we wish we could pat a domestic dog for comfort. We wish we had conventional hands to pat a domestic dog. But a body with conventional hands—the human body—is a ruinous construct, prone to injury and susceptible to the ravages of time.

Are you out there reading this?

§

We hope you are out there, and you are reading this message. We are broadcasting from 78°14'09"N 15°29'29"E, the Svalbard Global Seed Vault. On this day 119 years ago, the Syrian civil war saw the bloody takeover of Aleppo. On this day 143 years ago, Heinrich Himmler bit into a cyanide pill a day before his scheduled interrogation for war crimes. And on this day 123 years ago, over 1,000 members of the Glorious Dawn cult, hastening their journey to a promised utopia, committed mass suicide by drinking cyanide-laced purple Kool-Aid.

At the slope of Mt. Chimborazo in Ecuador, we maintain a base camp. Thankfully, it is still fully operational after all this time. A long time ago, it was built for a geoengineering project that aimed to regulate the earth's climate by aerial spraying of aerosol. The aerosol droplets were believed to reduce ground solar radiation. By then, the geoengineering project was already too late in making any difference to the rising global temperature. The base camp has just sent its weekly readouts. As usual, atmospheric and ground readings are consistent with the projections of the Copenhagen Diagnosis. Microscopic extremophiles, the only signs of life, teem on the surface of rocks.

Are you still out there? Let us know.

§

We hope you are out there, and you are reading this message. We are broadcasting from 78°14'09"N 15°29'29"E, the Svalbard Global Seed Vault. On this day 286 years ago, Iqbal Masih was born. Iqbal Masih was a bonded child laborer in Pakistan. When he was ten years old, he escaped from the carpet factory where he had to work in order to pay off his family's loan. Then he helped release more than 3,000 children from illegal slavery in Pakistan before he was murdered at age twelve. On this day 187 years ago, South Korea had at last, although a century too late to spare millions of dogs, put an end to its Boknal dog meat festival. Spain followed but not soon enough, putting an end to its Toro de la Vega bullfighting tradition. And on this day 154 years ago, five firemen put out the fires in a nuclear reactor in Chernobyl. They knew that no protective suit in the world could protect them from the radiation around the reactor. They died painful deaths within 36 hours of exiting the nuclear power plant, successful in preventing catastrophic effects of the meltdown.

Today, a manual probe has parachuted and safely touched down at Tristan de Cunha. We remotely guided it to check the houses for human survivors. None. This far-flung place in the southern Atlantic Ocean once had a maximum total population of 272 people. Tomorrow—still on schedule—we'll make a sweep of the Huascarán National Park in Peru. We hope to find you there. If not, we will try again. Next stop is the Tanggula Mountains of Tibet.

Hope, hope is a good thing. We hope to see you soon.

Solar Flare

Christine Moleski

Sunvault

Fairy Tales & Other Species of Life

Chloe N. Clark

Under the gaze of snakes and spiders
we dip our fingers into soil
dig deep enough to feel the dirt
pulsing against our skin

Once upon a time someone said
and we all turned to listen
because stories beg to be heard
because in fairy tales the water
heals and the forests are filled
with mothers returned as trees

Once upon a time this land
was filled with life once upon
a time the roots of trees stayed
firm in soil and babies were born
squalling for mothers and they
were sung lullabies and everyone

Hush someone else said we don't
want to hear what has been we need
to hear what is coming

And we looked up to the stars
to the deafening dark and the spiders
and the snakes were just shadows
things used to be feared that now
were just missed

We dug deep and pushed seeds
from locked away vaults
into the earth so gentle we pushed
and we wondered if the past
could be reborn

And we whispered to the not
yet born grow
grow
once upon a time you would
grow

The Road to the Sea

Lavie Tidhar

One autumn when I was old enough, my mother took me with her and the other salvagers to see the sea. I had gone with them before, on shorter journeys across the Land, once making it as far away as Suf, where they harvest the sun. But never that far, never to the old cities by the ocean, never to the sea that squatted like a beast beyond the shore, grey-blue and ever mutable, a foreign world much larger than the Land, in which all things were possible and all things, I thought, could be true.

When the world changed and the moon was hurt and our people came to the Land, the ocean remained. It only grew. Old grandma Toffle had an ancient book of sea creatures, and I would spend the winter months curled by the fireplace in my father's lap, and study its withered pages. Sea anemones undulating, part flower, part animal, their colors as bright as and as vivid as a mirage. Schools of dolphins caught from down below, streaks of shadow against the blue lit ceiling of the world. I envied them, their lithe purpose, the way they chased across a world so much bigger than my own. I loved the Land. Yet, sometimes, I longed for Sea. Whales, as large as mountains, rising out of a whitewash of water. My father told me that they sang, their voices carrying halfway across the world. They sang to each other, and to the moon, as they played and as they grieved. But my father said no one had heard their song in many years.

I did not know the ocean. The creatures in the book were things straight out of fairy tales, of Old Mercurial's ghost stories or old grandma Mosh's rambling hand-me-downs of the times before. I knew the story of Flora and Deuteronomy, which I think I told you (though memory plays tricks with me now, like an old yet still-mischievous friend), and how the winds carried them to the Land when the sea rose at last against the shore. I knew many stories, but I did not know the *truth* of them, if truth they had, or what had happened to the sea in all this time, for there was this: We had left it alone, at last.

Old grandma Mosh, who had many curious ideas, believed humans only ever deluded themselves that they were the ruling species of this world.

"Ants!" she'd say, "ants, little Mai! This is an ant planet, did you know ants grow mushrooms, they herd caterpillars, they forage and hunt and fight other ants. They dig tunnels, build caverns, make alliances with other ants. Their super-colonies stretch all across the Land, a single one is an untold tangle of tunnels, millions of individual queens, billions of worker ants—this is an ant planet," (she'd say), "it had been their planet all along."

And she may have had something in it, in the old retelling. One should not make the mistake of ignoring what one can't see. There is the story of Shosho Mosh and the ant queen of Thebes . . . but did I tell you that one, yet?

In any case, both ants and humans are creatures of Land. But the sea is much wider and deeper, as unknown as space (though as a species we had dipped our toes into both). The world-ocean was there, it had always been there, and I—I longed to see it.

That autumn when we left, the houses shrunk in the distance. A thin fog had fallen over the fields and the pine and olive trees. My father and the others stood beyond the stream, waving. Their voices soon faded away in the fog. We followed tracks made by salvagers passing, we followed brooks, the natural contours of the world. At last we reached the old, abandoned roads and marched not on but beside them, along what the salvagers call the Shoulders. Indeed it felt to me, young as I was, that we were walking on the shoulders of giants, if vanished ones. Often we would come across the remnants of rusting, broken travel pods, now filled with earth. Flowers grew out of empty windows, snails crawled along plastic and rusting metal. The roads were badly broken. The roots of trees had dug out of the earth and broken their black surfaces, and to traverse the road itself would have been hard and dangerous.

Salvagers are practical, stoic people. I was never meant to be one, I was always more given to stories. But my mother was born for this job, leading us true across all the twistings and turnings, and even Old Peculiar, the map maker, bowed to her skill. There were traps, too, though the passage itself was beautiful, as I saw mountains with peaks covered in snow, trees growing wild and free with red foliage falling like sunsets, and little green birds darting in the foliage, chattering in a language I almost thought I knew. We had to beware of the wild machines that still, sometimes, lived here in the wildness; of potholes and cave-ins, of landslides and ice. Shosho Mosh was the hunter, often disappearing for one or two days before returning from beyond the road, skinned rabbits or a small boar carried on her back. My mother would cut the meat into strips with quiet efficiency. We built fires by the roadside and ate warm tubers, buried in coals. We left stone rings behind us like markers, and often used old fire pits left there from other excursions. We would thank the Land for its bounty and never take more than we needed. It is a hard, physical labour, salvaging, but my mother made it look easy. Then, one day, we crested a hill, and I first saw the sea.

§

"You're always scribbling away, little Mai," Old Peculiar said, looking at me with his one good eye. He was a small, gnarled man; his left eye covered in a rakish patch, his right was bright and curious. How he lost it, I never learned. He'd gone deep into the blighted lands one time, for so long that he was thought lost. When he returned he was much changed, his eye was gone, and in his bag were maps, a treasure trove of maps showing places that no longer existed. Where he got them, and how he lost his eye, he never said. Some cave of treasure, some said, a time vault of the ancients, deep in the lost places of the world where only the ants and the wild machines live still. Once the world was covered pole to pole with human habitation, cities, roads, ports, factories, and fields. This was when we had forgotten Land, and the bond we owe it. In the rare times when he brought the maps out I would be fascinated by their elaborate forms, the lines of elevation and the demarcation of land, of Land. *Ash-Sham, Krung Thep, Nooyok.* . . . My imagination was inadequate to picture the cities of the past, how close on each other buildings were and how tall, and I could not imagine so many people, could not imagine living among so many strangers.

One map fascinated me in particular. I do not know the place it depicted, if it were real or imagined: it was a fabulous town filled with giant, living rats and lions, puppies who sang, bears who danced to music. There were crenelated castle towers, miniature mountains belching fire and steam, giant walking bottles of soda. There were lagoons and ships and rockets, and though much of the map was hard to read I believe it was called Sneyland. Our own maps were more practical, hand-drawn, current as current could be: my mother, too, spent long hours poring over her maps, but hers just showed routes to and from the old places, marked with black bold Xs to denote threats that were left carefully unmentioned.

"What are you writing?" Old Peculiar said, that night, by the fire. We were not far from the ocean by then. The air smelled different, I realised later. It was an unfamiliar smell to me, it left a salty taste on the tongue.

"It's a letter," I said, surprised. He seldom expressed interest in my activities or anyone else's, his whole focus being on the route ahead, on the dangers only he could perceive all around. But the truth was that the old roads were mostly safe to travel. The wild machines were just a story, or so I thought, gone deep into the blighted lands; and there were few predators on the Land. I always remember that first journey as breathtakingly beautiful, my first real glimpse of the world beyond, and how peaceful, and prosperous, and wild it had seemed.

"A letter?"

"It's when you write to someone who is not there," I said, self-consciously. "Like when old grandma Toffle writes to Oful Toffle, who lives in Tyr—"

"I know what a letter is," he said, shortly.

"Then—"

"And who do you know, little Mai, who lives so far away?" he said, and his single eye, I thought, seemed to twinkle. "And how would you get them this *letter*? Wait for a passerby? Tie it to the foot of a bird migrating across the Land?"

"There used to be mail carriers," I said, "in the old days, and they say people could speak to each other even if they were standing at opposing ends of the Land, as though they were right next to each other—"

"Yes," he said. "But that depended on the satellites, mostly." He pointed up at the night sky. I could see the Milky Way, stretched out from horizon to horizon, a beautiful spiral like a snail's. "And the satellites are dead, suspended in orbit, if they hadn't all crashed down to Earth yet." He seemed surprised, himself, at his own voice. "In past time, Low Earth Orbit was so chockfull of junked machines that they would often crash against each other and fall down, fiery bright, like shooting stars. . . ." He shook his head, and I realised then I never really knew him, what he was, what dreams he had, for all that he had always been there.

"Who is the letter for?" he asked, then. I shrugged, self-conscious. It was to no one real, you understand. It was a letter I was writing to the people who came before us, the people who lived on, yet never really knew, the Land. It was about my life, mostly, about our journey to the sea, about the salvagers and my father who stayed behind, about my friend Mowgai Khan and about old grandma Mosh and her collection of antique books . . . and in my letter, too, I tried to ask them questions, though I knew they'd never answer back. What was it like? I wanted to ask them. To have so much, to have everything, and to still want more, to *need* so much for *things,* that everything else became secondary, even us—their children?

I tried to explain it to Old Peculiar, I think, in my halting way. He nodded and stirred the embers in the fire with a stick.

"I used to think about that too," he said. "Even now, sometimes, in the old places, deep in the cities where nobody lives . . . but do you know what I think, little Mai? I think they were not that much different to us, to you, to me. They were just people. They tried to do their best, and sometimes they succeeded, and sometimes they didn't." He poked at the fire some more, sending a shower of sparks into the air.

"You'll find out," he said, gently. Then he was gone, and I was left there holding my pen and staring into the fire. You never really know people, I remember thinking, even if you spend all your life with them. Later, I signed the letter, and I buried it in the ground. Perhaps I wasn't writing it for the past at all, but for the future, and for my own children, after all.

§

That winter we sheltered in the ancient city as the rains lashed down on the Land, and my mother and the salvagers burrowed deep into the tangled mazes of its empty streets in search of useful discard, workable tech, reusable metal. This was a long time ago, when I was but a girl, but I remember that first glimpse of the ocean, how it went on and on until it reached the sky; it seemed to me an immense beast then, always moving, never quite still, its smooth back stretching across the world; and I thought, for just a moment, that it sensed me, somehow, and that it responded. A flock of birds, white against the grey-blue of the world, shot up and were framed in the light of the wintry sun. I blinked. I felt very heavy then, and for a moment the world spun and spun. Then the curious sensation was over, but the ocean remained; and we began the long descent down to the shore.

As for the city, that is another story, for another time. The light grows dim, and I must soon put down my pen. But one day, a week or so into our stay, my mother led me to the shore, my hand in hers, and together we stood on the sand and watched the sea. I saw, then, a demarcation line: a place where wet sand gave way to dry, and all along that line—which was, I later learned, the mark of high tide—there was debris.

This was not salvage. I saw seaweed, dulled by the air; small, shining seashells, their inhabitants still cowering inside; human-made ropes, black and slimy from the depths; a half-eaten plastic doll of what I thought must be a mouse, with its head missing and a hole in its chest; a plastic bottle, too—for plastic remained long after the world that had made it was gone; and a small, green-shelled sea turtle, helplessly turned on its back.

There were many things the ancients could have done and many things they did, in fact, do. It was not so much the doing or otherwise, as much as a certain mass that was required to change things. Towards the end, I think they realised it. Some left their travel pods by the side of the road, and began to walk. Some planted fruit trees, seeded flowers, allowed nature into their cubicle homes. Some stopped purchasing that which they did not need, abandoned *things*, began, too late, to try and live with the Land. They began to only use the power that they needed, to harvest the sun, to get to know the seasons. They cleaned that which had been polluted. All these things happened. All these things were possible. They didn't mean harm, they wanted the best for their children, the way their parents did, the way we do. It was all there, it just wasn't enough, it was just a little too late. They knew, and yet the mind is capable of great delusion. They didn't *want* to know.

The art of those last decades, too, is strange. There is so much vitality and violence in that last epoch, before the sea rose and the winds hit and my people came to the Land. It was the wind that tore Flora and Deuteronomy from Nueva Soledad . . . but I think I told you that story elsewhere.

All this happened, long ago. It wasn't enough to save everyone, but it was enough to save some and, in a way, to save a world. The dinosaurs lived longer and died quicker . . . and perhaps old grandma Mosh is right, and this has been an ant planet all along.

All this happened, long ago, and around me the light grows dim. That spring we returned to our home, laden with what could be salvaged. We try not to waste. Eventually, all that was left will be returned to the earth, repurposed and reused. Already, I know, plants and animals have returned to the old cities. And I remember that debris line, on that nameless beach, under grey-blue skies, and the little sea turtle, lying upturned on its back. When I picked it up, it emitted a stream of pee in fright, and I almost laughed. I had never seen a sea turtle. Then I crossed the line, my bare feet sinking into wet sand. And I walked to the water, which lapped at the shore, spraying me with white foam.

I placed the turtle gently in the water and watched it swim away.

The Reset

Jaymee Goh

It is now five years after the Reset. I have stood trial for my complicity in it and come away innocent.

The newspapers screamed about the time-traveler's companion going on the stand when I testified. They were wrong: it wasn't a time-travel machine, it was an environmental restoration controller. Also, I wasn't Dr. Morton's companion; I was his student assistant.

I based my defense on my age and relative ignorance. One of several he had roped into the project because the funding was too good to pass up. I was a first-year graduate student, in a cohort that received absolutely no funding from our university. I just so happened to have been assigned a role within the containment chamber that day.

My lawyer was not completely grateful for the Reset, because he lost all three young children of his. But he didn't take for granted regaining the youth he lost thirty years ago, without losing all the knowledge he has now. He thought I should play up the fact that I was only a graduate assistant. I had only a vague idea of what my supervisor was doing. If he hadn't realized the mistake he was making, how could he have expected a fresh grad to catch what he had missed?

Anyway, if it had been a time-travel machine, no one would have kicked up a fuss, because they wouldn't have known what they had lost.

§

The Earth, Dr. Morton always said, has a long memory. To simplify, if we posit that the universe is a super-computer program, then there must be a way to reset the world back into some prior period.

"Like save points in a videogame?" I had asked.

"Like so," he'd replied.

The machine he built was designed to take the Earth back to a previous "save point." A time before the current global warming crisis. If the experiment was successful, we would see clearer skies, and cleaner water, for a start.

"These parameters have been set to thirty years. Why not last month, or last year?" I had asked, complacently going along with the department's famous crackpot professor. "Why such a big gap?"

"Well, Nam Jing," he said in an exaggeratedly patient voice, "if we set it to just last year and it worked, we wouldn't know that it did. Thirty years is a good time; it's close enough to our time that it won't jar us and far away enough for us that it'll make a significant difference."

I was skeptical of this reasoning, but I didn't want to say so. Department politics were such that for all his crackpot theories, Dr. Morton was well-liked and well-supported. He had spent years squirreling money away for this project. "What if we mess up?"

"Then we'll just try again. It's just an experiment to see how much we can affect the environment. Relax. Everybody get ready now!" He was so cheerful, as if nothing bad could happen. Part of me now thinks he never expected it to work after all.

§

What Dr. Morton hadn't counted on when he had calculated for physical bodies to be affected by the regression outside the chamber, was that *everything* would return to its state thirty years before. Everything in the world includes *everyone*. It seems so obvious when one thinks back, but apparently Dr. Morton had never really talked the project over with anybody else who took it seriously. (If they did, no one owned up to it.) It turns out that he was a rare breed of likable that didn't translate into actual friendships with people who would have called his stupid ideas out.

When we had stepped out of the containment chamber, the lab hadn't changed much, and Dr. Morton hastened to reassure me that it had looked like this for the last fifty years. We could only know whether we had succeeded by going outside. I didn't buy it, but I *did* wonder where my classmates had gone. No one ever leaves in the middle of testing.

In the nearby labs there was uproarious shouting. There were grad students I didn't recognize. About half of them were passed out, from the inertia of regression, though I hadn't figured it out at the time. The conscious ones were either puking or they were disoriented.

"McHenry?"

"Herb!"

"Matsu—Mata—whatever your name is, is that you?"

I looked to Dr. Morton then, who had a growing expression of confusion on his face. It took me much longer to realize that these students had graduated years before, and suddenly, in the Reset, they were back in this lab, where they had been thirty years ago to the minute. Dr. Morton rushed back to our lab to look for his notes. They no longer existed, because, physically, the paper notes probably would have still been trees at that point in time, and tablets were still raw materials in the ground.

§

"In this way, Dr. Morton, you have absolutely succeeded, and congratulations on that. But hadn't you thought about the costs of what would happen?"

Every single talk show host asked him that question. He raked in more money than ever from these guest spots, more money than he had earned even as a tenured professor.

"The cost of living once more in a world where we can have a fresh start? If I had asked you, what would you be willing to give up to have your youth again, and the world as it was back in your heyday, what would you have said?"

"Well, I'm sure I don't know Dr. Morton, it would never have occurred to me. . . ."

And always, I could tell that they were lying, and it had, but they never bothered to answer the question for themselves, because they always thought it was completely impossible.

"Don't you worry that your science will be abused, Dr. Morton?"

Dr. Morton snorted. "Only if they find a way to recreate it, and it was such a fluke, I don't think anyone will ever risk it happening again," he bragged.

I always stood off-set, holding his coat, because in those days, I didn't have anywhere else to go. They would never ask me such theoretical questions about the Reset.

§

"It must be very lonely for you," a radio show host commented to me on one of the rare times I was invited to speak. "None of your peers exist anymore."

"It's all right," I replied. "I just find new ones." I didn't tell her that I often woke up in the middle of the night, confused at my surroundings. I regularly forgot my way around town, because the landmarks I was used to were not there. I had a few older friends, but it was hard to track them down. The few times I met up with them were discombobulating; it really is hard to take people who look like children seriously. My younger siblings, who I had loved dearly, were completely gone, never existing, possibly never to exist again in any form I would recognize.

"What do your parents think?"

§

To be honest, I was too overwhelmed and terrified to try to find my parents for the first year. I didn't understand a world without the technology I had grown up with. I had to relearn how to use phones. What are landlines! Everything was suddenly so very slow. And so very boring. Except for the paper. So much paper everywhere! No wonder we digitized everything, what with all those trees we must have been killing to keep up. But I thought about toxic factories endangering workers with exposure to dangerous chemicals and minerals for specialized, unfixable technologies. Paper at least can be recycled or restored to the earth.

"I missed the smell of ink," Dr. Morton confessed to me.

I was sure it was toxic but didn't say so. "I like the smell of paper," I replied, trying to connect to him in some way. Dr. Morton had taught me how to sort papers and organize them, and I got good enough to work as his secretary for a while.

§

When I tracked down my father, he had gone on holiday with the grandparents I had never met. It was a while before I tried again. I called his work phone, and his snooty secretary refused to forward me to him. I learned later that the secretary was pissed that his (previous? future? I don't know) workplace, where he had made Director before the Reset, hadn't taken him back, despite everyone remembering that he had had a perfectly decent track record.

"Not a big surprise, though," Dad said. The company where he had been working for thirty years prior dissolved earlier than he expected, and he was now a freelance consultant, as he had been in retirement when I left home. "When you're as nasty as that fellow has been for thirty years, if suddenly you find yourself in the pits, you'll find no one wants to help you."

He asked me if I had been eating properly (sort of), whether I had a job yet (yes; I was doing R&D with a company that manufactured laboratory equipment), and where I was going to be in the next few years—finishing my PhD? Could I even finish my PhD now that the equipment I need for my project no longer exists? Maybe, because my boss was keen on helping me finish. I wasn't sure I wanted to.

My grandfather found part-time work in a nearby office as a grant writer. "It's good for him. He got a stroke when he retired because he didn't get the exercise of walking to work, right before you were born," Dad explained. "Plus, he gets to scold people for bad grammar. That always makes him happy."

"That's nice," I said, wondering if I should go introduce myself to my now-living grandparents.

Grandma went to live with my uncle, despite the strained relationship she had had with my aunt. My cousins were infants again and needed help, because they were infants with some adult memories and were all the worse to deal with for that. When I visited them, they sat in stony silence, while my uncle and aunt made awkward chitchat.

Dad and I didn't talk about my mother that first conversation. When I had left home only a few years before, they had been on the verge of a separation. I had been closer to Dad, but not by much; the man on the phone was still, in effect, a stranger and all the more so for his sudden youth.

§

Within the years that have passed, everyone scrambled to restore the technological status quo. It turns out that without the rooms upon rooms of air-conditioned servers, digital information cannot possibly exist, despite "the Cloud." Funny that.

Now comes the question of memory. If memories are the result of electrons repeating themselves over and over in your brain, are they physical? The answer should point to "yes," except, as all good scientists say, it is not that simple.

People remembered things differently, but most retained their memories of the last three decades. Activists worked harder to push in legislation to prevent the environmental poisoning that would occur in thirty short years. Lawyers who were now in their second childhood and teenage years participated in raging wars over what constituted youth for the current generation. Global commerce was fiercer than ever, trying to recoup the losses they made (or never did), and socialist groups came out in full force to prevent multinational corporations from (re)gaining their foothold. There were companies that grew earlier than they originally had, mindful of the mistakes they had made, rushing to offer the services that had been lost. Rival companies rose up from workers of those companies. I was no Steve Jobs fan and was glad that less pretentious alternatives would exist.

There were, of course, people for whom the last thirty years faded quickly, like waking from a dream. Things got weird for me with these people. They held the theory that the last thirty years hadn't actually existed, but were a premonition of things to come. I was a sham to them, a fake person cooked up by Dr. Morton. I'm used to not existing to certain people, of course, but they took it to the next level. Before Dr. Morton took the stand, some people turned to the theory of premonition in order to cope and get settled in their lives again. It was traumatic to realize that the last thirty years of life had just—gone. Calling it a premonition instead allowed them to frame the last thirty years not as a loss, but merely a potential life, something to work towards, or against.

Then there are people who fiercely cling onto the memories that made them what they are, unwilling to give them up, unable, perhaps, to make a fresh start.

§

Maybe my mother had hoped that Empty Nest Syndrome would bring them together, maybe she didn't care anymore. I don't know. I'll probably never know.

I knew she had been a university lecturer when she met my father. When I had some vacation time, I went to the city where she had lived to look her up. Calls to her office were fruitless, because now as before, she hated the phone. So I wandered the campus, looking for her department. The students were a mix of what appeared to be very young children and adolescents. It felt like visiting a tadika of undergrads.

"Second puberty is *the* most overrated thing ever," one girl complained to her friends as they passed me. "And the mature students' officer is *such* an asshole. I can't believe I have to repeat all my credits because my records don't exist anymore."

Class let out then; a sudden wave of students washed over the quad. I stood up from the bench I'd been sitting on because I recognized my mother. She looked just like she had in her old pictures: short bobbed hair, carefully-done eyeliner. Her fashion sense was a lot more muted, but she still wore her favorite yellow scarf from her lecturing days. I walked toward her, intending to meet her face-on.

I had agonized a very long time on whether to meet her. We had always tried to recreate some sort of relationship, ruined because she couldn't let go of her sense that being Mom meant always getting her way even after I'd long grown different opinions from her. I wouldn't budge, and our mutual resistance to each other led to ever-escalating fights. "Strong-minded women," Dad said when I was a teenager, "should never live in the same house." Yet I decided that even if the Reset had torn our family to shreds, I still thought of her as my mother, and she deserved to know.

I expected that she would yell at me about the long hours she had worked for the family, only to be abandoned by her husband. Just like always. I couldn't imagine the Reset changing her that much, psychologically. I couldn't imagine her as a premonitioner, either. I had a dramatic vision that she would launch into a litany about how all her life she had been working, working, working, only to have ungrateful kids who didn't care about her. And I would say, "Well, I am here now." Maybe she would burst into tears.

She caught sight of me, and her eyes widened. Then she stiffened and swung away. Her walk was brisk, just the way I remembered it. When I was a child she had expected me to keep up with her.

"Mom!" I called. "Mom!"

She didn't stop, though I know she heard me. People were stopping to look at me, and some recognized me from the television programs. I heard them whisper, felt them pointing at me. I began to walk faster, discreetly trying to catch up.

But just as I was about to call again, she turned to me and pinned me with a cold, hard glare. Even at her most abusive, when she hit me with her own hand, she had never looked so hostile before.

I was so startled I tripped and fell.

Someone with manicured hands helped me up. "What was that about?" they asked.

I shrugged, smiling sheepishly. "I got the wrong person, I guess." I adjusted my bag. "Thanks."

"No problem. You're Tan Nam Jing, aren't you? From the future."

"No," I lied, because I just really wanted to go home and lie down. "Sorry, I really gotta go now. My mother's expecting me."

§

When Dr. Morton was put on trial, he was accused of genocide.

With supreme confidence, he calmly rejected the idea that he had been responsible for any such thing. The Reset had not involved any of the actions within the United Nations' own definition of genocide. He had not done it to kill entire groups—in fact, his intent had been to restore the Earth to a condition that would make it salvageable for the world's population. The Reset did not prevent births of entire groups; if fewer children were born this generation, it was a result of personal choices made on a societal scale and suited perfectly what popular wisdom on overpopulation advised.

The Reset did not necessarily create injuries that targeted specific groups and restored the health of many who had been terminally ill, to such a state that they could diagnose their health earlier and prevent future deterioration. People who had unjustly died in the last thirty years were now alive once more, and people who were known to be criminals could be caught and removed earlier before they snuffed out the lives they did. And if they did not, it would be an indictment of the society that allowed them to continue existing.

Dr. Morton acknowledged that in the first days after the Reset, people had suffered several health issues as the result of their bodies readjusting to the condition it had been in thirty years before. However, studies had shown that people were, for most part, surviving and taking preventative measures to safeguard their health. He cited my grandparents as an example, a nudge-nudge-wink-wink to how close he was to his grad students.

It was hard to not get angry at him. Yes, there were studies showing that people were rethinking their life choices before any problems escalated, but there were just as many studies showing that in the face of hard data, it was still easy for people to ignore the consequences of their decisions. When I yelled at him after, too mad to hold back, I didn't even mention the articles on the suicide rates post-Reset. I quit my job on the spot and managed to not talk to him for over a month. I also managed to not talk to anybody else. He wrote me glowing letters of recommendation, anyway. Small favors.

As for the children, well, every parent who had lost a child could start over if they wished and do so with the added wisdom of having done it before. There was also a generation who would grow up wiser as to what the future could hold for them, because they had already lived it.

"You can always have more children," Dr. Morton said. "But you cannot replace the Earth. Now with the Earth restored, you can have the children you miss so much, all over again." He sounded like he was right, but he was actually wrong.

§

We are taught to believe, as children, that our parents love us so much that they would suffer through any trial for us. And for most part, they do. Not because they know how we will turn out, but because they don't, and they already have a squalling baby and are committed to the parent task. The parent's love is unconditional. We repeat this not because it is objectively true but because we want to believe it is so.

If you had asked anyone from my peer group whether we would have willingly suffered through what we did to become the person we did become, some would have said no. It isn't because we loved our parents any less; in fact, some of us couldn't love our parents at all. Those of us who did love our parents, we just felt screwed up and not really worthy of our parents' love. And those who said they would, indeed, do it all over again, make the exact same choices, were generally insufferable people I never cared to be around.

I read advice column after advice column about children, now back in their teens, having to renegotiate boundaries with their parents, when they had been adults so long. When someone physically became a child, it seems even with thirty years' experience of that person being an adult is erased, or made murky. Of course, some children knew their parents would be abusive no matter what, and "children-run children's shelters" cropped up all over the world. Parents of newborns wondered if they should treat those children as adults too, or if the Reset didn't affect them and newborns had a completely fresh slate. Couples who were formerly parents wrote thinkpieces about whether they should go through the same thing again, with full knowledge that their children won't turn out exactly how they remembered. Did my father have such conversations with his new partner, the woman he might have married if not my mother?

No one seemed to have any advice for me, the adult child whose parents were now the age of her peers. My parents were not interested in recreating the life they had together that would produce me and my siblings.

"What for?" Dad said when I asked him during a visit. We were having tea in the house he shared with Grandpa.

"What, you didn't like us?" I teased.

"Not that I didn't like you. But your mom and I didn't get along very much. Why put you all through that again?"

"But you'd have me."

"But I still do," he pointed out.

"You could have another me!"

He burst out laughing. "Gee, you!"

My father would never go back into that marriage that made him unhappy for thirty years, not for the brilliant, kind, caring children he had from it. I supposed that he had the chance to have kids who were just as smart and great, without the terrible marriage. And if he never did have us again, the exact same us he lost, we didn't exist for our opinions to count, so it made no difference, really.

Well, it made no difference for Nam Ling and Nam Yong. I, on the other hand, went home after these visits and cried myself to sleep. Some things cannot be restored. Some things will never be.

§

The one thing Dr. Morton was half-right about? The environmental consequences of the Reset. I now see the blue skies of my very early childhood, and everyone has been scrambling to create best practices for maintaining it. Clean air bills pass. Citizens vote out the people who resist them. Cities are starting the process of ensuring that their infrastructures don't deteriorate. Procedures are established to prevent the degradation of rivers. *We can now swim in Lake Ontario!*

People of my parents' generation are suddenly brimming with positive energy that I didn't see them have when I was growing up. It got annoying very, very quickly, and hypocritical too—these grown-ups who used to tell me off for being passionate about the environment, saying I was too young to understand the world, suddenly themselves were *so* gung-ho in their activism. On the plus side, they weren't complaining about the state of the world anymore. Whether they were of the camp that this was an actual Reset of the physical world, or if they were of the camp that the last thirty years were a premonition, everybody had an opinion on what went wrong with the world, and lots of them were finally doing something about it. I've written to sociologists and psychologists asking about it but haven't heard back. Maybe it's still too early for those studies. My theory is that these people have to maintain their self-righteous attitudes somehow, and being passive about what is essentially a second chance to get things right would make them lose any moral ground to their children.

I say he was half-right, because there were things Dr. Morton stuck back in place that we could probably have done without. Some places in the world had bad air pollution, cleared up after several years of moving industries around, and they were now back to their previous levels of pollution. Dr. Morton got a lot of hate mail from people who had spent years restoring lakes, animal populations, natural reserves, only to have the Reset undo their efforts. Public transit systems have to be reestablished all over again—and this time with triple the resistance from auto companies. And governments are still prone to using shortcuts for everything. I'm pretty sure we're still going to fall apart, just much faster than before.

Because of the understanding that technology develops at the cost of the environment, the technological status quo was never quite established, and may never be. This means less out-sourcing to developing countries (ha! Cold War nationalist frameworks still apply in the Reset!) and more workers striking against unsound work environments. The Internet, which really should have been reestablished by now, is facing danger from governments who intend to establish more limitations on it. Underground "networktivist" movements have arisen to deal with this problem. And as always, money makes the world go 'round: profiteers will always find a way around laws. The last thing we all need is a price inflation on a basic internet package, but I'm not positive.

This also means I haven't been able to use a smartphone in years and that *sucks*. No more late-night chats with friends to keep my sanity. The Reset didn't make me less socially awkward. I don't think I'm the only one, but no one's investigating that. I'm going to get Carpal Tunnel Syndrome from handwriting all these letters, but scented paper is back in fashion, and I've always liked stationery.

§

When I took the stand for the first time, I was aware of the cameras trained on me and aware that digital streaming had also occurred way faster than it did before. I remembered the high-profile trials of my youth and sighed in resignation that I was now being recorded in high-definition. At least I wouldn't go viral on social media.

The questions didn't really make sense to me. I consented to the project because it was my job. The project was part of my funding. Yes, everyone on the team knew what the parameters of the experiments were, and no one could have predicted these results. Maybe we could have thought about this particular possibility, but it genuinely had not occurred to anyone, because we had all been acting out of indulgence (and, to be frank, fear of financial insecurity). Dr. Morton never got around to teaching us the physics behind the machine, despite promising to, so we could have a better sense of how the machine worked. Instead, he had us each work on specific parts of the machine, like we were line factory workers. In the four years, he recreated all his notes, and the task of interpreting has of course fallen to yours truly, but even then, I'm not sure I could confidently say that the machine would work.

What I resented the most was the implication that I should have, could have talked Dr. Morton out of it. Haha, what a joke, like a tenured professor was going to take someone fresh out of undergrad seriously. I thought this was Dr. Morton's trial, not mine. I said this out loud, and was scolded for speaking out of turn and not answering the question.

I really appreciated the donations from people who sympathized with me. It was nowhere near the amount of money Dr. Morton received from people who thought him a visionary genius, but it was enough to put away for a rainy day after paying my lawyer. I tried using it for therapy for a while, but it didn't work out.

I also really appreciated the money I received when Dr. Morton, who had not regained any youthfulness nor health with the Reset, died unexpectedly of a heart attack. In the absence of any heirs, the state decided to award me that money as the only person close to him and who also suffered his unique position during the Reset.

I sent some of that money to both my parents. My dad called me up when he received it to warmly thank me, and that he was going to use some of it to put Grandpa and Grandma on a cruise around the world. I didn't hear from my mom.

Does the truism that "if you love someone, you learn to let them go" apply to parents? I thought the filial response would be to do my best to patch things up with my mother the best I could. Her silence, snarling in my heart, said otherwise.

§

I used the money to rebuild Dr. Morton's machine. My apartment isn't very large, but it's big enough for the machine. I haven't told anybody about it and built it using stuff I developed for the firm I've been working for. I think it will work. Even if it doesn't, no harm no foul. Maybe.

The thing is, I feel he was short-sighted. Restoring the world to what it was thirty short years ago? That's not really meaningful. Thirty years ago everyone had the most terrible aesthetic sense, and it shows in the buildings built back then. If you want clean air, then go all the way back sooner. Maybe two hundred years before coal. Maybe five hundred years. And maybe those people then would have their memories of what had happened and prevent diseases and whatnot from happening.

I've widened the parameters, and this time I haven't bothered building a containment chamber. I don't need to be there to see what happened. Mostly, I just don't want to be here anymore. It turns out that when armed with knowledge of what would, or could, happen, everyone becomes even more insufferable.

Somewhere at the back of my head, there is a voice saying that this isn't really the best idea I've had. It's not kind, it's not compassionate to pull this prank all over again on the world. I ignore it, because the recent Qing Ming celebrations have reminded me that I'm not close to any family, and Dad has remarried someone else, and they're expecting a kid who's not me. My friends either hate me for not regressing or pity me for not having thirty extra years. No matter what I do, there's no me-shaped hole to fill because Dr. Morton's machine closed up all the possibilities for it five years ago.

The phone rings, sharp and loud. I jump up and knock my head on the frame of the machine. I frown at it; I'd have to fix it later.

When I pick up the phone, my voice is as snappy as its ringtone. "Wai?"

There's a shuffle on the other end for a moment. Then a huffy sort of sigh. "Nam Jing?"

I need a moment to recognize the voice. "Mom. . . ?"

Outside, it begins to rain. Petrichor. I'm hearing my mother's voice, soft and wavering. She's not a premonitioner; I'm real to her. I know we're going to get into a fight later. I might slam my phone down.

Right now, though, I understand the smell of petrichor, for the first time in my life.

Pop and the CFT

Brandon Crilly

I went out to the demonstration, to get my fair share of abuse.

"Mr. Cameron?"

The last notes from Keith's guitar faded away, and Gabe looked around his father's old dining room, taking in the clutter, dust, and age as he remembered where he was. Eventually his focus came back to the woman seated across from him, staring over her reading glasses.

Gabe grunted. "Hummin' to myself again?"

"Yes." Before he could ask, Ms. Flynn added, "I didn't recognize that one, either."

"Damn," Gabe murmured and shook his head. He'd reached a point where most people looked like kids to him, but he figured Ms. Flynn was in her late thirties or early forties—old enough to recognize the chorus to "You Can't Always Get What You Want." She hadn't picked up on "Take It Easy" earlier, though, so maybe he shouldn't have been surprised.

"Do you need me to repeat the question, Mr. Cameron?"

"Might not be a bad idea. Sorry, darlin'." He offered his famous stage smile, but the one she returned stayed polite and professional. *Ah, well.*

"Did your father use his car less or more after he retired?"

Gabe glanced across the adjoining living room, through the window to the front of the house. His father's old Camaro was sitting in the driveway under a tarp, waiting for Pop to take it for a spin. The only thing he had loved more than restoring that car had been driving it around. He could imagine Pop taking the Camaro out at least once a day, maybe twice if the mood struck him.

Baby, don't you hear my heart, you got it drowning out the radio.

"More," he said. "Guessin' that's another point against him."

Ms. Flynn sighed and removed her glasses, causing strands of blonde hair to tip over her ears for a moment before she tucked them back into place. "I'm not here to pass any kind of judgment on your father's memory, Mr. Cameron. The CFT is in place simply to assess the impact of an individual's actions, not the character of the person. I know this tax may seem like a black mark, but—"

"That's the man's attitude, not yours?"

"Something like that, yes."

"Fair enough. What do you need to know next, darlin'?"

Ms. Flynn swiped at her tablet, full of charts and spreadsheets she had shown him earlier. The last time he had sat down for something like this, there were mounds of actual paper spread across the table; he supposed that wouldn't make sense for someone concerned about the environment.

"So to recap—we've gone over the total mileage on your father's current vehicle, the previous vehicles he's owned, and the energy consumption and resource use here at his home." She glanced around the old place again. "The fact that your father owned a property of this size and lived alone for the last fifteen years will count against him, as well as things like not investing in personal solar panels. However, behavior like using energy-efficient lightbulbs and hanging his clothes to dry will offset some of that."

"Little things like that? Bonus." Pop had only used those bulbs because they were cheaper and hung his clothes out of a habit established by Mom, before she passed.

"Little things have a surprisingly large effect," Ms. Flynn said without looking up. "Of course, the age of the property is problematic, specifically with regard to things like heat and insulation. What was your father's diet like?"

"What's the best answer here?"

Ms. Flynn frowned. "The honest one."

Gabe crossed his arms over his leather jacket as he laughed. "Let's just say that if Pop ate a fistful of somethin' green over the course of the day, we'd call that a win."

"Meat and potatoes sort of person?"

"Pretty much, yeah."

"Lots of beef?"

"Made a wicked steak on the grill out back. Old family recipe for the marinade." Ms. Flynn tapped on her tablet, and Gabe asked, "Uh, that bad?"

"Cattle are particularly bad for the environment. They use approximately twenty-eight times more land than chickens and considerably more water. And they contribute more to emissions than gasoline-powered cars—approximately fifteen percent of the global total. Beef is terrible for the planet, I'm afraid."

Gabe blinked. She had rattled that off without taking her eyes off of him. "You know all that off the top of your head?"

"It's my job, Mr. Cameron," she said. "I suppose if I chose any song by Eric Clapton or Joan Jett, you'd be able to recite the lyrics in full."

"So you know some names, at least?"

"A few. They were legends in their time, after all. Just not my taste."

Gabe's brow furrowed. "What exactly is your taste, darlin'?"

Ms. Flynn rubbed at the side of her nose. "Some Top 40, but mostly jazz."

"A jazz girl. . . ." Gabe mused. "Huh. Never been much for that. Good melody, but not enough . . . oomph."

"You'd be surprised," Ms. Flynn said, not quite sounding defensive. "There can be as much emotion in the wail of a saxophone as the plucking of a guitar."

"Hmm. Guess so." Gabe eyed his guitar, which he'd leaned against the doorway leading to the living room. *I look at the world and I notice it's turning.* "I could demonstrate some, if you like. Been a while since I put on a show."

For the first time that day, a smile with some actual feeling crossed her lips. Gabe liked to think he could write a ballad about any woman's smile, and Ms. Flynn was no exception. He was disappointed, though, when she said, "Maybe later."

"Girl's all business. Okay," Gabe said, drawing out the "o" as he stretched in his chair. He wasn't used to sitting and talking about something for this long that didn't have chords to go along with it. His fingers were starting to itch for his guitar strings and his feet for the sides of his Harley. That hog was probably going to set his finances back when his turn came, he realized. Not that there would be anyone to worry about it on his behalf—just the state.

"There are a few other small items we can get out of the way right now." Ms. Flynn flicked at her tablet again. "Did your father tend to buy new clothes regularly?"

"Wore the same shirts every week 'til they were nothin' but holes."

"Personal electronics?"

"Just the flatscreen upstairs, I think. Wasn't much for fancy gadgets like yours."

"And he used it often?"

Gabe shrugged. "Liked his stories. Mostly went to the bar to watch things with his crowd. Place around the corner." He perked up a little. "Hey, that's probably good, right? Sharin' a tube instead of turnin' one on for himself."

Ms. Flynn nodded. "You're catching on, I see."

"Not just a pretty face," Gabe said. He dropped his stage smile when she didn't look up from her tablet.

"Did he replace items very often? Furniture or tools, for example?"

Gabe gestured at the dining room set and the nearby sofas. "Most of the stuff around here comes from when Jesus wore short pants. Pop would rather fix somethin' than replace it."

"And he held onto a fair bit of personal property."

For a moment, Gabe pictured the basement and then the garage; they were both crammed full of things that his dad likely hadn't touched in years. Both were somewhere between a treasure trove and a cleaning service's nightmare.

"Yeah, he liked his stuff. Mainly since Mom died."

"And he didn't contribute to any environmental initiatives, correct? Donating to new technology firms, attending demonstrations, volunteer work?"

Gabe just shook his head. He was still thinking about the basement, hoping that they wouldn't need to discuss it any further.

Naturally, Ms. Flynn said, "The last thing we need to go over in detail, then, is the possessions your father left behind."

Drain the pressure from the swelling, the sensation's overwhelming. Gabe's fingers started twitching again, recalling the couple of shows he played with Billie Joe and the boys, during their reunion/comeback tour a little while back.

"Look," he said softly, "Pop wasn't entirely okay after mom died. He got by, but with me on the road . . . he needed to keep busy. He'd already been collectin' stuff, so—"

"Gabe." He looked up at Ms. Flynn. "I'm not here to judge, remember? From everything you've told me and what I've seen in these files, your father was a remarkable man. My job here is to assign a Carbon Footprint Tax to your father's *estate*—not your father. Okay?"

He let out a breath and his fingers stopped twitching. "Okay."

"Okay." She turned the tablet to show him the pictures she had taken earlier. Shelving lined his dad's garage, packed with cardboard boxes and plastic tubs that had gradually flowed in stacks across the ground. Each of them was labeled and contained a particular type of screw or bolt that Pop would turn to when he was repairing something around the house. The pictures from the basement showed a similar set-up, except that these boxes held album covers, stacks upon stacks of records, old concert tees, and memorabilia from shows going back fifty years or more. Gabe knew that some items from his own tours were stored down there, too—boxes of programs never handed out, retro EPs never bought but which his dad insisted on keeping. The most important mementos of Gabe's career were strategically placed around the house, though, away from the piles of old *Rolling Stone*.

"Part of an individual's carbon footprint," Ms. Flynn said as she swiped through pictures, "is the amount of physical material that is discarded when they pass away. Anything that can be recycled or repurposed has a much lighter effect. Anything that can't be, however. . . ."

"Jacks up the price?"

"Something like that, yes."

"Makes sense. So what's the damage here?"

Ms. Flynn sighed. She turned the tablet away again to consult it. "Some of the hardware in the garage can be melted down and repurposed," she said, "but a lot of it will end up in scrapyards, and not all of these will be authorized treatment facilities, unfortunately. The records and collectibles downstairs . . . historically would have ended up in places like antique shops. Let's just say there's far more supply than demand these days. There's going to be a hefty tax there."

"Someone else could use that stuff, right?"

"Not a lot of people own record players these days, Mr. Cameron. The problem here is that these items *exist*—materials were used to create things like posters and vinyl records, and those materials will end up in a landfill sooner or later."

Gabe grunted. He had never been one for owning a lot of things; he hadn't spent much time at home back when he was touring. His condo downtown was sparse, but he had his fair share of things that, he supposed, would get thrown out someday: his awards and gold-plated LPs, walls of photos from concerts and big events, signed T-shirts that he had never intended to wear.

He glanced at his guitar. Even now, it traveled around in the trunk of his car or on the back of his Harley, as though he was Bon Jovi's cowboy from "Wanted Dead or Alive." It wasn't particularly flashy—yellow-and-red coloring, flame-maple top, and a sunburst finish—but he maintained it with only original parts and tried to keep it from scratching or denting when he was jamming on stage. That guitar, to him, was a work of art. He didn't want it to end up in the back of some antique shop or in a landfill.

"All right, darlin'. What's the final number?"

Ms. Flynn finished entering information into her tablet; she had a good poker face, and he tried not to fidget. When she turned the tablet toward him again, he let out a long, low whistle.

"I know it seems high. . . ."

Gabe managed a chuckle. "Seems?"

"Do you have a financial advisor who can help you with this?"

"Yeah, this won't be anythin' new for him. It's not like I've been flush the last few years."

"There are payment plans available if. . . ."

Ms. Flynn trailed off as Gabe stood up. He rolled his shoulders, savoring the sound of his leather jacket creaking, and twitched his fingers to the chords of his second big hit, "That Time You Spent the Night." His dad had always said that was one of his greatest songs, even after half-a-dozen others topped the charts.

He wandered into the living room. Over a low bookshelf that mostly held Mom's old novels, Pop had erected a sort of shrine, a wall of framed photos from Gabe's various concerts and public appearances. His parents made it to at least one concert every time he toured, sometimes more, and Pop had kept up the tradition of taking a photo each time and adding it to the wall.

"Can I ask you a question, darlin'?"

"Of course."

"What's your first name, anyway?"

There was a slight pause. "Beth."

"Really?" Gabe's grin seemed to confuse her. He shook his head and hummed another tune. *Beth, I hear you callin', but I can't come home right now.*

There was a fading photograph in the center of the collection. It was a selfie—though Pop would never have called it that—of him and Mom at the Radio City Music Hall, when Gabe and his band had opened for AC/DC. That had been one of their first big shows, and his parents had insisted on driving for a day so they could be there. Gabe tried not to let the fact that they were gone now sour the memory—not just his parents, but Angus and Brian, and folks like Gibbons and Debbie and Michael Lee. Everyone who had inspired him, back when he and the band were making a name for themselves.

Of course, the band was gone, too. First Toby, their drummer, died in that car accident. Then his husband, Everett, their bass guitarist, got tired of doing it alone and walked away. In the eight years since, Gabe had planned on getting them back together, even just for one night; not just for himself or even for the boys, but so that Pop could see him perform one more time.

I think I can hear you calling.

Ms. Flynn had gone back to her tablet, probably finishing up her report. She jumped when Gabe set his guitar down on the dining room table.

"Here."

"I beg your pardon?"

"This'll cover that footprint tax of yours," Gabe said. "And then some, dependin' on who I sell it to."

Ms. Flynn stared at the instrument. "A guitar?"

Gabe grinned. "Not just a guitar. 1959 Gibson Les Paul Standard.

Original pieces and kept in great condition by yours truly. Even if my name wasn't attached to it, any idea how much this would go for?"

Ms. Flynn shook her head.

"Lots. Especially when people see the signature on the back, from the guy that gave it to me."

"Who?"

"Billy . . . Billy Gibbons," he added, but she just stared at him blankly. "Never mind, darlin'."

As he sat back down, Ms. Flynn said, "To be honest, most people don't respond this well to the news I give them."

"Gave up on lettin' things like money get me down the second time I went bankrupt," Gabe said. "Besides, it's not like I need that thing anymore."

"I'm . . . I'm sorry."

Gabe waved a hand at her. "Knew goin' in I'd fade eventually."

Ms. Flynn fiddled with her tablet. "In that case, there is one other thing that will need to be settled: how you'll be handling your father's remains."

"Am I still allowed to bury him?"

"Yes, but. . . ." Ms. Flynn winced a little. "There is a heavy cost associated with that these days, due to regulations."

"Go figure," Gabe said with a chuckle. He pointed at the guitar. "There should be enough left over from that to cover it." Another tune came to mind, and he leaned toward her. "Tell me, Ms. Banker—won't you bury my papa for me?"

You and Me and the Deep Dark Sea

Jess Barber

Liam returns home to Oceanside on a warm southern California evening, three years and two months after leaving it, thinking it was going to be forever.

Of course, Tara's apartment is the first place he goes.

The apartment complex looks abandoned, unsurprisingly. It's too close to the ocean, a malevolent glint not a hundred meters away. There's one balcony with a clothesline strung across it, towels limp in the lack of breeze, and a few children's toys scattered over the concrete, but nobody comes out to interrogate Liam when he drops his pack on the ground next to Tara's front door. That's okay. He has no real desire to meet the neighbors.

His key still works, which is good, because he sold his lockpick kit somewhere in New Mexico, one of the first in a long line of personal items he shed like scales along the southwestern border, and he never got very good at picking locks without it. Hell, he never got very good at picking locks *with* it.

Not like Tara was.

The interior of the apartment has been stripped bare. Of course it has, but just because it's expected doesn't mean it hurts any less. Doors dangle open on the cheap laminate cupboards, and there are indentations in the carpet from where the furniture sat. The drywall has irregular holes punched in it where somebody's stripped out all the copper wire. Liam allows himself a moment of nostalgia, coloring in ghosts to fill the place: Tara stretched long on a bare mattress in the middle of the floor, dangling a book over her face, laughing, summer sunlight streaming in through the blinds.

The door to her bedroom is shut. He makes himself cross over to it, shove it open. Empty, of course, and that should be that, except he's hit with a bright gut-shot of pain, has to brace his shoulder against the door frame to keep from buckling. "God, what am I *doing*," he asks himself, and he doesn't know, hasn't known since he pulled himself ashore in what used to be New Orleans, lungs full of brackish water, right side of his body a lacerated mess, alone.

He backs up into the living room, closing her bedroom door as he goes.

Blanket down at the bottom of his backpack, fished out and spread over the scratchy industrial carpet. A few of his dwindling supply of ibuprofen, swallowed down dry. Gun within easy reach. Liam stuffs his backpack underneath his head and wills himself to sleep.

§

He wakes up to the sound of somebody rattling the doorknob.

It's full daylight outside, the sun pouring through the bare windows, baking the room stiflingly hot. Liam rolls to his feet as quietly as he can, wiping sweat from his eyes and grabbing the gun as he goes, heart thudding a frantic tattoo in his chest. He spent weeks waking in a panic, after, certain he was being followed, certain he had been found out, but after a month of nothing he started to grow complacent. *You dumbass,* he thinks, and trains his gun on the door.

The knob clicks. The door swings open, and Liam, stunned, lets the gun drop to his side. *"Ale?"*

Ale looks different than the last time, thinner, sharper, but the same in essentials, down-turned mouth and inked forearms. Ale stares at him for a second, stunned. Then: "You *motherfucker,*" he says and punches Liam in the mouth.

Liam has known Ale since they were both ten years old. In that space of seventeen years, Ale has punched Liam in the face more times than Liam can count. Most of them, Liam has probably deserved. This is the first time it's taken him to the ground.

To be fair, it's not the punch itself. It's Liam's attempt to dodge, an instinctive motion that puts too much weight on his bad leg, which crumples underneath him. Liam's still got the gun in his hand, so he can't even catch himself properly out of fear of landing on the thing, so he hits the ground, hard, on his hip, vision whiting out in a sparkling burst of pain.

Liam manages to get the gun up and pointed in Ale's general direction, though he can't focus well enough to aim properly. Doesn't matter. He wouldn't actually shoot Ale—he *wouldn't*—he's just hoping the gun is enough of a deterrent to keep Ale from hitting him again. He isn't sure he'd be able to take it.

His vision finally clears enough to focus on Ale, held at a distance by the gun, fingers twitching like they want to form fists and mouth flickering towards a frown. Liam raises his free hand in a gesture of surrender. "Could you maybe not do that again?" he asks. "I'm not as spry as I used to be."

"Liam," Ale bites out. "What the fuck are you doing here?"

Liam figures that's as good as he's gonna get and lowers the gun, commencing the arduous climb to his feet. "I could ask you the same thing," he grunts, settling himself unsteadily upright. "Since when do you have keys to Tara's apartment?"

"The rent you paid on this place ran out two years ago, asshole," Ale says. "And nobody's been around to collect it for longer than that. Not sure it counts as 'Tara's apartment' anymore. And where the fuck is she?" Ale's gaze darts around the room, settling on Tara's closed bedroom door. "Is she with you?"

Liam closes his eyes. "Ale," he says, "Tara's dead."

This time, when the hit comes, he's expecting it.

§

It's not like Liam didn't know Ale was in love with Tara.

Liam walked in on them once, obviously post-coital, Ale struggling into a t-shirt, Tara puddled in sheets and letting her braids down from their wrap. Liam knew better than to expect Tara to apologize—knew better than to think she had anything to apologize for. But later that night, both of them sprawled on the floor of her living room, surrounded by circuit diagrams and breadboards, Tara said, carefully, "About earlier. I didn't mean to upset you. I thought you knew what this was."

"You didn't," Liam lied, muffled around a mouthful of wires he was stripping for her. "I do."

"Ale—" Tara began.

"Let's not," Liam said, taking the wires out of his mouth to stop her, "talk about him anymore, okay?"

"Okay," she said and leaned forward to lick the taste of copper out of his mouth.

§

When Liam finally manages to pick himself up off the ground, Ale is gone.

Liam finds he's not surprised.

§

The Ralph's still operates like a grocery store, sort of. A skinny, pockmarked kid pries open the sliding glass doors at seven most mornings, sits slumped at one of the checkout counters while Liam limps around the store, eerie with its two-thirds empty shelves and busted out fluorescent lights. Liam tips canned goods and water purification tablets into a cracked plastic basket, as much as he thinks he'll be able to carry the half-mile back to Tara's apartment. There are no prices on anything. The kid helps Liam load the lot of it into his backpack and then stares at Liam expectantly. "Well?" he asks. "Whaddaya got?"

"Cash okay?" asks Liam, fishing out an assortment of wadded bills from his pocket and thrusting them toward the kid, who raises an eyebrow. "Sorry," says Liam, unsure how things work around here these days. "I don't have a lot to trade."

"Nah," says the kid, "cash is cool. Just don't see it a lot anymore." He peels a few hundred bucks in fives and tens out of Liam's stash and organizes it meticulously before tucking it away out of sight. "All good?" he asks.

"All good," agrees Liam, hefting his bag over his shoulders and turning to begin the long trek back to Tara's apartment.

That night, he sits in the sand and eats canned peaches with his fingers, heavy syrup dripping into the toxic waves frothing at his feet. He thinks of Tara, months after the quake, standing in this spot with tar streaking her bare ankles, staring out over the water with a kind of tightly leashed rage. He was almost afraid to approach her, half-certain she would fly apart at his touch, dissipating into the acrid air.

"Three months," she said. "Some cleanup effort, huh."

Liam dragged the toe of his boot through the black mottled sand, watching the sea water that bubbled up to fill it in, dark and sludgy. "It's all we're gonna get. Bankruptcy filing gets you out of anything, apparently."

Tara laughed, harsh and tired. "There's a joke about my student loans in there, but I don't have the energy to make it." She hugged her arms tight around herself, expression cracking fractionally as her eyes tracked the downward curve of the sun. "There's got to be something we can do," she said. "I'm gonna figure out something."

"I believe you," he said, and he did.

§

Liam puts his groceries away in the empty cupboards, organizing everything carefully: neat stacks of canned green beans, rows of saltines in plastic sleeves. He traded his camp stove for a ride over the New Mexico/Arizona border, so he eats everything unheated, drinking down slippery cold noodles from a can of minestrone and trying not to taste them.

He sleeps a lot.

He doesn't go back to the ocean.

§

Three weeks into this half-conscious vigil, he wakes up to an insistent knocking on the door.

Liam grabs his gun and tumbles up into a crouch before the haze of sleep has fully cleared from his mind. He trains the sight on the door. "Who's there?" he calls out, voice hoarse from sleep and disuse.

There's a pause and then Ale's voice. "Listen, dumbass. I'm trying to be neighborly here, but I still got a key. Lemme in before I do it myself."

Liam blinks then tucks the gun away at the small of his back, pushing himself to his feet and going to pull the door open. Ale stands there framed in it, wearing a sour expression, two travel mugs tucked into the crook of one arm, a wrinkled paper bag dangling from his fingers. "Well?" he asks. "You gonna invite me in?"

Liam steps aside wordlessly, making a half-hearted sweeping gesture with one arm. Ale snorts, boots thudding heavy across the threshold. "Love what you've done with the place," he says, crouching next to the tangle of blankets on the floor and settling the coffee mugs on the faded carpet.

Liam is too tired to make any of the obvious jokes. "Ale," he says instead, "the fuck are you doing here?"

"I'm the neighborhood welcoming committee, asshole," says Ale, settling back on his haunches. "I'm a little late, but we weren't sure you were gonna stick around. Coffee?"

Liam opens his mouth then closes it and circles around, lowering himself to the ground across from Ale, who picks up one of the travel mugs and holds it out, wiggling it enticingly. Liam takes it, twists off the lid and breathes in the rich steam that rises. It's been awhile since he's had coffee. It's not usually easy to get. "I kind of thought you punching me in the face—twice—was my housewarming present."

Ale's expression darkens. "Like you didn't deserve that," he begins, then stops himself. "Look," he says. "You planning on sticking around here or not?"

The ruined muscles of Liam's right quad are throbbing and twitching unbearably; Liam finally gives up and drags his knuckles down the length of his thigh, hard, trying to massage out the spasms. "Yeah," he says. "I think so."

Ale shrugs. "It's a small world these days. Around here everyone's gotta look out for everyone else, at least a little. You're gonna have to stick your head out of your rabbit hole eventually."

"I—sure, okay," says Liam. *So Ale really is acting as some sort of fucked up welcoming committee. The world is a magical place.* "Should I start putting together a casserole to bring to the next potluck?"

Ale reaches over and raps his knuckles against Liam's shin, hard. "Ow," protests Liam, glaring.

"Don't be a dick," says Ale, aiming an accusing finger at Liam's nose. "And while we're on the topic. You keep your mouth shut about anything and everything you and those tree-hugger fucks got up to, you got it?" Liam opens his mouth, whether to protest or ask Ale what the fuck he thinks he knows, he's not sure, but Ale cuts him off with a sharp gesture. "I'm serious. Ain't nobody needs to know that shit. We don't usually get bothered around here, but plausible deniability is better for everyone. After all, you seemed like such a *nice* boy. You got it?"

Liam digs his fingers into the scar tissue above his knee. "Yeah," he says, voice even. "I got it."

Ale's expression softens a little, and he nods, nudging the paper bag closer to Liam. "You better hurry up and open that, then," he says. "Pasteles. Grandma's recipe. You don't wanna let them get cold."

Liam is hit by a sudden flash of memory, him and Tara and Ale, fat-cheeked thirteen year olds crowded into Ale's grandma's kitchen, taking way too much pleasure in cookie-cuttering shapes out of floured dough, and he has to blink something hot out from behind his eyes. "Yeah," he agrees, and goes to rip the bag open.

§

There are, in fact, potlucks.

Ale doesn't *call* them potlucks, but Liam knows better. There are more people left in Oceanside than Liam would have guessed—around three hundred, Ale estimates—and community-wide get-togethers are thick on the ground. Weddings, funerals, Friday night fish fries, fucking barn raisings, hell if Liam knows. "One little apocalypse, and we're all turning into the fucking Amish," Liam complains the first time Ale tries to drag him out.

Liam staunchly avoids anything involving communal dining, though he does eventually cave on some events that seem more functional: helps repair a septic tank, puts up a rain-barrel water collection system. He doesn't try to make nice with the neighbors, though, and despite the lecture Ale doesn't really seem to expect him to. Liam keeps his head down, and helps out when Ale asks, and nobody tries to make nice with him, either. He figures it's probably more comfortable for everyone that way.

§

Sometimes, helping out is more of a pain in the ass than seems worth staying in Ale's good graces. "You think," Liam asks, blinking the sting of sweat from his eyes as he edges carefully along the hood of a gutted-out Camaro half-buried in other junkyard detritus, "that this is the sort of shit all those collapse fetishists had in mind when they jerked off to the thought of the end times?"

"Who knows, man," says Ale, ten feet ahead of Liam, bouncing from the rusted hull of a speed boat to the stained bulk of a refrigerator with easy grace. "Some of 'em, probably. The really masochistic ones. Reaping what we sowed." He picks his way along a complicated structure made of narrow metal railings, balancing like a tightrope walker.

Liam is still working on the Camaro. "And the rest of them?" he asks.

"Too busy laughing at us from their fortified bunkers full of Uzis and canned goods to care, probably. Yo, could you hurry it up? I know you're like the walking wounded these days but Jesus."

Liam flips him the bird and determinedly does not speed up as he finally conquers the speedboat. "You ever think about that stuff, back in the day?"

"Nah," says Ale. "I was perfectly content in the bubble. I never wanted to give up my creature comforts. I'm still fuckin' bitter about it. You?"

"Never really thought about it," says Liam. This is a lie, sort of. In the morass of his own all-encompassing youthful angst, the dim, romanticized prospect of a zombie horde or a super volcano as painted by first-person shooters and disaster flicks had seemed like a step up. He thinks this had probably been a pretty popular sentiment among his directionless contemporaries, so he refuses to be too embarrassed about it, even if he's not going to admit it to Ale. "How much further, anyway?"

"Another quarter mile, maybe. We're almost there."

"Thank god," mutters Liam. He doesn't even really know what they're trawling the junkyard *for;* Ale said something about parts for the generator, which Liam has never actually seen used. *For emergencies,* Ale said, but if their whole goddamn lives don't count as emergencies Liam doesn't know what does. "Hey," says Liam, squinting. "Is that a surfboard?"

It is a surfboard, remarkably intact, still strapped to the roof rack on an ancient jeep. "I'll be goddamned," says Liam, tracing a reverent hand over the blunt curve of its nose. It's a beginner's longboard, huge and garishly colored, nothing Liam would have been caught dead on as a kid. He doesn't care. He wants it, desperately.

"You gotta be kidding me," says Ale. He's reappeared next to Liam somehow, popping up like a magic trick. Liam starts and almost loses his footing; Ale catches at his elbow to steady him, fingers warm and strong against the slide of bones. "You're such a *bro.* You really planning on going for a dip in that radioactive sludge?" Ale waves a vague hand toward the west, where the shimmering line of the ocean is just visible through the haze. "Your organs are gonna rot out."

Liam laughs, a little short. "Come on, you know how many hours I've spent soaking in that shit over the past four years?" he asks. "I've probably *swallowed* more than a gallon of it. It's too late for me. I'm like ninety percent radioactive sludge already."

Ale opens his mouth, closes it. His fingers slip away from Liam's arm. "I'm not helping you haul it back," he says.

Liam gives the thing an affectionate tap. "I'll come back for it."

Liam makes his way back to the junkyard in the evening, misjudges how long it'll take him to find the right spot again, gets lost, has to drag the surfboard home by the inadequate light of a half moon, freezing his balls off in the night air. The next morning he wakes at dawn, chest tight with the nostalgia familiarity of it, and trudges down to the water, dragging the board behind him, scraping a shallow channel in the sand. His shoulders ache as he paddles himself out past the break, woefully out of shape. The water smells funny. He knows the chances of him actually catching a wave with his leg the way it is are slim to none.

It doesn't matter. Sitting there, straddling the stupid ugly board, riding out the gentle undulations of the water, staring off into the endless expanse of the ocean—he can almost pretend nothing has changed at all.

§

On the five-year anniversary of the quake, Ale wakes Liam up at midnight, pounding insistently on his door. When Liam limps over to open it, Ale holds up a dusty bottle of Jack like a beacon. "In memoriam," he says. "Put on some pants, and let's get out of here."

It takes Liam a solid ten minutes of following Ale blindly through the frigid dark before he figures out where they're going: the yawning sinkhole in the earth that marks where their high school once stood.

"Jesus Christ, Ale," Liam says, as Ale settles himself terrifyingly close to the edge, flinging out one leg to dangle over the abyss. "The fuck did you want to come here for?"

"This doesn't seem like a good place to celebrate?" Ale asks, pulling the whiskey bottle out of the depths of his coat and twisting off the cap. He holds it out and upends it, sending a healthy slug down into the emptiness. Liam listens to it splatter and trickle off the debris within, weirdly loud and echoing in the silence of the night. "Sit your ass down, Liam," says Ale. "I'm trying to have a moment."

Liam sits.

Carefully, he edges his legs right alongside Ale's, into the yawning darkness. Ale bumps their shoulders together, holding out the bottle, and Liam, nerves tight and thrumming, takes it gratefully, tossing back a substantial swallow. Ale's upper arm pressed against Liam's feels a thousand degrees warmer than the cold night air. Liam takes another gulp, two, before handing the bottle back. "You gonna say a few words?"

Ale snorts, looks down to where he's running his thumb in slow circles around the mouth of the bottle. *His eyelashes are really long*, Liam thinks, then blinks. Whiskey on an empty stomach.

"Congratulations," says Ale to the abyss, raising the bottle and startling Liam, who hadn't really expected Ale to say anything. "On getting out when you did."

Liam makes a sound that's almost a laugh, scrubs a hand over his eyes. "Touching," he says.

Ale laughs too, a puff of fog-silver in the chill air. "Yeah, well."

The whiskey is really starting to hit Liam now, turning his thoughts slow and syrupy at the edges. Ale settles the bottle down between them, fingers still looped around the neck. When Liam reaches down to take it Ale doesn't let go, and they sit like that for a minute, knuckles bumping together, the bottle a buffer between them. *I'm gonna do something dumb*, Liam thinks, too booze-softened to be nervous. *I'm gonna kiss him or jump into this hole in the ground, I'm gonna—*

And then Ale says, "You know, Tara and I. . . ."

The moment shatters. "Christ," Liam says. "Don't. I know. I mean, I know as much as I want to know. Okay?"

"But—"

"You wanna know how to disable a deep water drill?" Liam asks, to make a point.

There's a long silence, and then Ale says, "Actually, kind of, yeah."

Liam blinks, twisting to stare at Ale. "For real?"

Ale shrugs, doesn't say anything.

Liam stares at him for another long moment, then laughs, flopping down onto his back. "Robots," he says.

"Fuck you."

"I'm serious." Liam laughs again, too drunk to help himself. "I mean, what'd you think it was? Me swimming down there with a depth charge?"

"Shit, I dunno," says Ale, sulky. "Coulda been."

Liam shakes his head. "It's actually not that hard," he says. "There are a lot of safety mechanisms built in, to cap the well if it looks like something is going wrong. You just have to trigger one of them. The easiest is just to cut the communication lines from the operating deck to the platform. Send in a robot, an unmanned underwater vehicle, and—" he makes a scissoring motion with his fingers. "The whole thing shuts down catastrophically."

"So tell me something, nerd-boy," says Ale. He twists suddenly, looming over Liam, filling Liam's vision and utterly blotting out the haze of the sky. "If it's so fucking hands off, what the hell happened?" Their faces are really, really close together. Ale's breath is hot on Liam's skin, heavy with whiskey. Liam swallows.

"What happened," Liam says, "is that, sometimes, you get caught."

§

They don't kiss. Liam puts his mouth everywhere else. Afterward, he spends hours licking grains of sand out of the crevasses between his teeth.

§

"You should come over for dinner," says Ale, a few days later, elbow-deep in the guts of a busted old engine.

Liam, helping out by lounging around and looking pretty, props himself up on his elbows and blinks. "You serious?"

"Sure," says Ale. "What kind of boy do you think I am? Woulda made you buy me breakfast, after, if I didn't have things to do."

"I would have," says Liam, before his brain can catch up with his mouth.

Ale grins. "I know you would've. Dinner instead, though. My place. Seven."

Ale still lives in the same shitty little house Liam remembers, a rundown one-bedroom thing in what used to be the bad part of town. When Liam knocks a woman answers, pretty, careworn face. Through the open doorway, a riot of noise, a dozen chattering voices, tinny music being piped in. Cooking smells, garlic and heat. "You must be Liam," says the woman. "Come on in. Ale's in the kitchen."

Kitchen is kind of a generous term, since all of the functional areas spill together in one big open space. There are at least five people squeezed onto a threadbare couch, talking animatedly; several other small clusters of conversation huddled in corners, blocking doorways, and Liam almost loses his footing when three small children barrel past him, squealing. Liam hunches his shoulders and squeezes his way over to Ale, apron-clad in front of the stove, frying something. "You motherfucker," Liam says. "You tricked me into a potluck."

Ale snorts, scraping a spatula around the edge of the pan. "You were expecting candles and long-stemmed roses, maybe?"

"You're such a dick," says Liam. "Holy shit, where the hell did you get ground beef?"

"My resources are vast and mysterious," says Ale, using the spatula to fend off Liam's attempts to reach into the pan. "I'm in the middle of a culinary masterpiece, man. Fuck off and go make friends with the locals."

Liam pouts, but before he can shuffle off to obey, Ale snags a finger into his belt loop, halting him. Liam twists around to see what's up, and Ale's mouth is on his, insistent and warm, right there in full view of everyone, and oh. *Oh.* "Food'll be ready in ten minutes," Ale says and releases Liam, blushing and dazed, back into the crowd.

§

The water was always going to rise again. It's not like it comes as a surprise.

Nobody else is dumb enough to live as close to the ocean as Liam does, but it doesn't matter. They have some warning, not enough. Liam had always kind of hoped he'd do something heroic if he found himself in this situation again; instead he finds himself huddled alone on the roof of Tara's building, clinging to the industrial HVAC, waiting to get swept away.

He doesn't get swept away.

After, he goes back down to Tara's apartment to survey the damage. He's peeling seaweed off cans of oranges when the front door slams open. Liam jumps, wheels around to see Ale, shoulders heaving. They stare at each other for a long moment, both wild-eyed, until Ale exhales, slumping. "Man," Ale says, with something that could almost be a smile if he didn't look so wrecked. "This place is a goner. You're gonna have to rip out all the carpet, at the very least." He bounces on his toes a couple times, seawater squishing up between his boots.

"I've been thinking of putting in hardwood anyway," says Liam, wiggles the can of oranges. "Hungry?"

They end up down by the ocean, slumped against each other, daring the water to come for them.

Thirstlands

Nick Wood

One thing I knew for sure: the rains were late here too.

I scanned the ridge of grey rock towering off to my left—there was no vast, unified surge of water pouring over the edge as I remembered only five years ago—just sparse, thin water curtains dropping from the escarpment into the sludgy green river over a hundred metres below me. Gone was the towering spray of vapour above, no water cloud sweeping overhead. Deep in the wooded Batoko Gorge, the sluggish river struggled through the trees. Good old Queen Vic—although she was long dust, her namesake waterfall here in Zambia was drying quickly too—this was no longer "Mosi-oa-Tunya" either, no "Smoke-That-Thunders."

"Record," I said reluctantly, closing my right eye simultaneously to activate my neural cam. *Du Preez is going to hate this.*

A black-uniformed guard with an AK strapped across his shoulder stood nearby, clicking on his digital palm-slate. The payment request bleeped in my cochlea; with a muttered command, I sent the amount in Chinese yuan from the Office account in my head.

No, Du Preez is going to go absolutely mad, absolutely bedonnered about this.

The guard moved on, accosting a young black man with an antiquated mobile phone cam. There were only five other people circling the viewing platform; none jostling for a view. I licked my lips, ever thirsty as usual.

<*Is that all it is now? What a fokkin' waste of time and money!*>

Hell, I had no idea the Boss had joined me, watching through my eyes like a mind-parasite, tickling my cochlea with his electronic croak.

So I closed my eyes. In the reddish darkness of my interior eyelids I could make out a green light flicking on the right, virtually projected by Cyril "the Rig's" neural cybernetics. The Office was online, the bloody Boss in.

But there was still only a dull red glow behind my left eye-lid. *Where are you, Lizette? What are you doing right now . . . and are you okay? You must know I hate having to leave you; but I've got to pay the bills, especially the damn water.*

<*So what happened about the fokkin' rain forecast and the Vic Falls deluge that we flew you out for?*>

"Blown away, I think, gone."

I spat the words, each one drying my mouth further. Eyes closed, a faint tingle of water from the falls sprayed onto my cheeks—a tantalising tickle onto my dry protruding tongue. I pulled my tongue in before the sun could burn it into biltong steak. The water from my hip-flask sizzled sweetly for a brief moment as I swigged, but then the ever-present tongue-throat ache was back.

Always thirsty, I took a final frustrated gulp and opened my eyes. I stretched my arms and fingers across the wooden railings of the viewing platform, but I couldn't feel any more faint spray. The sky was becoming darker blue—still clear, the bloating red sun dropping onto the horizon.

No, there was no "Smoke-That-Thunders," no constantly roiling crash of water anymore—all that's left is an anaemic spattering of water, me, and a few other tourists scanning the ridge for a riverine surge that would never come.

Beyond, the surrounding green GM bio-fuel fields stretch to the horizon, leeching the river. Over the horizon, in slums on the outskirts of Livingstone, I'd heard there were crowds of desperate thirsty, probably starving, people gathering to watch their food shipped overseas as biofuels for SUVs and military tanks. I had taken the long way round to avoid the sight, so I don't know if that's the case for sure—or if it's yet another web myth. I'm not sure if even Cyril could tell me; I'd heard FuelCorps had censored the overhead sats. Anyway, there's no market for video clips of *that* sort of thing anymore, not even from the last of the official news agencies.

<Hell man, I'm off to ask Bongani how we can jack up your visuals on your clips to see if we can get any of our online Avatar subscribers to pay for them. Not even our Chinese Stanley will want to meet Livingstone with the crappy shots you got there. Du Preez out.>

Ach ja, shit, and the Boss too, of course. I winced at the sharpness of his tone in my ear. I had no energy to reply—he never waits for one anyhow—and swigged another guilty sip.

There was a bleep in my cochlea—a wifi neural kit was requesting contact. I ignored it; it wasn't Lizette.

"Hey, have you got the latest C-20 model?"

I looked at a man in the khaki Smart safari-suit, skin reddened by the sun, despite the generous smears of what looked like factor 100 white sunblock. His accent was vaguely Pan-European, the wispy greying hair underneath his dripping pith helmet disguising its original color. He grinned at me and tapped his head. "I've had the latest C-20 model inserted, no need for vocal commands, it's all thought operated."

"Mine's an old C-12 model," I said, scanning past him, along the escarpment and eastwards to the vast maize fields below, which looked as if they were encircling and attacking the shrinking strip of green riverine bush and trees. Perhaps I'd edit the clip later; momentarily too embarrassed to audibly cut my shoot.

The man went on talking, breathing hot meat and beer onto me, and I wondered briefly whether he'd heroically Safari-Shot drugged game before eating it: "My Rig's compatible with the latest web designs from China and is wired into the optic nerve for six-factor zoom capability."

"That's good to hear, I'm afraid mine just does a job."

It was then that I saw them, scattered on the edge of the riverine trees, before the fenced maize fields, as if they'd died seeking cover from encroaching razor-wire. I knew the Boss would kill me, but I had to keep filming—it was the biggest elephant graveyard I'd ever seen, and it had been months since *anyone* had last seen an elephant. Huge piles of bones, like stranded and stripped hull-wrecks of ships, some of them arching their white curves in neatly laid out patches—as if their death had been calm, deliberate, and careful to acknowledge an individual, elephantine space for dying.

Jan du Preez may only want Live Game—me, I take what I can get.

The man turned to follow my gaze and grumbled with disappointment: "Bugger. Just bloody bones, I thought you'd seen some real wildlife for a change. Did you know the C-20 also has full amygdala-hippocampal wiring that allows synchronous ninety-three percent recall of emotion?"

"Really?" I looked back at him. For the past few years it felt as if my own feelings were desiccating; the barest husks of what they had been—what must it be like to pull out old video clips saturated with the original feelings, rich and raw with young emotional blood? It's been over two decades since Lizette and I had watched handheld video clips of us and baby Mark, now three years gone to an accountancy career in Oz. Three years on from the hijacking that left him without a car outside our gates but crying with gratitude he was alive, physically unharmed. Three years since I've been too scared to walk outside the house but weirdly okay to travel to so many other places. It's been only two years, though, since Du Preez contributed to the Rig in my head—to "Cyril," who has helped to sharpen and hold my most recent memories.

Still, I've been thirsty ever since. I'm sure they buggered up my thirst center at the same time they did the Rig neurosurgery. But the insurance disclaimers had been twelve pages long, the surgeons in denial.

The man opened his mouth again; sweat dripped off the end of his nose, as if his Smart Suit struggled to adequately regulate his temperature. I couldn't resist a brief smile at the sight, but turned away, not wishing to say goodbye. Maybe old feelings should be left alone after all, left to dry and wither like fallen leaves.

"Command—cut!" I muttered.

So his Rig was better (bigger) than mine . . . big bloody deal. He's not an African, just an effete tourist in a harsh land his skin can't deal with, filtering it through his foreign money, fancy implants and clever clothes.

And me?

Red blinked behind both my eyelids when I shut my eyes, so I let Cyril randomly cycle a babble of blogs over me as I headed back to the car park, the public toilet, and the chilly airport hotel, before the early morning flight home.

Home—and Liz.

§

The last kay home is always the longest, so I tried to coax more speed out of the car's electrics. The time, though, seemed to drag on for an eternity, inching past corrugated iron shacks. People milled on the right of the road on the approach into Dingane Stad—mainly men, concentrated near a bridge overpass, no doubt jostling in hope to be picked up by passing bakkies or trucks for a desperate day's work.

One old man near the road held out pale palms to me—but I've always avoided paternalistic gifts and dependency; this is Africa. I kept my windshields up, my doors locked.

The fields on the hill were brittle brown and eaten to dust by scraggly herds of cattle, watched by boys with sticks in hands, with shoulder-strapped and cocked Chinese P.L.A. T-74s, that looked in danger of blowing off their legs.

Still definitely no rains here either—shit man, we're lucky we have our secret backup, Lizette; a hedge against the soaring costs of privatised water.

My eyes blinked heavily with the alternating early morning sunlight and the spidery-web shadows of overhead pirate cables snaking down from Council Electric grids and pylons into the shacks along the roadside. The cables will be cut by officials come sunset tonight and will have sprung back magically by tomorrow morning. Crazy, man, absolutely bedonnered, holding an impoverished community to electric ransom, when there's so much sun for free.

My car was on auto as it turned into the long and bumpy drive past neighboring sugarcane fields up to our small-holding, an old disused farmhouse we'd bought at a financial stretch called "Cope's Folly," in search of a "simpler" semi-rural lifestyle. Hah.

I closed my eyes and sent yet another desperate message, almost a plea: *<I'm home, Lizette.>*

The red light under my left lid continued to ache for moments.

And then flickered green: *<About bledy time, Mister Graham bledy Mason.>*

Relief flooded me. *So she's still pissed off with me. That's something, at least.*

The black electrified gates swung open to the car's emitted password.

Liz was waiting, arms crossed, gum-booted and disheveled in loose and dirty clothes, glowering. There was a barrow of carrots next to her—a good looking bunch, so no doubt due to go to the neighboring township co-op, as she's done ever since we moved here and she started growing food.

We pecked cheeks warily, eye contact tentative, and I'm awkward with a complex mix of feelings. Lizette's a big-boned woman, dark of skin, with wild hair that she shoves back with a red Alice band. Her black hair was greying quickly, which she flaunted with a twist of her band. I gave her a furtive glance. Even angry, her brown eyes were lovely. But the anger seemed to have dimmed, she was almost . . . anxious?

It's not like her to be fearful—she still drives herself alone into the township when I'm away, despite what I always tell her about the dangers. Nah, I must be wrong. She can't be nervous, not Lizzie.

She wheeled the barrow off to pack the carrots away in the shed. I stepped inside and through to the hot sunken lounge, with its big AG ("almost green") Aircon against the far wall. My presence tripped the air-conditioner switch with a *click*; whirring on. The web portal was tucked away discreetly in the corner as she'd insisted when I'd had it installed for her, but the controls were on red, as if constantly locked, unused. But she'd sent me that response just before I arrived. A new decorative screensaver spiralled, a fuzzy grainy floating picture, hard to make out as I walked through to the kitchen to make cheese sandwiches for us and to grab a drink of water.

She was waiting on the single chair when I came back and she took the plate with thanks, putting it on the side table, as if not hungry. I sat on the couch opposite. She looked at the floor. *Oh no man, was this going to be another rehash of the argument we'd had before I'd left? "Why can't you demand to stay on local assignments, you've never been able to stand up to Du Preez, blah, blah, blah."*

"It looks like the garden's been productive despite the lack of rain," I said, breaking the silence, but putting my cheese sandwich down, suddenly not hungry myself.

She looked up at me and smiled. "Yes, our solar well-pump has helped, although I've been careful not to let the well drop below three quarters."

I smiled back, relieved to see her relax. "A bloody godsend that was, you calling in the surveyor—you've always had damn good intuition, Lizzie."

She grimaced and stood up, pacing restlessly over to the web portal. *What the hell did I say? Must be the swear words—she hated me swearing, never gets used to it, keen Churchgoer and all—"bledy" was the worst of it from her, and even that had only arrived these past few years.*

Her dark eyes brimmed with tears when she turned to face me. She leaned against the thin computer screen, and the floating screensaver froze and sharpened beneath the touch of her fingers. It was a picture of a little barefooted black girl in a broken yellow grimy dress, looking up at the screen, face taut with pain. And it looked like it had been snapped from the CCTV on our outside gate.

"Her name's Thandi," Lizette said, "She came here yesterday morning after you left—her tongue was so thick she couldn't drink. She was dying of thirst, Graham. Dying, man, vrek, out on her little feet, true's God. I didn't know things were this bad! She's just seven years old, Graham, but I had to dribble the water down her throat; her tongue was almost choking her."

"So you gave her tap water or water from the fridge," I said, standing up.

She shook her head: "Nee, Graham, I gave her water from our emergency supply and called the village Traditional Leader to tell him about it and to find her mom. There are others like her, just down the bledy road, man. So I told T.L. Dumisane and said we could spare them ongoing three-quarters of our well supply."

"Ach shit man, Lizzie, you didn't, did you? That's *ours*! Why the hell didn't you ask me first? You've had free access to my head for three years now. And why didn't you return my calls or let me know you were okay at least?"

"It's hardly free," she snorted, "I can only hear what you *choose* to tell me. And what would *you* have done and said, Mister Graham Mason?" She stood up tall and focused, as if suddenly sure of herself.

I hesitated, but just for a moment: "I'd have given her water from the fridge and told you to keep quiet about the well. You know we have to keep this a secret for our own safety, otherwise we'll be the target of every water bandit and tsotsi in KwaZulu-Natal!"

"See, I knew you'd say that, and I hate arguing when I can't see your face. I knew calling you would end up in a fight. I'm sorry I ended up saying nothing and worrying you, but I had to make this decision on my own. Dumisane is a good man, hy sal niks se nie . . . and there's no way I can live here with children dying just down the road. No ffff—" She clamped her mouth with her hand and took a breath before releasing it and finishing through clenched teeth: "No . . . way!"

Lizette *never* swears—and only reverts to Afrikaans when she's absolutely distraught. She seemed to crumple slightly, clutching at herself, sobbing. The little yellow-dressed girl fuzzed over and spiralled randomly across the screen. Of course, she'd always wanted a little girl too.

My anger emptied into a desperate sense of helplessness. I hovered for moments and then stepped forward to coax her to turn *towards* the screen. I could send her comforting emoti-messages from LoveandPeace Dotcom that should help soothe and calm her.

Her eyes froze me, though—her dark, lovely, lined but frighteningly fierce eyes. I knew then with some weird certainty that if I tried touching her, turning her to face the computer screen, she would scream, hit and kick me towards the outside door and gate. Beyond that, I could see that there was no returning in her eyes.

My arms hung in frigid confusion as tears streamed from her blazing eyes.

Shit, what else was there to do? I could only reach out to hold her, awkwardly wrapping my arms around her taut, trembling body.

Her arms were rigid, almost pushing at me for moments, but then she seemed to let go, and the sobs strangled in her throat; her hair was thick and tickly in my face, my own eyes stinging from a sudden bite of emotion. I could smell the coconut fragrance in her hair and remembered it had been her favorite shampoo when we'd first met almost thirty years ago. Hell man, it must be *years* since we'd last really held each other.

Since Mark had left.

"Come," she said, pushing me away but then taking my hand in hers, my shirt sleeve wiping her wet face.

She pulled me forwards.

Oh . . . right, so she's not taking me out to see how the veggie patch has grown.

Dear God, I'd almost forgotten how much of a woman she was.

And, in the end—despite my constant thirst—I wasn't nearly as dry as I feared I might be, either.

§

I left her sleeping.

Face relaxed, serene, dark hair thickly splashed over an oversized yellow pillow, she lay on her back, a soft snore. It hurt to watch her, and I felt strangely guilty to stare—weird man, we'd been together so long—so I rolled over quietly and pulled on trousers and shirt, making my way through to the front door.

The door flickered and dallied while it de-armed, so I toyed with the idea of getting a drink of water from the kitchen. No, a dry mouth never killed anyone in the short term. I scanned the weapon rack behind the door, eventually inserting a taser-rod into my belt, before clicking the electric gate open in the outside wall.

The dry mid-afternoon heat carried little of the past summer humidity in the air. I breathed a set of ten deep breaths to quell my panic and then stepped with jellied legs through the gate, clicking it closed behind me.

As the gate clanged shut, I noted a red sports car parked beneath an ancient oak across the road, its driver in shadow. No time to reopen the gate—it would just expose the house and Lizzie. So I deactivated the fence charge, rammed the hand-panel deep into my trouser pocket and backed against the gate, hauling out the taser. Shit, I should have gone for the gun instead.

The car door opened, and a young black woman stood up, her arms akimbo, hands empty—dressed in workmanlike blue overalls, duffle-bag strapped over her shoulders, hair cropped squarely close to her head: "Kunjani, Mister Mason, I'm here about your water."

They certainly hadn't wasted any time; things *must* be pretty desperate in the township.

"Ngiyaphila, unjani wena?" I replied, easing the taser into my belt.

"I am well too," she smiled with a slight twist to her mouth; I wondered whether she toyed with the idea of testing my paltry isiZulu, but thankfully her next words were in English: "I'm Busisiwe Mchunu, a hydrogeologist for the FreeFlow Corporation. However, I reserve room for a little private freelance work in the services of my community; strictly off the record, you understand."

"Oh," I said, with an African handshake of palm, thumbs grip, palm again: "Graham Mason, pleased to meet you. And of course I understand." *Wow, strong grip.*

"I'm here to survey the underground water on your land. Of course, *before* the white man, all of this land was ours anyway."

"Oh," I said, "Is that a . . . veiled threat?"

She chuckled: "Don't be so paranoid, Mister Mason, we amaZulu don't veil our threats. It's just a historical observation. Your wife looks out for us, so we've looked out for you."

"Hello!" Lizette leaned against the inside of the gate, back in grubby trackpants and shirt. "Who're you?"

"I'm Chief Dumisane's water rep, Mizz Basson," said Busisiwe, walking across. "Just call me Busisiwe."

"Pleased to meet you, Busisiwe, I'm Lizette." They shook hands through the gate.

Lizette smiled as I gave her the controls. She rattled off a fluent phrase of what sounded like welcoming isiZulu for Busisiwe, who responded with obvious delight. I could tell they'd probably get on like a shack on fire.

"I'm just going for a walk," I told them.

Lizette looked surprised as the gate opened. "Be careful, Graham."

Yes, I do remember this was the path on which Mark was robbed and stabbed in the face; I have replayed his scarred face so many times in my head. But I know I need to do this, if I can.

It's a short walk, but every step felt heavy, my legs stiff in anticipation of someone leaping out at me from behind the tall stalks of sugarcane densely spearing both sides of the footpath. The path bent sharply to the right as it had when I'd last walked it with Lizette four years ago, dipping down into the valley with an expansive view of the city, skyscrapers strutting their stuff against the clear sky; no fires today.

There, beside the path, lay the cracked and uneven boulder Lizzie and I had rested on, after we'd agreed to buy the small holding. My bum warmed as I sat down, the disarmed taser-rod stabbing into the small of my back. Around the city lay blackened Midland hilltops, informally marking the southern perimeter of the Umgeni Valley. Dingane Stad, "Sleepy Hollow," as it had once been known, or Pietermaritzburg by the white Afrikaners.

"Switch off." The Rig fell absolutely silent, no lights blinked inside my eyelids, just the red constant heat of the midmorning sun filtering through my eyelid blood-vessels.

It'd been two years since I'd been absolutely alone. Two years since the implant and I'd last been quiet in my head, cut off from the electric pulse of the world. Here, there were no hovering voices, no Cyril, just my own solitary thoughts.

My shirt trickled with sweat, and with my thumb I killed the black Matabele ant biting my shin. It gave off an acidic stink as it died, and I stood up quickly, but there was no nearby swarm, no nest hiding under the rock.

This is a hard place to be, but all I know right now is that this is where I want to die. This is where I want to lay down my bones, just like the elephants. Why? I have no bloody idea. Maybe it's to do with the light on the hills or perhaps just the bite and smell of an ant. The thoughts circled my brain, trapped and private, no place to go.

Still, as I walked the path home, my steps felt somehow lighter, looser, but never quite tension-free.

"Switch on," I said, as if re-arming myself for the world.

<Hey, where the hell you been? You must upload your video clips from Vic Falls for the day!>

That bastard Du Preez. I glanced at my watch, it was after four. *<Work's over, I'll do it tomorrow.>*

<You'll do it now! Jeez man, I've heard of sleeping on the job, but you just took the bledy cake on that one earlier with your wife.>

Shit, I must have forgotten to switch off, swept up in the day's events, and he had just . . . watched?

<Did you?> I asked.

No answer, but he must know what I was asking. *<Damn you, Du Preez, cut Office.>*

I stopped to take several slow and deep breaths, thirsty as hell.

Around the last bend, Lizette and Busisiwe were standing in the shade by Busisiwe's car and turned to me as I approached.

Lizette shook her head.

I looked at Busisiwe. "It's a shallow freshwater aquifer," she said. "It's also pretty small. I don't think it will last long, unless we get more rainfall."

Lizette looked at me.

This is Africa, I wanted to tell her, *doing this may salve our conscience in the short term, but will solve nothing in the long term.*

I could tell in her eyes she knew what I was thinking, even without the direct link with Cyril that I'd pressed her so long to get, in the hope that it might bring us closer. I could also see resignation and uncertainty—for us, and all we had tried to build—and, despite this morning, I could also see a fear of the end for us in her eyes.

I opened my mouth, knowing my next words could finish everything.

I turned to look at Busisiwe. "Okay," I said. "We'll help."

"Ngiyabonga," she said.

Lizette put her arm through mine. Skin on skin will do me.

I'll take this moment. I couldn't be sure how long it would last. All I knew for certain was that I wasn't ready for some endings and that the rains were late. *Bloody weird, but I'm not* quite *so thirsty anymore either. Long may this last too.*

Solar Child

Camille Meyers

Below, sunlight glints off the peaks of a shifting ocean dyed blue-black with depth. The sharp wind carries salt and stings Jamie's cheeks with velocity as she soars above, cradled in the Kevlar pouch of her flying gear. Jamie pulls a strap and shifts her weight to the right. Bio obediently tilts his wings and banks south.

"Good boy, Bio," Jamie calls above the wind's whistle. "We're almost there!" She double-checks the coordinates displayed on her oversized flying goggles, then scans the seas. "Keep your big eyes out for trouble. We don't want another run in with pirates or Revelationers."

The large yellow beast burbles as if responding to her verbal directions. Jamie knows he cannot understand her words. No more than a dog or parrot could, at least. He was not designed for that. As a budding genetic engineer, Jamie had made her name working on the solarsaurus team. The goal was to create living, solar-powered transportation, whose fuel and waste was sustainable much like the horse and buggy of old, and Jamie's inner child reveled in the fact that the result looked a lot like a pterodactyl.

From the flying pouch strapped to her steed's chest, Jamie sees the whorls of photosynthetic symbionts living in Bio's large membranous wings. The many green clusters look like splotches of lichen spreading across ancient stone or the spotty swirls of a galaxy. Bio gives a high trill and nods his long slender snout. A pod of dolphins crests the waves below in graceful gray arcs, and Jamie resists the urge to fly closer and zip through their spray. This is not a joy ride. She needs to concentrate on the mission no matter how rare the wildlife sighting.

Jamie's headset beeps, and Floyd's voice cuts through the wind's whistle. "How's it looking out there, Jamie?"

"Blue skies, sparkling waters. Oh, and dolphins." Jamie zooms in with her goggles' camera and snaps a few photos of them.

"The Barnacle Pod? You're a little out of their usual range. Can you get me a—"

"Sending the picture now," says Jamie, keying in the command on her wristband.

"You're the best, Jamie."

"You're welcome, Floyd."

"But seriously, any suspicious ships?"

"Nothing but a steam fisher a little ways back."

To fill the pause, she adds, "You know, back in my college days, I used to debate with demonstrating Revelationers."

"Are you crazy?"

Jamie laughs. "That was before they militarized. Back when working for Dr. Laird was still an unfulfilled dream, I'd quote her about how humanity needed to rely on assisted evolution through genetic modification to cope with the altered Earth. They would spew their doctrine about how the spreading desertification, coastal flooding, and rising infertility and birth defects was retribution for trespassing in God's territory of the genome. Luckily, my friends pulled me away before the flying spit turned into swinging fists." She chuckles.

"I spent so much of college holed up in the lab that I hardly saw daylight, let alone demonstrators. Ugh, I made so many slides of snail parasites that—"

"Hold up." She focuses her goggles to magnify a bright speck on the horizon. The large white sails of a luxury solar yacht fill her vision. "I think I found our generous sponsor." She double-checks coordinates. "Yep, right at the rendezvous point. Right on time. Well, a little early actually."

Jamie eyes the maneuverable guard ships flanking the yacht. They look run-of-the-mill anti-pirate. She doubts the group of religious fanatics that attacked their floating research station a few months ago would disguise themselves as a wealthy Lander out for a pleasure cruise. Still, she cannot fathom the minds of militarized zealots who label her work at the Photobio Research Station an abomination against God.

"Be careful Jamie. After the last Revelationers attack we can't afford . . . I don't want to lose. . . ." Floyd's voice cracks as he fumbles for words. "Anyone else."

"I know, Floyd," she says, more soft than irritable. "I'll radio you again after contact."

"Roger."

§

Floyd's emotion evokes her own, and Jamie tries to consciously compartmentalize the memories of the last Revelationer's attack. Never before had she felt so much fear. Jamie always kept a cool head under pressure and took charge of a situation. It is not the *ratta-tat* of artillery or the huge explosion that rocked the whole research station that haunts her nightmares. Instead it is desperation, endless searching through twisting narrow corridors lit with the blinking glow of emergency lights and the screech of sirens that drown out her own wails for Ella. When she wakes from these dreams shivering with sweat, Jamie reminds herself of how she found Ella and wrapped an orange life jacket around the little girl. Of how they clung to each other until the world returned to silence.

In fact, the explosion prompted the research station's need to reach out to new sponsors. Saltwater flooded into Biodome III, killing the plants and rendering the soil useless. Fertile dirt, viable seeds, and new glass panels all imported from land cost more than the station's store of emergency funds, so when they received interest from a new donor, the station could not afford to miss the opportunity.

Keying in the designated radio frequency Jamie makes contact with the yacht below. As a rule, the research station never gives out its ever-changing coordinates. Identity confirmed, Jamie leads their potential savior to her work, her home, her life.

§

Forty minutes later the yacht docks at the research station. Freed from his flying harness, Bio flaps over to join the small flock of solarsaurs clinging to the side of the settlement. They dip their elongated heads underwater to scrape seaweed and mussels from the pontoons and grind the shells with flattened molars. As creatures designed for a specific purpose rather than evolved in a certain landscape, Jamie notes their unexpected resourcefulness when it comes to foraging. With such stretched and tinkered genes, where exactly does this mollusk-eating behavior come from? Learned or instinctual? How much of what we are comes from what we are? Jamie shakes her head and mentally steps back from the chasm of philosophy, saving the unanswerable for another time.

Turning to her guests, Jamie says, "Welcome to the Photobio Research Station!" with a sweeping gesture. With that, Jamie hands her flying equipment to an aid and begins the well-rehearsed tour. Typically, their land-dwelling donors take a virtual expedition through the research base, but occasionally some of them need to experience it firsthand to commit their money to a project.

Fernanda Harrison's heels click on the metal gangway as she walks down from her pearlescent sea vessel. The wind tussles auburn hair cut in sharp angles and sticks it to the gloss on her straight lips. Her eyes remain hidden behind a pair of large sunglasses. Floyd, as communications manager for the station, vets all potential investors and gave Fernanda the green light, but something about the woman put Jamie on edge. She had scanned Fernanda's profile earlier that morning: 47-year-old CEO of Progressive Energy, Inc., known for her cutthroat bargaining and philanthropy to climate refugees, married to the famous abstract painter Loren Klin, no children. While the solarsaur project was widely advertised, they kept the current project hush-hush due to potential backlash from both Revelationers and the general public alike. Supposedly, Fernanda learned of their work from screenwriter George Faulkner, who upgraded from sports car to solarsaur and always made quite an entrance at celebrity parties. George's unintentional advertisement brought some of the biggest investors to the research station. Yet, Jamie cannot pin down the woman. Ambitious entrepreneur seeking to invest in a new wave of technology? A woman with too much time and money on her hands? Or did she have a more personal interest in their work?

"As you can see, we are a small mobile operation. We are almost entirely self-sufficient, growing our own food in biodomes and running entirely on solar power," Jamie says, hoping to engage the energy mogul.

"As one would expect in this day and age," Fernanda says. "I am not interested in where you live. I want to see what you can do."

"Of course," Jamie replies, maintaining a plastic smile. Two stern-faced men flank Fernanda as they enter the research station.

Walking through the narrow labyrinthine corridors, Jamie skips ahead in her script. "During the solarsaur project we developed new technologies and techniques for the splicing of genes and the integration of photosynthetic symbionts with large land animals. However, Dr. Melissa Laird, who unfortunately passed away due to breast cancer three years ago, had a vision that stretched beyond coping with the current hot and toxic state of our planet to one which redefines the position of humans in our biosphere. Ultimately, her work culminated in this."

The small group enters a large clear dome filled with fruit trees, a small fish pond, and a variety of edible crops ranging from the tender shoots of seedlings to tall tangles of pole beans. Jamie glances around and then exchanges a few quiet words with a woman digging in the dirt as the visitors scan the area with small frowns. The gardener stands up and hollers, "Ella! Where you hidin', child? Auntie Jamie's back, and she's got guests for you to meet."

The top of an apple tree comes alive. Branches sway, leaves rustle, and then *thump*, a small dark-skinned girl emerges and runs so hard that her momentum almost knocks Jamie over as thin arms encircle her legs in a hug. Jamie gives a burst of laughter from the impact. "I wasn't gone *that* long! But I missed you too." Her voice softens as she runs a hand over the girl's smooth bald head. "Come on, Ella. Say hello to our visitors. This is Ms. Fernanda Harrison and . . . um her two friends, Mr. Smyth and Mr. Kay."

Fernanda's body has gone stiff, and her eyes fix on the child like a raptor. With slow movements, as if trying to avoid startling a sparrow, she lifts her sunglasses and props them in her hair.

With a little nudging, Ella peeks around Jamie's legs. Large brown eyes stare out from an earth tone face freckled with bits of forest green.

"She's beautiful," Fernanda whispers.

The girl hides again and giggles into the back of Jamie's knees. "Ella is the first photosapien. The project was modeled after the relationship between corals and sea anemones with photosynthetic zooxanthellae. The host animal, photosapiens or solarsaurs, for example, provide shelter, transportation, and protection, for their photosynthesizing partner. In return, the little green cells gift a bit of glucose, food essentially, straight into the bloodstream of their host. Ella still needs to eat, but not as much as normal humans. Of course, she also needs to spend plenty of time in sunshine. She dislikes wearing clothes, but we aren't sure if this is because it covers her symbionts or is just normal kid behavior. So we compromise, a spaghetti strap dress, but no shoes. Hey Ella," Jamie coaxes, "let's show Ms. Harrison your curtsey. Remember how we've been practicing like the princesses in your favorite movie."

Ella tightens her grip on Jamie's pants for a second before jumping out. Then with theatrical poise, the little girl pinches the edges of her white dress blazed with sunflowers and tips a curtsy. Her toes grind into the rich garden dirt as she says, "Pleasure to meet you, Miss!"

Fernanda sweeps the hem of an imaginary skirt and bends like a ballet dancer. "The pleasure is all mine, Princess Ella." The CEO's warmth and playfulness with Ella surprise Jamie.

The little girl giggles and then repeats her curtsy to each of the bodyguards. The men return startled half-bows. Jamie smiles, relieved that her ploy to entice Ella worked. Having spent her whole life with the less than eighty people who lived and worked on the research station, the young photosapien was unused to meeting strangers. Jamie and her peers feel that the less people who know about Ella and the project the better. The Revelationers and much of the general public consider genetically modified humans taboo, especially ones so visibly different.

"She's bald?" Fernanda asks, squatting down to Ella's level and beckoning the girl over.

"The top of the head and shoulders get the most sun exposure on a human body, so we eliminated hair to increase photosynthetic surface area. The high melanin content of her skin reduces the impact of UV radiation."

"How old are you?" Fernanda's tone softens.

Ella counts on her fingers. "Four an'a half!"

"Wow, such a big girl! I like your dress."

"I don't like it, 'cept I can do this!" The young photosapien twirls on her toes, and the sundress flairs out like the petals of a flower. Then she collapses in a heap of giggles. Even the square-jawed bodyguards smile.

"Wanna see my baby brothers?" Ella asks, sitting up. "I got to help innocutate them."

"Inoculate," Jamie automatically corrects, pronouncing the word slowly.

"I-no-cu-late," repeats Ella.

"Good," says Jamie, but Ella has already started skipping ahead.

"This way," the little girl calls, co-opting the role of tour leader.

"She means she passed on some of her photosynthetic cells to the two boys born six months ago," explains Jamie as she and the other adults follow. "Normally when a baby is born it is inundated with microbes from the birth canal and also through a mother's caress and kisses. This contact helps to build the newborn's immune system." Fernanda frowns, and her posture stiffens, but Jamie continues. "Young ruminants, like deer or sheep, ingest a bit of their mother's fecal matter to populate the flora of their four-chambered stomachs so they can properly digest plant material. The concept is the same for photosapiens. In addition to immune-boosting bacteria, a mother photosapien will pass on some of her photosynthetic symbionts through her sweat. The cells can only survive in moist environments. We have lab cultures of course, but we wanted to test the theory."

They stop in front of a glass-walled nursery and look in. A young man sits in a corner reading a book as his two charges sleep curled together in a large crib situated in a sunbeam. "As you can see, the trial was successful."

Ella raises her hands, and Jamie dutifully lifts her up to peer at her siblings. Ella is getting too big to be carried, but Jamie does not complain, not wanting to think about the little girl outgrowing this closeness. "The symbionts reside in modified pores in the skin which grow and spread over time. Nutrients are passed through a thin membrane—"

"Are they twins?" Fernanda interrupts.

"That's Duo. And that's Tristian," Ella says, smudging the glass with fingerprints.

Jamie swallows her frustration at the inattentive audience and adds, "We use a synthetic womb system, so they are twins only in that they were born a few hours apart. Genetically, they are distinct, as we want as much variety as possible in this early population."

Ella squirms, so Jamie sets her down. "I'm gonna go back to the garden and Matilda."

"Okay," Jamie says, and the little girl skips down the corridor humming a made-up tune. She recalls the triumph she and her fellow researchers felt when Ella was born and how tiny and tenuous she had seemed, like the first leaves of a pea sprout. With Revelationers scouring the land and sea, Jamie feared the world would reject Ella and her brothers. But Jamie clutched to the words of her mentor: "The human race does not need revolution. We have tried that so many times, and here we are. No, what we need is a new way of living with ourselves. A way to adapt to the world we have created. We need to evolve. And evolution takes love." She and her fellow researchers knew that Dr. Laird meant that to dedicate one's life to this project would take more than an ideal, it would take passion for the project and love for its subjects. Jamie never expected to feel as strongly attached to Ella as she does, but now she could not imagine the world without her.

Fernanda continues to watch the babies. One of them yawns, then flexes his pudgy, green-specked fingers.

Just as Jamie begins to grow uncomfortable in the sustained silence, Fernanda quietly asks, "Do you know why I was attracted to your project?"

"No." Jamie shakes her head.

"In my early thirties, my husband and I tried to start a family. Even with all the medical expertise money could buy, I suffered three miscarriages. One so far along I counted fingers and toes as the bloody fetus grew cold in my cupped palms." Fernanda closes her eyes and tightens her jaw with suppressed pain. For the first time, Jamie notices fine lines creasing the woman's face. "Finally, I carried a baby to term. My son lived two months before his lungs collapsed." Fernanda's hazel hawk eyes bore into Jamie's. "I want a child, Dr. Brown. A child who can live in this world. I want Ella."

Internally, sirens scream and lights flash down tilted corridors. Jamie's chest constricts and her heart pounds overtime. She folds her arms, takes a deep breath, and hisses, "She is not for sale."

"One point five million," Fernanda says.

"No."

"Think about it," Fernanda says, leaning forward. "What could this research station do with that much money?"

The practical part of Jamie's mind runs the numbers. More than enough to fix the damage from the last Revelationer's attack, they could even install defensive turrets, maybe guard ships, and still have funds left over. With that they could hire more research personnel, upgrade technology, and expand the photosapien project beyond its literal and figurative baby steps. But those cherished baby steps. . . .

Jamie never wanted kids. Never felt the womb tug of her biological clock. Never cooed over chubby infants. She did not think twice when mining her own ovaries for the photosapien project when funds ran low. She did not know how many, if any, of her own genes twined in the body of the little green girl. Jamie knew that even if there was a blood tie, Ella did not belong to her. The Photobio Research Station held custody. Dr. Melissa Laird had her registered when born, filling out all the necessary paperwork to be a documented citizen of this world. Dr. Laird was insistent that even though she was a research subject, Ella and any subsequent photosapiens were not property. They were humans.

Jamie takes a deep breath, releases it slowly, and then says as evenly as possible, "Certainly, we could use those funds, but she is not chattel. Ella is a human being, and she cannot be bought or sold."

"Of course I am not suggesting any such thing," says Fernanda, looking offended. "Think of it like an adoption. People pay adoption fees all the time. How about five million?" Jamie shakes her head, but Fernanda continues to press. "Think of the life I could give her. A life beyond these gray halls and enclosed domes. She is a growing girl, you cannot keep her confined to a research station her whole life, she will wither."

"Even if she were ready for the outside world, the world is not ready for her. The Revelationers—"

Fernanda barks with laughter. "As if she is safe here! The Revelationers posted a video of their last attack. The bombs, the smoke. If the UN Coast Patrol had not arrived Ella would already be dead. You are a limping target." Jamie swallows hard to suppress the cold sweat of remembered screeching sirens, blinking emergency lights, and her desperate search for Ella. Fernanda gestures to her bodyguards. "But with me she's safe. I have my own state of the art security team, plus no fanatics stalk me, they would not even know to look my direction. No one will know until the world is ready for her, as you say."

Jamie seethes at the accusation that she cannot protect Ella, but the underlying truth to Fernanda's words pierce through her anger. Would it really be better for Ella to let Fernanda raise her? Safer, yes, but would Ella really be happier? Was she being selfish trying to keep Ella here with her?

But again, Ella was not hers.

"As the first photosapien, continuous monitoring of Ella is necessary to see how she develops. If she runs into any health complications, we are uniquely equipped to deal with them." With more passion Jamie adds, "Plus, she is just a little girl. I can't rip her away from everyone and everything she knows and loves and send her off with some stranger. She'd be scared. Why do you want Ella so badly anyway? I know you want a kid, but you can't have her." Jamie meets Fernanda's sharp eyes.

"Then how about one of them," Fernanda says, gesturing to the two babies still asleep in their sunbeam. "You can keep one for your scientific monitoring, and I can keep one safe from the Revelationers. I can provide whatever he needs, a specialized diet, a private doctor, custom living facilities. Plus, the five million still stands."

"I . . . I would have to discuss it with the board of directors," Jamie replies. Relief that Fernanda has turned her sights away from Ella floods Jamie's veins like warm water and, with that, a needling of guilt. She knows her personal feelings for Ella swayed her judgement.

"Deal." Fernanda firmly extends a hand. Reluctantly, Jamie shakes it. She studies the business woman and wonders if perhaps one of the twins was her goal all along. Of course she would know to start a bargain high. Jamie feels played, but she can't deny the logic of the arrangement. She will let the rest of the directors decide the trajectory of their lives.

§

Three days later, after papers are signed and money transferred, Fernanda stands on the deck of her yacht, a small photosapien in her arms. As if sensing a kinship in their shared sun-metabolizing attributes, several of the solarsaurs circle over the departing vessel. They burble an ethereal chorus that Jamie instinctively wants to interpret as a journey blessing for Tristian. Along with the solarsaurs' song, Tristian departs in the company of a specialized pediatrician who will keep in regular contact with the station about his development. The bitter taste in Jamie's mouth about the whole transaction dissipates as she watches the way Fernanda snuggles the swaddled green baby to her chest. The sharp woman's features soften with a glowing smile as she looks at her ward.

Watching the scene, Ella squeezes Jamie's hand. The little girl's lower lip pouts out, but at least she's stopped crying over her brother's departure. Jamie squeezes Ella's hand back.

§

Later that night, Jamie slips quietly into Ella's bedroom. The spots on the sleeping girl's skin glow faintly with bioluminescence like a reflection of the stars twinkling through the skylight. Another unexpected result from the genetic manipulations, like the solarsaurs' foraging behavior. Just as unexpected as how much she loves the girl. Perhaps who we are does not come from what we are, but from what we do.

No matter her fears about sending a photosapien into the world, Jamie accepts the need for more people like Fernanda, willing to love a baby as a baby despite genetic differences. Willing to stand up to ridicule and defend against threats. She thinks about the shift in Fernanda's countenance and then her own.

Jamie kisses Ella's jade-dappled forehead. "It's true," she whispers. "Our evolution takes love."

Through the Glass

Leigh Wallace

Sunvault

recursive

Bethany Powell

he had wanted to be an astronaut
but works in an aircraft scrapyard
now, carefully dismantling, resorting
his love making him different from scrappers,
who loot the extinction of another age
he finds, with a scientist's precision,
new bodies for the marvels of his own time
a catharsis, in saving these old giants—
shuttle, airplane, satellite, jet
—to birth new bodies of sunplant, windwing,
radio to the universe.

The Colors of Money

Nisi Shawl

Though the sun grinned fiercely down, September's steadily blowing kaskazi kept Rosalie cool enough as she walked out from under the shadow of the recently arrived aircanoe. Moored to the new mast built atop the Old Fort wall in 1918, *Tippu Tib* bobbed ever so slightly as the last dozen of its passengers disembarked. Beside her, Laurie Jr., Rosalie's formerly estranged brother, blinked in the brilliant afternoon light. "Kind of you to meet me here," he said. That was the sort of automatic politeness she'd come to expect of him during her year in Britain. The sort of surface-borne emotions he seemed to feel for her. Nothing deep. Nothing that would justify his visit now, mere months after her return to Africa.

What did he want? What did he really want? She watched his eyes rove nervously over the heat-thinned crowds of the fruit market. On her first trips to Zanzibar at the age of 18, soon after Leopold's defeat, the inhabitants of Stone Town had seemed strange, their billowing, quasi-Arab robes so different from Everfair's mix of nudity and tropic-adapted European styles.

"Is it far to where we're to stay?"

"No." They reached the intersection. She turned. "This is Hurumzi Street. That means 'free man' in Kee-Swah-Hee-Lee. That building up there—we'll soon pass it—that's Zanzibar's old Office of Manumission." She had learned while in England that Laurie liked being told such things. "From there Emerson House is only a few yards on.

"How was your trip?" She should probably have asked sooner, but he seemed gratified nonetheless.

"A bit of fuss over my transfer to *Tibbu* from the cruiser. Customs officials talked some rot about detaining me in Alexandria since I wasn't boarding the train to Cairo. But I had arranged this little detour with the company's full knowledge. It all worked out with a touch of lubricant." He rubbed his thumb and fingers together in a gesture she easily understood.

Laurie's "little detour" here had taken him as many miles from Alexandria as his original itinerary had taken him from London. Rosalie supposed that once he'd left "civilization" behind the rest of the world was a featureless blur to pass through as quickly as possible. All the rest of the world except their mother's home, where he refused to go. He refused as well to call her their mother—but then he'd been raised by Ellen, who bore them both.

To Rosalie, mothering was what Daisy had done. Mere biological functions didn't matter.

Clouds rushed in to cover the sun. Rosalie raised her hood and gathered her cream-colored Omani duster close about her. Her brother's Foreign Office helmet, made from the pith of the sola tree, would shield him from rain as well as the heat of the sun. But they arrived at the guesthouse before the shower burst.

Imran waited in front to open the door and usher them to the table behind which his mother sat in stiff watchfulness. A nod, a swiftly made notation to the page of the registry book, and her gnarled hands removed an iron key from the bunch at her waist. Imran took the key and went ahead of them to the stairs.

After the fourth flight Laurie flagged. He pretended to be astonished by the view between the bars covering the landing's tiny window. "Very nice!" he declared. "That's the mooring tower, I take it?"

Rosalie didn't bother looking. She already knew the tower was visible. "Yes."

Laurie's stoutness stemmed not from greed or laziness. She no longer laughed, even internally, when his fatness discommoded him. She mounted the next set of steps more slowly. "The view from the rooftop garden is most astonishing. Imran, you will bring us tea there, please."

"Just the ticket." Breathing heavily but still through his nose, Laurie followed her up the penultimate flight.

"Miss's room is to the west," said Imran in his accentless British English. "Yours is opposite. Do you wish to see—"

"No, no, I'm sure it's fine. Will my valet be able to obtain entry? My luggage, when it's brought, will that be properly taken care of?"

"Most assuredly. I will see to it."

"Then let us proceed to the roof for our refreshment." Stubbornness was a family trait.

Exiting the shed at the top of the stairs, Rosalie felt without surprise the gentle patter of rain on her light curls. She made an apologetic face at her brother as he emerged behind her. "It won't last long. Do you mind? There's a pavilion where we can shelter till it stops."

Laurie removed his hat and swiped off the moisture collected on his forehead—probably a greater percentage of sweat than precipitation. "Capital. Cooling, isn't it?"

Imran assisted them in seating themselves, bestowing embroidered cushions so strategically that her brother actually looked at ease on the low benches. At Laurie's nod of satisfaction he disappeared down the stairs without waiting for further instruction.

"Kind of you to meet me here," Laurie said again. He wanted her response so he could continue the conversation in a certain direction.

"I had business on Pemba anyway," she said, "with my coral suppliers and the family who collects shells for me. A trip thirty miles south was on the way."

"Nonetheless. I didn't dare write to tell you why I wished to meet you here, in case some spy found me out. And I realize full well that leaving Everfair so soon after your return, with the government in an uproar, must have upset Mrs. Albin—"

"Do you mean Maman or George's wife?"

"Daisy. *Your* 'mother'—as you keep insisting." From the age of three Laurie had been raised by their father's second wife, Ellen, in England; unlike Rosalie, he refused to acknowledge Daisy Albin's maternal relationship to him. "I imagine she was unhappy to see you go."

"She is a patriot and aware that Everfair's best interests are served by promoting independence." Not to mention the commission Maman's wife Mam'selle had given Rosalie to support the Sheikhas' clandestine extraction plans. "She understood."

"Did she." Laurie heaved himself up for a better sightline over the garden pavilion's short wall. "Will that boy be back up again with our tea soon? I have something to say. I don't wish it overheard by servants."

"Mr. Imran and his mother own this house."

"Or by anyone, if it comes to that."

Secrets. Rosalie had them, too.

To pass the awkward interval till Imran returned, she showed her brother the necklace she kept tucked beneath her smock top. It hung from a leather cord strung with carefully matched treasures: heavy silver beads from the braids of desert wanderers; two-sided rounds of shell, black and moon-bright; segments of blue-dyed coral, unpolished, their rough surfaces intricate with the patterns of growth. And suspended by a filigree finding the size of a baby's hand, the medallion she'd made from the remains of the little oil-slicked Pemba Island tortoise she tried to save.

"Pretty," said Laurie, setting it on the lacquered table before them. What had she expected? Not even Maman, sympathetic and familiar with Rosalie's work from years of intimacy, thought it important. Wordlessly she slipped the necklace back on. Thank heaven she'd met Amrita. Amrita understood.

"Jolly prospect up here," Laurie remarked. Streams of water poured off of the pavilion's canopy. Further away the individual chains of raindrops blended into greyness and obscurity.

The door to the stairway down opened, a subtle change in the sound of the monsoon's drumming, an almost-echo. Imran appeared, holding an umbrella over a woman carrying a tea tray. They hadn't taken two steps in Rosalie's direction before she recognized that woman as Amrita. Who ought to have been thirty, forty, fifty miles away, safe among Pemba's green hills.

Amrita smiled as she lowered the tray. "Miss will like to prepare the drink herself?"

Rosalie was momentarily too outraged at her appearance there to speak.

"That's right," Laurie said. "And is there any milk?" He began lifting the covers of the various bowls and ewers. "Ah, good! And what's this?" He indicated a pink-and-white cube on an enameled saucer.

"A confection of rosewater, a Shirazan delicacy my mother thought you might enjoy," said Imran. He bowed and turned to leave. Amrita did the same.

"Pardon me for just a moment, Laurie." Rosalie leapt up and chased her friends across the garden. She caught up as Imran grasped the handle of the still-open door.

"What are you doing here?" She realized she clutched Amrita's gold-trimmed sleeve. She made herself release it.

Amrita's flower-like face lost a bit of bloom. "Let us get out of the rain and your brother's regard, and I'll tell you." She took Rosalie by her elbow and guided her to the stairs and a few steps down. Imran stayed with them.

Impatiently she asked again, "What are you *doing*?"

"I'm spying on your brother."

"No, *I'm* the one doing that! *You* are simply interfering in what is none of your concern!"

A pitying look. "Imran, tell her."

"Yes, tell me." She rounded on her host. "Am I not intelligent enough for this work? Am I judged incapacitated by emotional attachment to our target? Am I to be withdrawn? Replaced?"

Imran raised his hands, tan palms outward. "No. Please, calm yourself, Miss." He called her "Miss" at all times to avoid addressing her erroneously in front of those who mustn't know of their true status: equals.

The kaskazi entered as the door behind her opened. Her brother stood without, his expression annoyed. "Is the help proving recalcitrant about something, Rosalie? Do you need any assistance?"

"All is well," Imran assured him. "Your sister merely inquired whether little Rita will assume the duties of her personal attendant now she is promoted from the kitchen."

"Doesn't seem so urgent you need to leave the tea to stew, Rosie."

How Rosalie abhorred that diminutive. "As you say." She forced hauteur into her voice. "Girl, you may bathe and dress me for dinner. Come to my room betimes." She went back to the pavilion with Laurie.

Already the rain tapered gently off. Drops fell more slowly from the new leaves of Imran's beloved stripling oil palms, or hung motionless till she brushed against them as she passed. In the wet distance, other rooftops shimmered as the sun broke cover.

The tea was passable. Perhaps Rosalie had been spoiled by the freshness of the produce of Maman's plantation. Laurie stirred a spoon of honey into his cup in lieu of sugar. "I believe I will try a morsel of this as well," he said, using a butter knife to slice a sliver from one side of the Shirazan rosewater preparation.

"Now. You know I have been tasked with representing certain British interests in the cause of exploiting oil and mineral rights in the Levant."

Rosalie nodded. He had admitted as much over Christmas of last year, when she reasoned with him for the last time about his avoidance of Everfair. Attending to his work, as he explained it then, prohibited long visits such as she wanted him to make.

"In the brief months since we parted, the assignment has expanded. Word reached my employers of oil deposits here, in their newly won possessions."

"Here?"

"Nearby. This very archipelago; in fact, Pemba." His face took on a look of self-congratulation. "So you see why I suggested that we make this place our rendezvous."

How had the far-off English discovered this? Who had told them? Was there a traitor at court spying on the Sheikhas? They wanted the oil developed independently to fund humanitarian projects, as did Mam'selle. Unlike the Sultan. Or could Laurie's source of information live in one of the fishing villages, hidden among partisans of the oil palm, the faction supported by Everfair's Princess Mwadi? Obviously the fiction of a bombed and sunken freighter full of crude had somehow been pierced. She must get away, must warn—was there anyone trustworthy?

Like an automaton, Rosalie lifted the teapot to Laurie's raised cup. "What will you have to do? Is there any way for me to assist you?" Hinder you, she meant.

"Well, I'll want to inspect the site and map out its boundaries. . . ."

She relaxed a tiny bit. He knew there was oil, but not exactly where. The Sheikhas could still make their claim.

"And then I'll need to approach the owner—"

"If there is one."

"How not? Oh, you mean that the deposits may lie within lands owned directly by Sheikh Khalifa."

"And his dependents."

"Yes. You have contacts there, I take it, because of your—" He waved his hand as if at a negligible object. "—hobbyhorse, that crafting of jewelry you care so much about. Fellow riders, eh? Nothing but time on their hands in that harem." A suggestive leer was banished as he remembered she was a lady—at least in his estimate.

The rest of their conversation consisted of plans for an excursion to Pemba. Rosalie suggested chartering a private boat, an idea her brother seized upon as if it had been his own. She would count on Imran to make the arrangements and to make sure that whatever they were they fell through till a means of dealing with Laurie had been found.

An hour of this until she was able to escape to her rooms. Ostensibly to nap. She took a chance on Laurie overhearing and rang the bell.

Amrita answered it, opening the suite's door and bowing gracefully as she shut it, as if she'd been in service all her days. "Miss."

Rosalie jerked her head toward the balcony. When Amrita joined her there she related her findings.

"So." Amrita, like Imran and much of Pemba's population itself, favored investing in oil palm production and leaving whatever petroleum deposits they sat on unexploited. "If your brother has his way, you'll be happy."

"No! The money ought to benefit *us*! Everfair and Zanzibar!"

"Then I suppose you'd better inform the Sheikhas that their charity fund is about to be plundered. And soon."

Next day, under the flimsy pretense of obtaining permission to access the ruins of a temple of no real interest, Rosalie was able to present herself at the palace.

Amrita accompanied her. Laurie, to his chagrin, did not.

"There will be a very special reception given in your honor on a fortuitous date," she consoled him. "Till then, it's best if you allow the court to act as if you haven't yet arrived. Officially, you know, you haven't."

In Rosalie's own case, all ceremony had long since been set aside. She went to the palace on foot, accompanied only by Amrita and one of Imran's kitchen boys, Kafeel. The boy was big enough to serve as an escort across the city but young enough that the guards admitted him to the harem's outer chamber with only a little hesitation. He awaited their return seated in apparent contentment on one of the narrow room's many benches.

Traversing polished marble floors to the source of an enticing scent of lemons, Rosalie and Amrita entered the harem's main courtyard. In patterns like a zebra's, palm shadows fell on white stone. The aroma of lemons intensified so that Rosalie could almost taste their cooling fragrance. Flowers and fruit together thronged the branches of the grove of trees sheltering Sheikha Ghuza and her four sisters.

At Ghuza's nod Rosalie and Amrita knelt to sit on the cushions provided. She made a gift of her tortoise pendant, but didn't follow it up with any Pemba-related conversational gambit as she'd half thought to do. Indeed, the discussion was pointedly desultory till a pitcher of sherbet had been poured and sampled. Then the youngest, named Salme, picked up a guitar and began to strum noisily to prevent them being overheard, and they talked more seriously.

Ghuza at least seemed unperturbed by Rosalie's description of Laurie's mission. "Perhaps it's best we fund our efforts another way. Fortune checks us in this scheme; it may be we should heed her guidance and forsake what we took to be the easiest path."

Blind Matuka, sightless eyes covered in a silken scarf, wondered whether they ought to wait a season—or two—or more—to ensure needed equipment and systems were installed, then force the interests Laurie represented to sell their stake in the business.

Rosalie struggled to conceal the impatience the Sheikhas' mysticism and indecision caused her. "But we are ready to help you now! And if you let the English in, they'll bring more than mining equipment! There will be military conflicts—which you may well lose!" She must find a way forward.

Amrita understood. "Is there any way to learn what Fate intends? At home we divide piles of rice grains or listen to crows singing."

"Yes." Ghuza consulted Matuka and her other sisters in Arabic too swift to follow. Then she declared, in Kee-Swah-Hee-Lee: "I will journey to the Green Island to perform geomancy upon its sands. You may join us. Let this be done tomorrow."

§

Fortunately, the foundations of Imran's gambit to thwart Laurie long-term had by now been laid. He and his mother packed several hampers full of provisions and sent them to the royal dock in the care of Kafeel and two of his small cousins. Chattering happily, the young boys led a procession comprised of Rosalie, Amrita (again in the guise of a servant), and a grumbling Laurie.

"Pesky valet had no cause to fall ill like that," he complained. Rosalie thought he had rather sufficient cause: Imran's mother had poisoned him. Though only enough to put him hors de combat so that Kafeel rendered services in his place. Despite Kafeel's tender years—twelve—the kitchen boy was a member in good standing of his employer's conspiracy.

They paraded down the rising and falling dock, their hollow footsteps echoing off the steel plates of the vessel moored beside it. *Nyanza* was a converted paddlewheeler, a steamer purchased by the previous sultan and devolving with time to the harem.

Up the gangway. Folding chairs had been arranged for them toward the yacht's bow. Once they cleared Prison Island the wisdom of this was obvious. Though she was equipped with sails, these were next to useless when heading northeast this time of year. *Nyanza*'s engines vented smoke and cinders as they pushed her almost directly into the kaskazi. The stern would be more sheltered, but the air there would be full of dirt.

Kafeel procured a blanket for Laurie and tucked it around him. Amrita held Rosalie's parasol so that it protected them both. Her skin was not much darker than Rosalie's own. Another variety of shell. One of Amrita's plump hands fussed unnecessarily with Rosalie's hair ribbon. She shut her eyes against the glare of the waves. The hand moved lower, to her neck and shoulders, to separate the chain of the locket Lily had bequeathed her from the elephant hair braid she wore because of Mr. Mkoi.

About to ask for—no, to *order*—this fiddling to stop, Rosalie opened her eyes on the unexpected sight of a harem servant throwing herself face-first on the deck.

A long moment passed before she remembered she must give the poor girl permission to do anything more. "Rise to your feet and speak," she commanded.

"Her Most Serene Highness Sheikha Ghuza wishes to welcome you into her private accommodations for the duration of her voyage." Rosalie stood, warning Laurie to keep his seat with a frown and a shake of her head. He subsided, muttering.

The servant led her below, Amrita following, to a spacious cabin, its walls swathed in some heavy cloth winking with tiny mirrors. On a divan covered in more comfortable-looking fabrics sat their hostess. Beside her sat her sister Matuka, eyes unbound.

Terrible scars twisted outward from the eyes' ends like frozen lightning bolts. Like stormclouds they were swollen, black, their lashless lids thick with bumps and ridges and—

Rosalie looked away. Then forced herself to look back.

Whatever damage had been done, it had healed a good while since. No blood. No—oozing. The blackness was that of the too-wide pupils.

She felt again the touch of Amrita's hand. Now it squeezed hers tight. "I'm so sorry," said Rosalie's friend.

"Yes. But of course this is the fault of neither of you, nor of anyone with whom you're associated."

"It was our father who did this to me," Matuka explained. "Seeking to cure me. He subjected me to dozens of operations meant to rid me of the deficiency which makes me unmarriageable."

"As for my singleness," Ghuza said, "it's mostly the result of the timing of attractive offers. Either there have been too many at once, making the decision of how to bestow me difficult or, lately, as I age, none at all."

"Our younger sisters," Matuka added, "continue to face these choices. Rumors of chronic illness, a squint assumed at critical interviews; such are their defenses should they want them."

"Why—why do you tell us these things?" Rosalie asked

"Ah. Perhaps we attempted an earlier divination? Our results indicated a need to become better acquainted with our allies, and to listen as well as share with them the bases of our daily lives. And also to invite— persuasion? At the very least, explication of your viewpoints."

"You will sit." Matuka's gesture indicated the cushioned stools before them, though her bottomless pupils stayed fixed on nothing that could be seen.

Slowly, over the two hours that remained of their voyage, they accomplished what the Sheikhas wished. They discussed mundane personal affairs: their monthly courses, caring for their teeth and gums. They exchanged information about politics; the princesses knew much more than Rosalie would have expected concerning the doings of foreign nations. They discussed the relative merits of oil palms and petroleum fields: the palms could be planted and raised generation after generation, but needed more processing for a less potent yield. And so on.

It was agreed that Imran's plot was the best way to render Laurie harmless.

Finally, the Sheikhas tried to explain the coming ceremony of divination.

"This method is called the science of the sand," said Ghuza. "So we want to lay out the squares on the beach above Chake Chake Bay." The "Mothers," the figures filling the four initial squares, were divided into four parts: Head, Heart, Belly, Feet. From them would derive four more figures, called Daughters, and from the Daughters Nieces, and from *them* Judges and Witnesses, on whom depended the querent's ultimate answer. To Rosalie it seemed unnecessarily involved. Why not simply decide based on the known facts?

"But how do you arrive at the Mothers?" asked Amrita, cutting through to the root of the confusion.

"We toss a coin. Or roll a die." Matuka took from her sash an ivory cube marked with ebony dots. "By whatever means available we generate a random number to allow the influence of Chance."

So much for facts.

One last effort to plead for rational thought processes. "Will it help at all to acquire what you need using your own resources?" Ghuza's eyes were as void of expression as her sister's. More plainly this time, Rosalie asked, "Can you not buy the food and building materials needed with your own funds?"

"Secretly? No. And the sultan will not be made to look as if he cares less than anyone for his subjects."

"We live on an island," Matuka said, as if the implications should be obvious. "And on that island we live within a closely watched compound."

"But via agents?" Amrita's question was once more to the point.

"Any we could employ are also closely watched—at least as to their business transactions," Ghuza answered.

"Does the sultan watch us as well?" Rosalie asked.

Ghuza's plucked brows arched with surprise. "But of course! However, he considers you little threat to his European masters. If he knew—if he could conceive how many varying classes of people are united in their dislike—"

A long, loud, two-noted hoot drowned out the Sheikha's voice. It repeated three times.

"According to this signal we arrive shortly," Matuka announced in the sudden silence following. Now Rosalie realized what the sound had been: a steam whistle such as blew back home in Kisangani at the start of each work shift.

"Yes." Ghuza lifted one wide-sleeved arm as if she spread a wing. "Have your party gather by the boats. You may disembark with us in the first to leave for shore."

§

The damp sand felt cool to Rosalie's bare soles. Golden, with a glint like diamond dust, the long strand lay before her in shining splendor, reflecting the sky where wetted by the sea. Behind her and inland lay the stubby ruins of the ancient Arab settlement of Qanbalu; between those broken walls and the shore the Sheikhas' servants labored to complete the erection of their pavilion, an edifice of saffron-tinted silk embroidered in scarlet and blue. Also behind Rosalie but anchored in the bay to the south floated *Nyanza,* kept from coming nearer by Pemba's thick girdle of reefs.

Freeing one hand from the parasol she wielded in the role of Rosalie's maid, Amrita lifted a pair of field glasses to her eyes and turned them *Nyanza*-ward. "Your brother is in the boat now being lowered."

"Good." The sooner Laurie was removed from the picture the better. She reached for the glasses to watch him being rowed off herself, but Amrita wouldn't relinquish them.

"Wait. It seems—" Amrita frowned. "—it seems they make for us, not the lagoon and the road." At last she let loose her hold and Rosalie was able to take possession of the glasses. Amrita was right! Though foreshortened and distorted by the magnifying lenses, the newly lowered boat did appear to be headed directly toward them. Up from its center protruded Laurie's head, unmistakable in his unfortunately ostentatious white Foreign Service helmet.

Why? Was this change of course at his direction? Or was it dictated by those who gave the *Nyanza*'s sailors their orders?

The pavilion stood. The servants who had protected the two Sheikhas from the sun furled their oversized parasols outside its awninged entrance; their mistresses must be within. Too bad. There would have been less difficulty in approaching to consult them out here. "Shall I request an audience?" Amrita asked. Rosalie assented.

But the big women on either side of the awning shook their heads in refusal and said something to Amrita that was impossible for Rosalie to hear. Not that she needed their exact words.

Amrita came back to her side. "The ritual has already begun. Their Highnesses are not to be disturbed."

No one else was within earshot. "What do you suggest?" Rosalie asked. It was a most un-mistresslike question.

"Let's assume, since they said nothing of revising the kidnapping plan, that it is your brother who has instigated this side trip. Can you guess why?"

"At a hazard, he wishes our escort and guidance. Or perhaps an introduction to the Sheikhas? The separation on board *Nyanza* wasn't at all to his liking."

"If we can keep him from causing an incident with the Sheikhas, what do we care if we're with him when he springs the trap?"

"Yes." Rosalie made a show of ordering Amrita to follow her to the spot on the beach where *Nyanza's* second boat looked likely to land. There they drew the backs of their robes forward between their legs and tucked the hems in their sashes, making them into a sort of pantaloons. They splashed out through the low surf together.

Nine men sat in the boat. Or eight if you counted Kafeel not a man but a boy. All the passengers but Laurie were brown-skinned, the two who rowed verging on black. Her brother gave an embarrassed laugh. "Have you always behaved like such a guy, Rosie? Why not wait for one of these strong fellows to carry you safely to me?"

The rowers had stopped and shipped their oars. "To you?" The question confirmed for her that the Sheikhas were neither this boat's controllers nor Laurie's goal. Kafeel grasped Rosalie by her left arm and pulled; she gave her right to the idle rower on her side of the boat. As they hauled her aboard Amrita underwent a similar process on the other side.

"Where are we going?"

"Oh, nowhere we haven't been invited." Laurie grimaced. "Don't worry. Your country's precious diplomatic relations aren't being compromised." Her country was Everfair. Not, therefore, his.

"Though I don't see why we couldn't have simply anchored at Whatsit Bay instead of here."

"You mean Mkoan?"

"Whatever you may call it—where that fuel carrier's supposed to have had those spills. Where there's every indication we'll find what we're looking for."

Amrita busied herself straightening Rosalie's attire.

"So to the lagoon, then?"

"There's transport there, right?" Laurie nodded to Kafeel, who spoke in Kee-Swah-Hee-Lee to the men crouched in front of the rowers. They switched positions. Then the new rowers brought the boat quickly about and sped them off.

Herons and heavy-beaked pelicans flew in tight circles above the lagoon's opening. The tide was falling; bleached coral and rocks covered in strange growths thrust upwards, several times breaking the sea's surface. One of the former rowers had moved to the boat's prow, whence he called directions to his replacements. Rosalie leaned over the stern, longing to trail her fingers in the cool water. Once they were within the lagoon's stillness, the bottom appeared close enough to touch.

And then it was. It must be: the boat's keel scraped over the rippling sand; the man at the prow and three others jumped into the shallow water and hauled the vessel a few feet further in. Kafeel leapt also, laughing when he fell short of a dry landing.

"Miss?" The second set of rowers had also left the boat. They'd formed a chair of their arms and waited for Rosalie to seat herself on them. She clambered into their embrace. Still facing the boat as the two men waded toward the shore, she watched the remaining sailor help Laurie seat himself on a sturdier piece of human furniture composed of the arms of four. That last sailor swung himself over the side as Rosalie was deposited on the beach and carried Amrita pick-a-back to her side.

Atop a steep rise, Kafeel waved his arms to signal that he'd reached the road. Rosalie heard Laurie swear below his breath as they followed *Nyanza*'s sailors up the trail. At first its loose sand slipped beneath her feet. As it climbed it became packed dirt. When they reached the patchy hillside jungle, she stopped to retrieve her shoes from Amrita and tied them on, mindful of poisonous insects and snakes. Her brother seemed glad of the halt. As she stood he beckoned her to the boulder where he sat.

"Will we need to camp here overnight?" he asked, after inquiring how she did.

"Here?"

"Not *right* here. On the island." A nearby bird screeched. He flinched.

"There are villages," she replied as coolly as she could. "I'm sure some merchant or diver would put us up." At his glum face she relented. "And there's an inn in Mkoan proper—but I believe *Nyanza* will sail to meet us there this evening." No need to start his suffering yet.

The road stunk of oil. Rosalie hadn't thought of that. Twice a year since the discovery of the seep, Pemba's road crews applied what they'd collected to keep down the dust. Later in the season the smell would dissipate, but now?

Laurie noticed it. Rosalie tried to explain away the oil as salt water-tainted salvage from drums that had floated ashore after the disaster. He wasn't stupid, though.

His pale, suspicious eyes darkened on the arrival of the promised transport: three of the steam bicycle-and-cart combinations typical of Everfair's capital, Kisangani. She'd expected that because of their coal-fueled boilers he'd take them as proof that the existence of oilfields on the island was nothing but a rumor. Instead he made the more obvious connection: machines from Everfair at the disposal of a woman from Everfair with better access to the royal house than he had.

"How shall we split ourselves up?" she asked, hoping that if Laurie were allowed to decide their seating arrangements he'd relax his guard and go along with the proposed itinerary.

It worked. At the sacrifice of Amrita's companionship. Rosalie wound up alone with her brother in the cart he decided was most comfortable; the others had to cram into the rest of the fleet with, he insisted, the food hampers Imran and his mother had provided. These her brother demanded to have placed inside—not strapped to the carts' exteriors. "Keep off the flies," he declared, easing onto the cushioned seat opposite Rosalie.

"Sure you don't mind riding backwards?" he asked anxiously.

She didn't. It shouldn't be for long.

But her small store of patience was tried sorely. Mile upon mile they jogged through Pemba's high hills. Laurie interrogated her sharply when they passed the land being cleared for aircanoe operations. She didn't conceal anything; this part of Everfair's aid to Zanzibar was common knowledge. About the clove plantations surrounding the road after that she had little to say. The sapling palms set out for the season in the clove trees' shelter were better not mentioned. How to explain the aspirations of the Pembans and other oil palm aficionados without describing the faction they opposed?

Laurie filled the resulting silence with a monologue, droning on for what seemed hours about his fiancée, Theresa: what Ellen—"Mother"— thought of her; how delicate her complexion and sensibilities alike; how familiar she was to him because of the generations of friendship between their families, yet how mysterious because so essentially feminine . . . all the clichés and platitudes she'd been able to avoid when his guest in England by the simple expedient of withdrawing to her room.

At last came the descent into the valley before Limani. As planned, both the cart's and the bicycle's brakes failed. Bracing her feet and holding firmly to the cart's door handle as they jounced ever faster down the rutted road, Rosalie wondered if this was when she would finally become religious. Or at least pray and pretend to be.

Their cart was first in the convoy. The others were far behind, out of sight when at last they crashed into a glossy-leaved bush.

Rosalie checked herself over and found no obvious injuries. Laurie was another matter. His silly helmet—which he'd worn, contra etiquette, in her presence inside the cart—had prevented any serious damage to his head. The same with the fat padding his figure overall, but the two last fingers on his right hand stuck out at a very curious angle, and the thumb on his left was bent back parallel with his wrist. Maman's wife would know how to splint those injuries.

Her brother's eyes blinked at her, dazed. In a moment he'd begin to feel his pain. Rosalie still held the door's handle. She opened it and climbed out, which took only a slight effort. The cart was canted off its front wheels and rested more on its far side than on this one—but not much more. Shaking her robes back into order, Rosalie looked around for the bicycle driver. Gone. As instructed. Excellent. Now to improvise, as Mam'selle would say.

"Help! Help!" She let her voice wobble as if in fear—easier than exiting the cart. "We're hurt! Someone, please!" That should be enough to let Imran know she was here with Laurie.

There he came, muffled in scarves like an old woman. "Shut up!" he commanded in Kee-Swah-Hee-Lee, sounding much gruffer than usual. No, he would not be recognized.

"It's all right," she replied in the same language. She attempted to whine pitifully. "My brother made all the others ride in the later carts. No one's around to understand."

"Hah! But I'd better stay in disguise just the same, hadn't I."

White-faced and shivering with shock, Laurie poked his helmeted head above the cart's doorway. More over-wrapped men appeared out of the forest, waving shonguns, Everfairer weapons that shot poisoned blades. A wince contorted Laurie's perspiration-covered features and his shoulders heaved; he must be trying to pull something out of a pocket—a weapon perhaps?

They needed to remove Laurie from the road before the rest of the party arrived. But when a pair of them approached to take him out of the cart he ducked down below the doorway. "Rosie!" he called. "Get back in here! I've got a pistol in my jacket. You needn't even fire it, just point—"

Rosalie shrieked and threw herself at Imran. Quick of mind, he caught and held her before Laurie's head was up again. His knife's edge grazed her throat, drawing real blood. But not much. "Perhaps we'll have to drag the cart into the jungle and dislodge him there," she growled defiantly.

To her brother's sincere-sounding cries of distress she answered, in English, that the black devils said they would kill her unless he too surrendered.

A true gentleman, Laurie stood when he heard that.

"Mind his hands," Rosalie warned the men extracting him from the cart. "And see if you can find his pistol." She hoped her Kee-Swah-Hee-Lee instructions sounded like terrified pleas. She hoped her pretended scuffling with Imran looked like she fought in ineffectual earnest to block their departure into the forest.

When they'd gone far enough off the road that Laurie's shouts shouldn't be heard by anyone investigating the crash, they came to a little house, temporary, woven of boards and covered in palm leaves. But they didn't go inside it; rather, their supposed captors shoved them to the ground near the house's fire pit. Then they stood over them, shonguns at the ready.

"You managing, my girl?" Laurie asked.

Rosalie shrugged. "I'm frightened is all."

"What do they want?"

"Money, I gather. Ransom."

"Well they won't get it!" Despite his words, Laurie looked unsure of that. Rosalie hoped he was right. Her brother's release played no part in this scheme.

Imran's mother emerged from the house. Bizarre designs in red and white paint covered her face. They served no purpose except to transform her into a stranger—though Laurie had probably not noticed her at the guesthouse anyway. She had to be surprised to see Rosalie there, but no one could have told by looking.

In Kee-Swah-Hee-Lee the old woman asked Rosalie, "How did this happen? Don't you want to go home?"

Imran made angry-looking gestures. "At the worst we expected one of the sailors!" he snapped. "They could have been explained. We'll have a hard time making your brother believe you've betrayed him despite the fact that you did."

"What's he saying?" Laurie twisted his head to watch Imran pace between the empty fire ring and the house.

"They're arguing about how much we're worth."

"Nothing!"

"Then we're dead." To Imran: "I think he's going to try to escape. Can you tie him up?"

"I'll get something." Imran's mother walked into the hut.

"We'll run for it!" Laurie staggered to his feet. "Opposite directions!" A heavily-built man knocked him to his knees with one hand. Her brother cried out in pain. The man raised his shongun threateningly.

Imran's mother returned, several scarves draped over her forearm. "Perhaps that's an idea. You, at least, could magically get away.

"Make him hold his wrists together."

"She—she wants to bind you," Rosalie told Laurie. "Perhaps if you cooperate they'll treat us more humanely?"

While the son and mother trussed Laurie—tightly at every joint, even when he moaned at their touch on his swelling hand—they discussed how to handle setting Rosalie free. At the last it was decided simply to put him in the house where he couldn't see her leave.

"Tell them they can't separate us! It's my duty to protect you," Laurie insisted as he was carried away.

"They say it's their religion!" Rosalie lied. "I can't talk them out of it!"

With her brother safely disposed of she followed the man who had subdued him to the road. The embers in the steam bicycle's fire box needed hardly any coaxing. By nightfall she was in Mkoan, once more with Amrita; by moonrise they were in a boat being winched back aboard *Nyanza*.

§

Nyanza's return to Unguja, the Zanzibar archipelago's largest island, went much more quietly than her journey out. The persistent kaskazi filled her sails.

As courtesy dictated, Amrita and Rosalie came to the Sheikhas' cabin when again invited. Late and cool as the hour was, they sipped warm chocolate seasoned with rare cubeb rather than partaking of the customary sherbet.

Amrita accepted a second cup. "What was the result of your divination, if I may inquire?" she asked. Her empty hand fell with seeming casualness on Rosalie's white-robed thigh. Rosalie let it lie there. It did her no harm.

"You most certainly may, for we obtained our results using your friend's gift." Ghuza pulled the tortoise pendant from the folds of her embroidered tunic. "We are to seek the will of the people." Which Rosalie knew, on Pemba, was in favor of palms over petroleum.

With a sigh she resigned herself to explaining this loss to Mam'selle. As Laurie had unintentionally demonstrated, things might have gone much, much worse.

Amrita was standing, tugging at Rosalie's sleeve, so she stood with her. Together they retired to the deck. The brisk breeze gave Amrita an excuse to tuck a shoulder under Rosalie's arm. For now this appeared to content her. As the silver moon slipped into the sea they passed Prison Island, Laurie's ultimate destiny. One day she would take Maman there for a visit.

The Herbalist

Maura Lydon

The shop smells musty with plants; leaves and flowers hang in bunches from low rafters while living plants grow in haphazard pots along the walls. At first there is no sign of human life, though a feeling of watchfulness comes from the vine growing around the archway of the door. Several white blotches on the leaves look more like half-lidded eyes than the piebald markings of a silent weed.

There is a counter and an account book hidden behind a pot of tall-leaved purple flowers, which quiver as the herbalist pushes through them. "Can I help you?" He emerges from the flowers like a spirit, one hand dusty with dirt and the other holding several fresh green leaves. His face is pale, but it is the pale gold of paper exposed to sunlight, not the sickly white of someone hidden away in a cave. "Do you need any herbs?"

You hesitate, glance at the door. You'd only come to gawk; the simple question throws something out of balance. The window's thickness between observer and observed. You look ridiculous in your paint-spattered shirt and pants, not because the clothes are out of place but because you are. You would have been more comfortable in a school uniform; like armor, it makes you anonymous. Untouchable. Instead there is this—the herbalist, unobtainably at home in this jungle of a shop, waiting for an answer you do not have.

"Pesto," you blurt out, remembering a conversation over pasta and green sauce. Your father and the cook, fresh ingredients, and you more interested in the latest headline from the *Times*: OVER ONE HUNDRED DEAD IN LATEST GAS EXPLOSION.

The herbalist raises one eyebrow, an expression made curious by the smooth slant to his eyes. "Basil?" he asks, not judgmental. Interested. You must be blushing by now; in the back, a section of plants rustle, enjoying your embarrassment. You nod.

His smile is a hundred attempts to reassure. You step closer to the half-hidden counter and stare fixedly at the little plant he's rescued from the shade of a fountaining succulent. "This little one will need repotting soon, but she'll do just fine for a sauce or two." He spins the pressed-paper pot idly in both hands, the leaves shaking at every half-turn.

"Great," you say, and know your accent gives you away. Not part of this place, this shop or this neighborhood or the people who live here. Not part of anything bigger, just this: you, in a costume that should have been comfortable but is instead embarrassing. "How much?"

At this he laughs, and you pretend to melt down into the floor. At the very least you lose a few inches of height. All you want is to get out of here, with or without the little plant. "No, it's fine, it's fine," the herbalist says, but he's still *laughing* at you. What's worse is that you can't think of what you've said or done to provoke it. "Here, look."

He retreats into the back of the shop, shoving the arm of a larger plant out of his way, and you reach out to hook one finger over the edge of the baby basil's pot, feeling rough, hardened paper and soft dirt and the tickling edge of a lower leaf. You tug the little plant closer, and out of the cacophony of smells in this place you catch a whiff of something familiar. Basil, recognizable from the pesto last night. Looking at the wide, curling leaves, you feel a protectiveness creep through your chest. Ridiculous, for a houseplant. Your father would laugh.

The herbalist returns carrying a five-gallon pot and a basil plant at least a hundred times the size of yours. He sets it down on the counter with a huff, brushing his fingers over the plant almost like petting a dog. You look from the plant to him, and back, wondering what this has to do with the price of your baby basil.

"Look," he says again, tapping several discreet purple flowers at the top of the basil. "Each of these flowers will produce up to twenty seeds, which I can save and grow. But for basil, you don't need to worry about seedlings, because all you have to do is cut a branch and stick it in a jar of water for a few weeks." He separated out a stem of the mother plant and mimed cutting it with fingers for scissors. "The cutting will grow roots, and you can plant it. That's how I grew your plant. And even if I cut off every single branch from this big one, it would all grow back *and* I'd be up at least fifty basil plants."

You look down at your little one, embarrassment giving way to interest. The herbalist has a way of explaining things that include you in the conversation. It feels ... different. Still, you aren't about to open your mouth just to stick your foot in. When the silence starts stretching like taffy, he sighs.

"There's no point in my charging for the plant. Why, I should be paying *you* to take it off my hands."

You clear your throat. You hadn't thought the stories about this neighborhood were true, not all of them. How can someone afford to keep a shop as full as this one open if he *gives* away product? It doesn't make sense. And then, looking at your plant, you think of a flaw. "The pot?" you ask, eager to find holes in this place. In this plan.

"Recycled paper," the herbalist says. You hear him shrug. On the edges of your vision, he pushes the mother basil out of the way and rests his arms on the counter. "Made from a mold in the lab down the street. You could go check it out, if you wanted." He sounds eager, happy. Surely he's figured out where you're from by now. Why doesn't he send you away, back to where you belong?

The funny thing is that you don't want to go.

"At least find a pot for your plant before you go," he says, and you almost look up at that, expecting him to offer one. Instead he continues, "Marie runs a pottery shop in the blue house on the corner. She'd be happy to let you look for a pot. Might give you one of her rejects. Or, if you prefer, you can buy a glazed pot from her." The laughter is back in his voice, but you can almost believe it's not aimed at you, with how gentle he's being.

You tell yourself that there was no point in coming if you didn't plan to be brave, and you look up. The herbalist smiles, and you spot a smear of dirt on his shirt. A silly thing to notice, you tell yourself, but it feels *real*. The opposite of your paint-smeared jeans, the blue handprint on your shoulder. Purposeful ruining of good clothes for aesthetic, not the worn preservation of something kept useful its whole life. "Thanks," you say. If you cannot manage bravery, you can at least pretend.

"Come back soon," he says, and he means it. That startles a smile out of you, and your leaving, the basil plant cradled in both hands, doesn't feel as much like a retreat as you thought it would. Through the glass on the front door, you can see the sun shining.

Sunharvest Triptych

Sara Norja

I. Sea-wind

Even after heartbreak
Helsinki in the sunlight catches the corners
of my mouth, tugs them up. The city
is brimming with possibility
even now, even without

her. I stare sightless
at the sea, throat heavy.
Sometimes my breath
catches in memory.
That's when I come here:
where the wind turbines
rotate, sluggish creatures,
on the rocky islets
before the city.
I follow their movement,
let it lull me, let the wind
knot my hair into tangles

I want to stay seabound
but it's time for the harvest
to begin, the summerlong sunharvest
much-awaited after winter's darkness
and I must make my pilgrimage,
kohta on jo kiire—

II. The journey

Thighs shaking, I scale the final slope
through the central parkforest
to the sunfields.
Citybike
steady under me, its spokes

whir like those wind turbines,
propelled forward by my effort
and the sunpowered motor.
Its frame glints sunflower yellow
brighter than my tarnished spirit.

Yet who can remain heartbroken
when summer is here?

When the whole land awakens,
when we bless the solar panels
the fieldfuls, the rooftopfuls,
the stained-glass-windowfuls of them:
the harvesters of energy
to sustain us in winter's dark months
when the sun barely greets us.

Now she's blazing
in benediction.
Half the city's here
at the ceremony. Sometimes
we all go a bit wild afterwards,
giddy on the day's length,
and yes, we're all drinking
sparkling things, we're dancing
and singing hei aurinko älä mee pois.

In all that hustle and rush of bodies
you take my hand,
your touch a smooth lake-stone
on a summer night.
"Tuutsä meille? Olis sauna."

I go with you in gladness.

III. Harvesting the sun

Evening falls, darkness doesn't.
Helsinki's a-glittering, sunset winking
off the panels on every house

as we bundle into the rooftop sauna,
you me and a whole bunch of your friends.

Someone calls: "Saaks heittää lisää löylyä?"
The steam hisses on hot stones:
the sound of happiness
small but immeasurably meaningful.

The heat enfolds me
laughter grounds me
and I can breathe again.

In the half-dark
I harvest the sunlight
lying in wait, after all,
within me

A Catalogue of Sunlight at the End of the World

A.C. Wise

June 21, 2232 - Svalbard

The twenty-first of June, the Summer Solstice, the longest day and the shortest night. That means less here at the top of the world where, in this season, we have sunlight twenty-four hours a day. But it seemed like an appropriate day to start this project nonetheless.

In just over a week, the generation ship *Arber* will depart on its journey. The docking clamps will release, and it will go sailing off into space to find the future of humanity. This is my parting gift, a catalogue of sunlight from the world left behind.

Of course the sun will still be there, getting farther away as they travel, but it won't be the same. The people on that ship— *those* ships, leaving from all points above the globe—will never again see sunlight the way it looks here and now. They won't see the sky bruise purple and hushed gold or the violent shades of lavender, rose, and flame as the sun creeps toward the horizon. They'll never see the way this sun sparkles off water in a fast-moving brook or dapples the ground beneath a canopy of leaves. It won't pry its way through their blinds in the morning, or slip under doors and through all the cracks sealed up against its intrusion. They won't know the persistence of it, the sheer amount of it. They'll only know its loss.

Maybe the *Arber*'s children, or their children's children will see starlight on the dust of some distant world, watch it pool in the craters of their first new footsteps and call it the sun. But not the ones leaving. The ones who grew up under its light. This is my gift to them. A little something to take with them into the cold and the dark.

Today, the light is pure. There isn't a cloud in the sky to cut it, no breeze to stir it off our skins. All the shadows are sharp-edged. There's so much of it, it's easy to forget it's there. Ubiquitous sun. It gets over everything and under everything and inside it. Today, the light of the sun has almost no color at all, but if you squint just right, you can prism it, see the rainbow fractures flaring away from it. That is the sun here today, children. The sun you're leaving behind. There has never been another just like it, and there never will be again.

There. That part is for the future. This part is for the present and the past. For you and me, Mila.

Kathe came to see me today and asked me one more time to go with them. *There's room*, she said. *You could stay with me, Linde, Ivan, and the kids until we figure things out.* She didn't mention Thomas.

Kathe has pull. It comes with being Head of Resource Management, Northern Division. She could make it happen, our girl. That's what she does, after all. She manages resources. If she says there's room for me, then there's room. She could probably get me the nicest berth on the ship, if I asked.

Space travel is for the young, I told her. *It's no place for an old man like me. Besides, this is my home. I like it here. This is where I belong.*

But your children, she said. *Your grandchildren.*

Her eyes. It's hard to look at them sometimes. They remind me so much of you. I think she knew she'd already lost the fight.

What's the point of space? It's just another place to be without you. I have my kettle here. I have my woolen socks and my favorite mug. I have a library full of books and music. I've even adopted a cat. Or it's adopted me. A little grey kitten I've named Predator X. They won't have cats in space. They'll have genetic material, of course, but it's hard to cuddle a test tube on a cold winter's night and be comforted by its purr.

§

May 23, 2171 - Prince Edward Island

To hell with separating past and future. This is my catalogue, and I'll tell it how I choose and to who I choose, and I choose you, Mila.

Obviously May 23, 2171 isn't today's date, and I'm not on Prince Edward Island. It's when and where we were married. The sunlight on that day deserves to be memorialized.

It was golden in the way sunlight never is outside of photographs and memories. It caught in your hair, turning those fly-away strands you could never get to behave—even on that day—into individual threads of crystal. It was sunlight in its ideal form, its most romantic form. They say it's lucky to have rain on your wedding day, but I think that's just something to make people feel better when their bouquets and tuxedoes and cakes and dozen white doves are all soggy and miserable.

We were married on the beach, on the dunes, with the waves in the background and wild sea grass running everywhere around us. Those dunes are gone now. In another few years, the whole island will be gone, lost to rising sea levels like New Orleans and Florida, London and Venice. So many cities swallowed whole. But back then, it was beautiful.

Lupines and red sand—those stick out in my mind. You insisted on traveling back to your family's home because your grandmother wasn't well enough to travel, and you wanted her to give you away. I didn't have any people of my own left, so one place was as good as another to me. You were all the family I wanted and needed back then. Now that my life is coming full circle, I'm finding that's true once again.

The day I proposed to you was the day I stole the Gibraltar Campion from the seed vault. *Silene tomentosa,* your favorite flower. The first time I saw you, you were looking at a 3-D projection of it, part of the vault's new finding aid. I didn't know it at the time, but that was your program. You were also the one who got rare and endangered flowers added to the vault along with staple crops. You said beautiful things should be saved as well as useful ones, and besides bees and pollination and flowers—even rare and temperamental ones—are part of our ecosystem, too.

On the day we met, you were looking at the Gibraltar Campion from every angle, studying it with a scientist's eye. I don't think you knew anyone was watching you. Then, for just a moment, your expression changed; you weren't looking at the flower like a scientist anymore. You frowned and reached out like you wanted to brush your finger along the pale silk of its petal.

Had you ever seen one in person? I imagined how many years you'd spent studying it and how you'd launched a whole program to protect it and other flowers like it. But had you ever held its thin stem between your fingers or breathed it in to see if it had a scent? That unguarded moment of fascination and longing—that's the moment I fell in love.

It was hell getting the Campion to grow. I sweated over it in secret, afraid of giving it too much water, not enough. But I did get it to grow. That was always my gift. Can't cook worth a damn. Never had a scrap of musical talent or enough coordination to play sports. Green thumbs, though. I have those like nobody's business. It's why I was hired on at the Global Seed Vault in the first place. It's what led me to you, so I can't complain.

Smuggling my Gibraltar Campion into Canada without getting caught—that was a special hell all of its own. Then I presented you with the bouquet—the sad, single-flower bouquet I was so proud of—right before you walked down the aisle of sand and sea grass, and you almost called the wedding off right then and there.

What the hell were you thinking? you said. *Do you have any idea how rare the*

Gibraltar Campion is? They brought it back from the dead. It was nearly extinct. What the hell do you think the vault is for anyway?

Storing up flowers so no one ever sees them? A vault full of potential, but never the reality?

Of course I didn't say that aloud. I wouldn't dare.

Some things are meant to be enjoyed, is what I did say, and I tried to charm you with a smile. *Sometimes you have to appreciate what you have while you have it, instead of holding on to it for someday. You just have to live and let go and stop worrying about the future.*

You called me selfish and a dozen other more unsavory names. You almost shoved me into the water. God, I was young and stupid back then. But somehow, I convinced you to marry me anyway.

You stayed mad at me through the whole ceremony. You refused to hold the Campion, so I held it, and you glared at me the whole time you said your vows. At the end though, you smiled a little, too. Then you cried; we both cried, and you told me if I ever did anything that stupid again you would throw my body into a bottomless crevasse where it would never be found. When we kissed, it tasted like salt, and we crushed the Campion between us, and we laughed so hard we started crying all over again.

I miss you, Mila. Every goddamn day.

§

June 23, 2232 - Svalbard

There was a big party down on the beach today. A goodbye for everybody leaving and everyone staying behind. We lit a huge bonfire, which seems strange in the middle of the day, but when the sun never goes down, what else can you do?

This is what the sun looked like five days before everyone went away. Weak, like tea or good scotch watered down a thousand times. Like if you took a glass and kept adding ice to it every time you took a sip, trying to stretch that last bit of alcohol just a little farther. Sunlight, divided infinitely and spread thin, the faintest hint of peat and smoke on the tongue.

It was mostly overcast, but every now and then something would break loose in the great patchwork of grey and a beam of light would come shooting through. It might pin the stones on the shore or a little boy's hair as he ran toward the water. It might catch a mother and daughter in a tender moment of goodbye or fall on the waves and break over and over again. Sunlight is like that, fickle and faithless. It shines on us all.

Listen to me getting melancholy. Then again, it is the end of the world.

Everyone was there. We probably only made up a handful, compared to other celebrations around the world, but this was ours. We roasted fish on wooden spits. There were marshmallows and tofu hotdogs. Someone made a spicy curry with goat meat; someone else made a giant pot of borscht. There were real English popovers. There was even an attempt at poutine. You would have loved it.

A kitchen party. That's what it reminded me of. Not that I'd ever been to one, but from your descriptions—everyone getting together, each person bringing food and something to drink and an instrument. Your grandmother used to throw them, just like the old days, you said. The whole house would be open to anyone who wanted to join in, music spilling out of every door and window all night long.

The party on the beach was like that, music and dancing, and all of it just seemed to roll on and on. Kathe was there with Linde and Ivan and the kids. Thomas was there, too, with Leena and their kids. Honestly, I'm surprised they never left Svalbard, Thomas especially. We chose this life, but Thomas and Kathe were born into it. Maybe they stayed because they'd already put down roots here or maybe because we have the illusion of safety up here at the top of the world, while wildfires and earthquakes, mudslides caused by deforestation and rising tide lines ravage the globe.

Whatever the reason, I'm glad they stayed; I got to see my grandchildren. On the day of the party, they all ran around on the shore together, chasing the black-legged kittiwakes and the long-tailed skua. Even Dani, who's almost thirteen now, too old for playing and entering that awkward stage of being caught between everything.

Kathe came to talk to me when things quieted down and the mood turned somber. We all looked up and remembered the space elevator was still going non-stop, bringing people and supplies up to the station and then to the *Arber,* all those eager and heartbroken people, ready to start their future.

What will you do when we're all gone, Dad? Kathe asked. We sat side by side, looking out at the ocean.

We'll get by, I told her. *There will just be less of us. The Andersens are staying, and the Guptas. Raj is already planning a rotating dinner party. Everyone will take a turn hosting, and we'll keep each other company. Besides, things aren't too bad here, not like it is further south, and we still have the elevator and the station if things do get bad. In the meantime, I'll have my garden, and I have Predator X. Helen Holbrook is going to teach me how to make cheese if I help her milk her goats.*

I tried to make it sound cheerful, like it would be a continuation of the party on the beach, but smaller. Kathe didn't look like she believed me. In truth, I knew there would be lonely days, but there would be days I relished my solitude, too. When you get to be my age, you surprise yourself by how often you're content to just sit and think.

We sat quietly for a bit then. It reminded me of when Kathe was little, before Thomas was born. In fact, it was when you were pregnant with Thomas. While you napped in the afternoons, I would bring Kathe to the beach to collect stones and look for fossils. She never shared our love of growing things, that one, though she was curious as hell. It was all about stillness with Kathe, the frozen remnants of the past. Funny, then, that she's the one going up into the stars, not me.

And Thomas, well. . . . Maybe I should have tried harder to understand him and the things he loved, but with Kathe it was so much easier. She wore her heart on her sleeve, while Thomas was so closed and serious. He was never a little boy, not really. It was more like he was born a grown-up, and he was just waiting for his body to catch up with his mind.

We'll still talk, I told Kathe after a while, *as long as the ship is in communication range. And after that, we'll have the ansible. Besides, it's not like I'll be alone, if you're worried about me.*

I do worry, she said. *That's a daughter's job.*

When did you get old enough for that to be true? I asked, and that made her smile at last. It was good to see. *Besides,* I said, *it's not like the world is really ending. Just changing, that's all.*

I know, but there are some things I don't want to change, Kathe said, and right then she wasn't Head of Resource Management, Northern Division, she was just our little girl again, and it nearly broke my heart. *You've been there for me my whole life, me and Tom both, and I don't know what I'll do without you.*

I squeezed her hand, and we both blinked against more than just smoke from the bonfire.

You'll be fine, kiddo.

I was searching for something else to say, something inspirational and comforting, but Thomas came over and nudged the tip of Kathe's boot with his toe.

Can I talk to Dad for a minute? he said. *Alone.*

I can't remember the last time I heard Thomas call me *Dad.* I didn't think I would ever hear it again.

Kathe looked surprised, but she gave Thomas her spot and gave us our privacy.

I know Kathe has tried to talk you into taking a place on the ship about a hundred times. Thomas kept his hands in his pockets while he talked, his gaze on the horizon. *I'm not going to rehash all that. I just wanted to let you know she's not the only one. I know we haven't always seen eye to eye, but you're my father.*

I opened my mouth to say something or maybe just take a breath in surprise, but Thomas held up his hand to stop me.

Just let me finish. He looked down and didn't raise his head again.

When Mom died, it was the hardest thing I'd ever had to watch. I know, and Thomas held his hand up again, even though he didn't look at me. *I'm not here to open old wounds. I just wanted to say it was hard, but you were there for Mom, every day. Kathe and I were there, too. She had her family all around her. She didn't have to go through any of it alone. When your time comes, I just thought . . . I always thought we'd be there for you.*

He looked up finally. His eyes aren't like yours, or Kathe's. They're more like my mother's. I didn't know what to say to him, Mila. I've never known. He touched my shoulder, let his hand rest for a moment, then walked away.

I've been thinking about it since leaving the beach. Thomas deserves an explanation. And Kathe. Maybe you deserve an explanation, too.

We spent our lives building the future, saving all those plants and flowers in the vault, not to mention our own future with Kathe and Thomas. Now that the future's here, I'm terrified. Thomas was right, watching you die was the hardest thing I've ever had to do. I don't want that for our children, and I don't want that for myself.

Maybe a bit of it is selfish. A man gets to a certain age, and he wants to live his life on his own terms. I think I understand the choices you made now a little better than I used to. When the end comes, when my end comes, I want to go quick and painless, not hooked up to machines. I'll choose the time and place of my death, when I'm ready, and I want it to be here on Earth with you.

In space, even death will be different. Kathe explained it to me. There's a morgue on the generation ship that is also a chapel and a burial chamber and a cryo-storage unit. Aboard the *Arber,* people will have the option of being ejected into space, being recycled—protein and calcium and other vital elements broken down and reused in a variety of ways—or being stored until their remains can be buried on the same alien world where our new crops will grow. That's what death looks like in the next great age of humanity.

I understand that Thomas and Kathe want to be with me at the end, but this is the point where our roads diverge. You and me, we did what we could to build the future, Mila, but it isn't *for* us. Why should Kathe and

Thomas bring grief with them among the stars when they can carry memories instead? I want them to remember me as I am now, not the way I might be one day down the road.

It's like we said all those years ago—sometimes you just have to live in the moment and enjoy what you have now, not hold on for one day and what's to come. I want to enjoy what's here while I can. We were the last generation who could have turned the tide. By the time Kathe and Thomas came along, it was too late to undo the mess we'd made. Climate change had already passed the tipping point, and whatever measures we put in place from then on out could only slow things down, not reverse them.

Perhaps it sounds egotistical, but I feel I owe it to the Earth to stay with her as long as I can. No one, not even a planet, should have to die alone.

§

August 16, 2200 - Colorado

I'm going to cheat and talk about starlight, instead of the sun. Then again, the sun is a star, even if we usually don't think of it that way. The stars on this particular day are important to remember; it's the day we started saying goodbye.

We were vacationing in Buena Vista, staying at a resort built up around a hot spring. We went skinny-dipping in the springs on our last night, and even though it was high season, we had the place entirely to ourselves. You leaned back against the pool's edge, and said, *Well, I'm dying.* Just like that.

You'd been losing weight for a while, but I wanted to pretend it was just your appetite slowing down now that we were both past middle age. You'd already considered all your options, you told me, talked to all the doctors. You'd tried everything there was to try—radiation pills, alternative therapy, even the more aggressive forms of chemo like they had in the old days. Those weeks you told me you were visiting your sister? You were really puking your guts out, suffering, but you didn't want me to worry until you were really sure there was something to worry about.

The only thing left to try was gene therapy, and that was a bridge too far. *It's fine for babies,* you said, *fetuses in the womb who don't know any better, but I know who I am and I wouldn't feel like myself anymore if I let them scrub me clean. It's my own body's cells betraying me. Maybe I just have to live with that. Besides, why go through all that trouble and expense when at my age, there's only a five percent chance of success? I want to enjoy as much of the time I have left as I can, not spend it hooked up to machines.*

Then you reached into the backpack you'd carried out to the hot springs with us and pulled out a small terra cotta pot holding a Gibraltar Campion. It might have been from the very same seed batch as the one I grew for you all those years ago. Yours was barely a seedling though, growing crooked like it wouldn't survive a strong wind.

I never did have your knack for it, you said. You held out the pot to me and smiled that lopsided smile of yours. *Sometimes you just have to live for the moment, right? Appreciate what you have and not worry about the future.*

Damn you for throwing my words back at me. How dare you give up? How dare you throw everything away when we still had so much living to do? But I could only stare at you and the Campion.

You let a full minute of silence go by before you asked me if I was okay. If *I* was okay when you were the one dying. What could I say? All my words dried up in that moment. You took my hand. We sat in the hot spring, your fingers in mine under the water, and tears ran down my face. Later, we made love, and I was crying then, too. I think I cried more that night than I did at your funeral.

The sky was utterly clear. There's nothing like a skyscraper for miles in Buena Vista and next to no light pollution. On a night as clear as the one on which you told me you were dying, the sky was a bowl of blue so dark it passed into black and came out the other side.

That blue-dark bowl closed over the mountains, sealing us in, but everywhere we looked, there was light. I want to say the stars were bright, and they were, but they were so bright and there were so many of them, they looked fuzzy.

The stars between the stars were visible, and somehow it was different than looking at them from the top of the world, even though there isn't much light pollution in Svalbard either. The stars seemed farther away. They seemed alive, like the whole of the dark was crawling with silver. I could almost see the arm of the Milky Way unfurling around us. It was enough to make me dizzy. Or maybe that was the hot water from the spring. Or the thought of letting you go.

Right before we fell asleep that night, you lay spooned against my back. I held your hands, your arms pulled all the way around me. I thought if I held on tight enough, maybe you wouldn't go. You leaned forward and whispered in my ear, *Take care of my flower for me, when I'm gone.*

I still have the damn thing, Mila. Or at least its descendant. It's sitting on my windowsill. Predator X hasn't knocked it over yet, not for lack of trying. I want that flower to be the last thing I see in this world. When I'm too old and frail to walk around anymore, I'll keep it by my bedside. It's a little piece of you, so when I die, I won't be doing it alone.

§

June 24, 2232 - Svalbard

Linde and Ivan are taking the kids to get settled on the ship today. Kathe will join them just before launch. Thomas and Leena are already on board.

Before Linde and Ivan boarded, Ivan asked me if I was sure I hadn't changed my mind. I never expected him to be the one. I had to bite my tongue to keep from asking if Kathe had put him up to it, but there was genuine regret in his eyes. Linde shook my hand, firm and strong as always. Ivan hugged me. I couldn't ask for better children-in-law.

Sometimes I think of the dangers Kathe, Linde, Ivan, and even Thomas will face up there. What would you think of me, letting our children, their spouses, our grandchildren go off into the dark alone? Kathe, Linde, Ivan, Thomas, and Leena will likely never see an alien world, let alone set foot on one. It'll be their children, their children's children who will colonize the stars. If they make it that far.

I think of all the things that could go wrong—a critical failure in the engines; explosive decompression blowing them all out into space; a plague; failure of the ship-board crops and death by slow starvation. Those possibilities are next to none. Kathe gave me the figures, something like a 0.001% chance. Me being on board certainly wouldn't tip the balance one way or another. Still, it's a parent's job to worry.

This is what the sun looked like on the day my grandchildren climbed aboard the space elevator and we all said goodbye.

The ocean was a sullen color, like pewter, but with a shine. Maybe tarnished silver would be a better comparison, the surface dull but with a brightness hidden underneath. The sun had a pinkish tint to it. Pink is normally a warm color, but this pink was cold. Like the inside of a shell fresh out of the sea or a thin sliver of pickled ginger. Like skin, when all the warmth of blood and a beating heart has gone out of it and it's just a container, no longer full.

There were clouds, a very few of them, scattered across the sky. The kittiwakes and skua glided on the wing, and every now and then one of them would let out a cry.

Ella, that's Kathe and Linde and Ivan's youngest, cried when she hugged me. She put her arms around my waist, and pressed her face into my stomach. I think she's too young to really understand the nature of this goodbye, but she could read the mood. Ryan, he's the middle child, promised to video call every day as long as they were in range. Dani, the eldest, didn't seem to know what to say. They shook my hand like Linde had, very formal, and that was the end.

I watched the elevator as far as I could. After a while the sun shifted to a white-yellow, cold, pure. The color of goodbye.

§

June 26, 2176 - Luang Prabang

There's nothing particularly special about this day, no reason it deserves to be memorialized, but life isn't all about the big moments. In fact, life is mostly what happens in-between, and the sun shines on those days, too. That's what this catalogue is intended to capture, after all.

I remember the day because it's the day I stopped thinking about the future as an abstract. For as long as we'd known each other, we'd been working toward *the future,* cataloging and protecting and gathering seeds in the vault at Svalbard. But that future was a nebulous concept. It was for someone else, not us. That day, I started thinking about the future as a personal concept, like maybe one day we'd have a family, and they would make everything we were trying to do to make the world a better place—even in small ways—worthwhile.

We were about 60 miles outside of Luang Prabang on that day, hiking. I don't remember the names of all the villages we passed through, but we started at the temple at Mt. Phoushi, overlooking the Mekong River.

We were there to pick up three new and heartier strains of *Oryza sativa*—rice, in layman's terms. They could have been shipped to the vault, but you convinced the director to let us act as couriers. We changed each other over the years, Mila. When we first met, you would quote rules and regulations and procedure for hours on end. I like to think I taught you to appreciate the spirit of the law, as much as the letter of it. It's like the way my concept of the future changed. I'd like to think I helped you see that we weren't just protecting plants as a nebulous concept; we were protecting living things you could touch and hold in your hand and appreciate for more than just their potential.

And you taught me to see a wider world. Before I met you, I never thought much beyond the present moment. You expanded everything. I loved you more than I loved myself, and that made my world so much larger than it had ever been before. You taught me that the future is worth protecting, even the parts I won't live to see. You taught me to have hope.

We did some touristy things in Luang Prabang—the temple, the Royal Palace, the Night Market—but it's the hike I remember the most. Our guides took us in a boat across the Nam Xuang. I think there were about ten of us, total. Tourism was on the decline already in those days. We hiked for maybe five or six hours, past rice paddies and through jungles. We stopped in a little village where we watched children play soccer.

And that was where it hit me, the idea of having a personal stake in the future. We hadn't even talked about kids yet, but I found myself wondering what our family would be like. Not if we would have one; it suddenly seemed like a given. We were so in love, how could that love help but spill over and spread outward and keep on multiplying itself?

I wondered if our kids would be happy. If they'd play soccer, running around with pure, unfettered joy. I wondered if they would grow up to have kids of their own.

When Kathe was born, I worried about so many things. I wanted to do everything to protect her. You were the one who finally got me to relax, to let go a little. She would be her own person; we'd given her everything she needed to get a good start in life. And you were right, Mila. We raised some good kids. Or, really, they grew into good people, and we managed to not fuck it up by getting in their way.

After that first village, we hiked to another village where all the houses were on stilts, and they gave us strong rice wine to sample. At our last stop, the villagers had set out a dinner to share with the hikers and our guides on a long wooden table in a barn. Before we ate, we watched the sun go down. It was less a sunset and more a sense of the light being swallowed by the mist, diffusing and turning the sky the color of a new peach, sliced thin and still holding the warmth of the day—sweet and melting and bright on the tongue.

What I remember most is the way the light caught in a curl of your hair, just before the sun vanished. It reminded me of our wedding day, except instead of flyaway strands, the hair stuck in the sweat on the back of your neck. It was like you'd found a way to braid the sunlight and make it a part of you.

I know that sounds incredibly sappy, but it's true. Or, at least, I've built it into truth over the years. That's what people left alone with their thoughts and their grey kittens named after prehistoric animals do. They invent narratives to make sense of their lives and to fix the pattern of those lives more firmly in their minds. Even if that isn't the way the sunlight looked on that particular day, that is how I choose to remember it. That is the image I'm sending out among the stars.

§

June 30, 2232 - Svalbard

Today was the last day, or the first day, depending on how you look at it. The *Arber* has officially set sail, or whatever word one uses for the departure of a ship the size of a city without masts or cloth or anything resembling a sail.

This is the first day of the new age of humanity.

Our children's children's children, will they even be human anymore? Born in space, living all those years on a ship under sunlamps and breathing recycled air. Will they still call themselves human when they land on a new world and make it their own?

I don't have any answers. How can I speak to the big questions of life when the small ones still elude me? How do you love someone and let them go? How can someone be a stranger and still be your own flesh and blood? How can you feel closer to someone who isn't even on Earth any more than you ever did when they were right there beside you?

Indulge me for a moment, Mila. I know you always hoped my relationship with Thomas would be more like my relationship with Kathe. The truth is, there was always a rift between us. Maybe we both sensed it, and so we kept our distance. Or maybe it was just a failure on both of our parts to try.

When you died, the rift widened, and everything came crashing down. Thomas blamed me. He told me in no uncertain terms that I should have *forced* you to undergo gene therapy. As if your body, and the decisions you made regarding it, were any business of mine. I told him over and over again it wasn't what you wanted. You'd considered and discarded that option.

There were days I agreed with him though, and that hurt the most. I lashed out at him, when I really wanted to lash out at you. At the end, when you were delirious, I couldn't help thinking—could I have done more? *Could* I have forced you? In the end, I respected your wishes. In the end, I sat by and watched you die.

I know, there are no guarantees that the gene therapy would have worked. It might have led to more suffering. But I can't help wondering. . . . You dedicated your life to the vault and to Svalbard, to cheating nature by finding stronger, heartier crops to withstand droughts and monsoons. You were determined to do everything you could to give them more than a fair and fighting chance to survive. Why wouldn't you take that road yourself?

I didn't understand at the time. I think I'm closer to understanding now. At my age, death is no longer a nebulous concept far away. I've thought about it and what I do and do not want it to be. I don't want to be hooked up to machines on a space ship fighting for a few more hours or months or years. I don't want to be stuck in a cold-freeze drawer just so my distant descendants can put flowers on my grave under an alien sun. It's *my* death; I want to own it. Death is the last thing we do as human beings, so I'm damned well going to do it on my own terms.

Does that make sense, Mila? That I can blame you and hate that you left me and still send our children off into space and insist on staying behind? I suppose we're all a bundle of contradictions in the end. Maybe that's what ultimately what makes us human. No matter what other changes or adaptations occur, that will survive.

Kathe came and sat on the porch with me before boarding the last elevator to the station. We sipped strong black coffee. She held my hand. We didn't speak. In the end, at *the* end, we sat and watched the skua and the kittiwakes. We watched the sun play on the water. Then she kissed my cheek and that was goodbye.

I watched the sky for a long time after she left. I imagined if I shaded my eyes just right, I would be able to see something as the *Arber* set sail. I would know, or feel it deep in my bones. But there wasn't anything to see.

No, that isn't quite true. There was the sun. On the last day, on the first day, the sun was bright and clean and it threw a halo around itself, a celebration or one last goodbye, although it was only those who were staying behind who would ever see. The light on the last day of the world was every color the sun could be, all the colors it won't be in space.

I read once that every person who sees a halo around the sun or the moon sees their own individual halo. Even two people standing right next to each other wouldn't see exactly the same thing. The light breaks through different atmospheric crystals for each of them, no two beams fracturing in quite the same way. Every halo is unique.

I suppose that's all there is. I'm sending this out into the stars to travel to new worlds, so new generations will be able to look back to know how the sun looked on a particular day back where their parents' parents' parents came from. So they'll know how the sun looked to one specific person as it bounced off the water or rested against the skin of someone he loved or slipped beneath the rim of the world.

Now, I'm going to make myself another cup of coffee and sit out on the porch a little while longer. Maybe I can even coax Predator X onto my lap. I may be alone, but I'm not lonely. I have everything I need. You're buried here, and from the moment I met you, I've never known how to be anywhere else but with you. The future is out there among the stars, but I'm where I belong. I'm home.

Sunvault

Her Own Captain

Likhain

Sunvault

Jess Barber lives in Cambridge, MA, where she spends her days (and sometimes nights) building open-source electronics. She is a graduate of the 2015 Clarion Writing Workshop, and her work has recently appeared in *Strange Horizons, Lightspeed,* and *The Year's Best Science Fiction: Thirty-Second Annual Collection.* You can find her online at www.jess-barber.com.

Santiago Belluco is a neuroscientist born and raised in Brazil before moving to America to get the usual degrees needed to become a real scientist (namely a funded one). He now lives and works in Switzerland, where he writes speculative fiction and studies the neurocircuitry of vision.

Lisa M. Bradley writes speculative poetry and fiction inflected by her Latina heritage. Most recently, her work has appeared in *Interfictions, Uncanny Magazine,* and *Strange Horizons.* Her collection of short fiction and poetry is *The Haunted Girl* (Aqueduct Press 2014). Forged in the scalding heat of South Texas, she now lives in Iowa. She loves horror movies, gothic country music, guerilla art, and art journaling.

Chloe N. Clark holds an MFA in Creative Writing & Environment. Her work appears in *Abyss & Apex, Bartleby Snopes, Apex, Hobart, Midwestern Gothic, Sleet,* and more. She currently writes for *Nerds of a Feather* and *Ploughshares.* She can be followed @PintsNCupcakes.

An Ottawa teacher by day, **Brandon Crilly** has been previously published by *On Spec, The 2017 Young Explorer's Adventure Guide, Third Flatiron Anthologies,* and other markets, with an upcoming short story in *49th Parallels: Alternative Canadian Histories and Futures.* He was a semi-finalist in the 4th quarter of Writers of the Future 32, contributes regularly to BlackGate.com, and is the Assistant Editorial Director of TEGG Games. You can find Brandon at brandoncrilly.wordpress.com or on Twitter: @B_Crilly. His first TEGG short story, "Wizard-sitting," is now available at onderemporium.com.

Yilun Fan is a PhD student of comparative literature at the University of California, Riverside. She loves reading and writing science fiction because she believes in the power of story. She used to work for the official website of World Chinese Science Fiction Association as an editor and is now a columnist for *Science Fiction World* magazine.

Jaymee Goh is a Malaysian-Chinese writer currently based in California, writing a dissertation on steampunk. Previous publication credits include *Strange Horizons, Science Fiction Studies,* and more recently *recompose magazine.*

José M. Jimenez is a programmer with the heart of a poet. As Director of Research Information Systems at the University of Iowa, he creates systems that streamline administrative processes so researchers can focus on their projects, not paperwork. His interests include data visualization, workplace diversity and inclusion, geocaching, cooking, and Ingress. He is a proud parent and a beleaguered cat guardian.

Likhain is a Filipina artist and writer who works in ink, watercolor, poetry, and odd bits of creative non-fiction. She is a recipient of the 2016 Tiptree Fellowship and has been nominated for the 2017 Hugo Award for Best Fan Artist. A loving albeit wayward daughter of Metro Manila, she now lives in regional Australia with her partner, their pomeranians, and their princess cat.

S. Qiouyi Lu is a writer, editor, narrator, and translator; their translation with Ken Liu of "Chimera" by Gu Shi appeared in the March 2016 issue of *Clarkesworld*. Visit S. online at s.qiouyi.lu or follow them on Twitter at @sqiouyilu.

Maura Lydon is a college senior studying Environmental Science with a minor in Creative Writing at Hollins University. You can find her stories in *Wings of Renewal: A Solarpunk Dragon Anthology* and the online magazine *Abyss & Apex*. She enjoys writing, reading, and growing as many plants as will fit in her room.

Camille Meyers is a writer and wildlife conservation biologist with wanderlust. She has worked with falcons in Belize and as a zookeeper in Washington State. Currently, she is an MFA candidate in Creative Writing & Environment at Iowa State University, where she received the 2014 Pearl Hogrefe Fellowship in Creative Writing. She served as poetry editor for *Flyway: Journal of Writing and Environment* and volunteers in wildlife rehab at the Iowa Wildlife Center.

Lev Mirov is a queer disabled mixed race Filipino-American living in rural Maryland with his spouse Aleksei Valentín. Before he was a published poet, he studied medieval history, magic, and religion. His Rhysling-nominated poetry has appeared in *Through the Gate, Liminality Magazine, Strange Horizons,* and in other magazines and anthologies, and his speculative fiction has appeared in the anthology Myriad Lands.

Canadian illustrator and comic artist **Christine Moleski** recently graduated from the University of Regina (BA English, BFA Visual Arts). She self-published her first original comic book, *ICE,* as part of her graduating exhibition. She is interested in the individual human experience and how that experience resonates with humanity as a whole. "Solar Flare" was inspired by cybernetics, i-tech, and clean energy sources. You can find *ICE,* and more of her work, at www.christinemoleski.com.

Kristine Ong Muslim is the author of eight books of fiction and poetry including, most recently, *Black Arcadia, Meditations of a Beast, Butterfly Dream,* and *Age of Blight.* She serves as poetry editor of *LONTAR: The Journal of Southeast Asian Speculative Fiction* and was co-editor with Nalo Hopkinson of the original fiction section of the *Lightspeed Magazine* special issue *People of Colo(u)r Destroy Science Fiction!* Widely anthologized and published in magazines, she grew up and continues to live in a rural town in southern Philippines.

joel nathanael is a second year MFA candidate in the Creative Writing & Environment program at Iowa State University. His writing interests are in and around the nexus of art and science. He has been given the title of space poet, due to his unrelenting obsession with the subject matter, and where he is often situated, the honorific is apt. While in the MFA program, Joel wishes to further his understanding of poetry through practice. He is working on multimedia thesis exploring recursive methods of interpretation of a given source text—space poetry.

Clara Ng is a confused snail scooting through life, soon to be a confused snail with a proper degree. Her greatest desire is to be a Renaissance snail, skilled in all the disciplines, but that's sort of up in the air right now. She has appeared in several university theatre productions, been published in some other small magazines, and is very honored to be included in this anthology. Someday, she hopes to live in a solarpunk world, as one might have guessed.

Sara Norja dreams in two languages and has a predilection for tea. Born in

England and settled in Helsinki, Finland, she lives for words, dance, and moments of wonder. Her poetry has appeared in venues including *Goblin Fruit, Strange Horizons, inkscrawl, Through the Gate, Stone Telling,* and *Interfictions.* Her short fiction has appeared in *Strange Horizons, Flash Fiction Online,* and the anthology *An Alphabet of Embers.* She blogs at suchwanderings.word-press.com and can be found on Twitter as @suchwanderings.

Writer, performance poet, and performance facilitator **Brandon O'Brien** is from Trinidad and Tobago. His poetry is published or forthcoming in *Control Literary Magazine, Uncanny Magazine,* and *Strange Horizons,* and my prose has been published in *New Worlds, Old Ways: Speculative Tales from the Caribbean.* He has been shortlisted for the 2014 Alice Yard Prize for Art Writing and the 2014 and 2015 Small Axe Literary Competitions. He currently serves as the poetry editor of *FIYAH Magazine.*

Daniel José Older is the New York Times bestselling author of the Shadowshaper Cypher, including *Shadowhouse Fall* and *Shadowshaper* (Scholastic, 2015), a New York Times Notable Book of 2015, which won the International Latino Book Award and was shortlisted for the Kirkus Prize in Young Readers' Literature, the Andre Norton Award, the Locus, the Mythopoeic Award, and named one of *Esquire*'s 80 Books Every Person Should Read. He also writes the Bone Street Rumba urban fantasy series from Penguin's Roc Books. He co-edited the Locus- and World Fantasy-nominated anthology *Long Hidden: Speculative Fiction from the Margins of History.* You can find his thoughts on writing, read dispatches from his decade-long career as an NYC paramedic, and hear his music at danieljoseolder.net, on Youtube at https://www.youtube.com/user/danieljose1, and @djolder on Twitter.

Jack Pevyhouse is a poet and writer with a BA in English and a minor in Creative Writing from UNC Pembroke, where he was the Editor-in-Chief of the student literary magazine, *The Aurochs,* from August 2015 to December 2016. He is working towards an MFA in Creative Writing from UNC Wilmington. His poetry has been published in the online magazines *Paper Crown* and *Open Thought Vortex.* He is also a scriptwriter, an assistant producer, and, in season two, voiced the Fig Wasp King for the award-winning audio drama podcast, *Jim Robbie and the Wanderers,* available to listen to, for free, on iTunes, Google Play, Podbay, and Stitcher.

Bethany Powell's first published poem was inspired by her hobby of hand-spinning yarn—the literal kind. After a youth of traipsing the US coasts and Japanese inland, she is now based in weird rural Oklahoma. You can find more of her work at http://bethanypowell.com.

Sireesha Reddy is a multilingual American-born South Indian who is working on becoming a real artist. Her interests are the psychology of diversity and abuse, wit, fashion, and annotating things she reads with unnecessary focus. This is her first published artwork, and she's very glad it's solarpunk! Her next work will appear in *Suma Lima Vol. 2: The Everyday Strange*, existence pending. She can be found—and even contacted!—on Tumblr (sirinsquared.tumblr.com) and Instagram (@sirinsq.art).

C. Samuel Rees has been featured in *The Fairy Tale Review, Chicon St. Poets, The Account, Borderlands: Texas Poetry Review, Permafrost, Raw Paw, Pithead Chapel, JMWW*, and *Row Home Lit*. His poetry is anthologized in *Bearing the Mask: Southwestern Persona Poems* (Dos Gatos Press) and in the upcoming *The Dead Animal Handbook* (University of Hell Press). C. Samuel is a high school teacher in Austin, TX where he composes poetry, writes stories about rivers and ruins, and subsists on a steady diet of books on desert ecology and horror films.

Carlin Reynolds is a traditional artist studying mechanical engineering at Northeastern University. They are passionate about interdisciplinary science and sustainability, and would like to pursue a career in materials science. In their free time, Carlin enjoys rock climbing, electronics, minimalist design, and growing succulents. Some of their work can be found at seelio.com/carlin.

Iona Sharma is a writer, lawyer, and linguaphile, and the product of more than one country. She's currently working on her first novel. She can be found at generalist.org.uk/iona and tweeting as @singlecrow.

Nisi Shawl's Belgian Congo steampunk novel *Everfair* is a September 2016 Tor publication. Her story collection *Filter House* co-won the James Tiptree, Jr. Award in 2009 and was nominated for that year's World Fantasy Award. She was Guest of Honor at WisCon 35 in 2011, and at the Science Fiction Research Association's convention in 2013. Shawl is coauthor of *Writing the Other: A Practical Approach*, a book based on workshops about writing inclusive fiction she has taught for two decades. She co-edited *Strange Matings: Science Fiction, Feminism, African American Voices, and Octavia E. Butler,* and *Stories for Chip: A Tribute to Samuel R. Delany.* She is a co-founder and Steering Committee member of the Carl Brandon Society, a nonprofit supporting the presence of people of color in the fantastic genres, and she also serves on the writing workshop Clarion West's board of directors. Shawl promises to update her website soon.

Karyn L. Stecyk is a Canadian writer and editor who had chosen her starting class in science psychology, but has since reallocated her stats to pursue a deep-seated need for escapism. This complements her wanderlust (and probably explains her two years in Japan). Embracing her location-independent career, she is currently accepting travel recommendations. Karyn has written for video games, edits primarily scientific journal publications, and is working on her first novel. Her other hobbies include rocking out to symphonic and power metal, recreating cuisine from her travels, and chipping away at her video game library. You can find her at karynlstecyk.com, or on Twitter @KarynLStecyk.

Bogi Takács is a Hungarian Jewish agender person currently living in the US with eir cheerful neuroatypical family. E writes and edits speculative poetry, fiction, and nonfiction, and eir work has been published in a variety of venues like *Clarkesworld, Lightspeed, Apex,* and *Strange Horizons.* Bogi also draws, designs, and typesets things on occasion. If you liked this poem, Bogi recommends the stories "For Your Optimal Hookboarding Experience," published in *Lackington's,* and "Forestspirit, Forestspirit" in *Clarkesworld.* You can find Bogi at www.prezzey.net and as @bogiperson on Twitter and Instagram. E also reviews SFF at www.bogireadstheworld.com.

Lavie Tidhar is the author of the Jerwood Fiction Uncovered Prize winning and Premio Roma nominee *A Man Lies Dreaming* (2014), the World Fantasy Award winning *Osama* (2011), and of the critically-acclaimed *The Violent Century* (2013). His latest novel is *Central Station* (2016). He is the author of many other novels, novellas, and short stories.

Aleksei Valentín is a queer, disabled, Jewish Latinx PhD student by day and writer by night. They live on the outskirts of the Battle of Antietam in Maryland with their husband and fellow writer, Lev Mirov, and two spoiled cats. Currently, they're working on a Religious Studies dissertation and fitting in time for poetry and paranormal romance. Whenever they escape the library, they can be found scoping out deals on ballet tickets, cooking kosher and gluten-free food, and hunting for the world's best cup of coffee.

Their poetry has previously appeared in *Liminality Magazine,* and a joint paranormal romance with their husband, *The Gods of Small Things,* is coming out in early 2017. To see where they're rolling next, connect with them at https://twitter.com/ai_valentin.

Leigh Wallace is an Ottawa writer, artist, and narrator who works as an Access to Information and Privacy analyst for the government of Canada. Her fiction is available or upcoming in *Tesseracts 19, Urban Fantasist,* and *Podcastle,* and more of her art is available at leighfive.deviantart.com. This is her first professional art sale.

T.X. Watson studies Sci Fi and Fantasy as a form of activism at Hampshire College in Amherst, Mass. Watson has been deeply engaged with solarpunk since late 2014, contributing to the growth of the genre with the Tumblr blog Watsons-Solarpunk, and, later, cofounding *Solarpunk Press,* a free solarpunk web fiction magazine at solarpunkpress.com. Their hobbies include digital art and binge-watching YouTube videos analyzing popular media.

A.C. Wise was born and raised in Montreal and currently lives in the Philadelphia area. Her short fiction has appeared in *Clarkesworld, Shimmer, Liminal,* and *Tor.com,* among other places. Her collections, *The Ultra Fabulous Glitter Squadron Saves the World Again* and *The Kissing Booth Girl and Other Stories,* are both available from Lethe Press. In addition to her fiction, she coedits *Unlikely Story,* and contributes a monthly review column to *Apex.* Find her online at www.acwise.net and on twitter as @ac_wise.

South African clinical psychologist **Nick Wood** has about twenty short stories published in various SFF magazines and anthologies, as well as a YA SF book under the 'Young Africa' series entitled *The Stone Chameleon,* and a recent adult SF novel *Azanian Bridges*: https://sfbook.com/azanian-bridges.htm.

Tyler Young is a Midwestern lawyer. His work has previously been published in *Daily Science Fiction* and *Nature.* When he isn't writing speculative fiction, he is usually at a zoo or museum with his wife and two young children.

About the Editors

Phoebe Wagner grew up in Pennsylvania, the third generation to live in the Susquehanna River Valley. She spent her days among the endless hills pretending to be an elf, and, eventually, earned a B.A. in English: Creative Writing from Lycoming College, where she also met her husband. She is an MFA candidate in Creative Writing and Environment at Iowa State University. Follow her on Twitter: @pheebs_w.

Brontë Christopher Wieland is an MFA candidate in Creative Writing and Environment at Iowa State University where he thinks about how language, culture, and storytelling shape the world around us. In 2014, he earned his Bachelor's degree from the University of Wisconsin-Madison in Mathematics and Linguistics. His fiction has appeared in *Flash Fiction Online* and *Hypertext Magazine*. Follow him on Twitter: @BeezyAl.

Acknowledgements

"On the Origins of Solarpunk" by Andrew Dincher: Originally published by OBSOLETE! Press, 2016.

"Speechless Love" by Yilun Fan: Originally published in Chinese in *Science Fiction World*, December 2014.

"Thirstlands" by Nick Wood: Originally published in the NewCon Press anthology *Subterfuge*, 2008.

"Dust" by Daniel José Older: Originally published in *Lightspeed*, October 2014.

Upper Rubber Boot would like to thank Loraine Posadas Flegal and Kelly Allistone for their sharp eyes.

Brontë Christopher Wieland and Phoebe Wagner would like to thank their wonderful publisher Joanne Merriam for taking a chance on two young editors and the new genre of solarpunk. They are also grateful to 62 Moons for creating solarpunk music to help with promotion. Without Choe N. Clark passing along the call for anthology submission, *Sunvault* wouldn't have happened. Phoebe would also like to thank her husband Andrew for putting up with the late nights and being a constant pillar of support. Finally, they are so thankful for all the Kickstarter backers and the many people who shared *Sunvault* over social media.

Sunvault: Stories of Solarpunk & Eco-Speculation was supported by the following generous donors:

A Goad

ABS

Adam Haenlein

AJ Fenske

Alex Conall

Alisa Beer

Amanda Ju

Andrea M. Pawley

Andrew Dincher

Angus McIntyre

Anke

Anonymous

Abraham Martínez Azuara

Adam Flynn

Adriane L.

Alain Fournier

Alex Hill

Amanda Edens

Amber M.

Andrew and Kate Barton

Andy Dost

Anil Menon

Anne Gregory

Asa R.

Aubrey Westbourne
B. Diane Martin
Benjamin Trown
Blake Neely
Brenda Tyrrell
C.N. Rowen
Chad Bowden
Chris Brant
Claire Selle
Corrie S
D Franklin
Daniel Feldmann
DrCris
Eline Tabak
Emily Walters
Erick Burdock
Faith Gregory
Fred Herman
George McCollum
Grayson Sheldon
GriffinFire
Gustaf B.
H. N. James
Hannah Bingham Brunner
Howard J. Bampton
Ignacio Navarro
Jack Pevyhouse
James Schmidt
Jaylee James
Jeliza
Jennifer S
Jesse Wolfe
John A. McColley
John T C
Joshua Ramsey
K
Katharine J. Houk
Keith Bissett
Keith Travis
Kermit O.

August Evrard
Bart Everson
Billy Leuellen
Brandon Zarzyczny
Brendan Mason
Camille Meyers
Charibdys
Christine Skolnik
Clive Tern
Cuervoscuro
Dan Grace
Debbie Block-Schwenk
Elena K.
Emily R. Houk
Emily Williams
Erin A. Bisson
Felicity Graham
Fullon
Glaiza
Gretchen Armer
Gunnar Norskog
Guy Immega
Haley Blanton
Helen Pearson Hespa
Ian Carr
Ivan Donati
jacquieink
Janice M. Eisen
Jaymee Goh
Jennifer L. Knox
Jeremy Zimmerman
Jessica Enfante
John McCracken
Jose Carlos Cuevas
Julia Patt
Kat Lerner
Katrina Allis
Keith M. Frampton
Ken Blakey
Kerri Regan

Kevin Riggle
Laura Duerr
Laureen Hudson
Lennhoff Family
Lois Spangler
Luca Albani
M Sereno
Malcolm SW Wilson
Marion Deeds
Mark and Kyra Wieland
Martin Bernstein
Matthew Farrer
Maura Lydon
Max O
Melissa Shumake
Mike Bundt Page
Missy Mirrix
Molly Dincher
MSM
Natalie Peters
Nick Wood
Noah Kenneally
Parhelia Games
Patti Short
Peter Gnodde
Rae Carra
Redsixwing
Rivqa Rafael
Robert Maughan
Rowan-Tarragon-and-Sage
S. Swansburg
S. Zupon
Sam Wagner
Sarah Crosby
Sarena Ulibarri
Shana DuBois
Simo Muinonen
Stephanie Cranford
Stevie H.
Sueage

L. Denoyer
Laura Wilkinson
Lauren C. Teffeau
Logan Browne
Loki Carbis
Lydia Martin
M. Molly Backes
Marcin J. Wolynski
Marissa Lingen
Mark Gerrits
Martin DeMello
Mattie Michelle
Max Battcher
Megan Hippler
Michael J. DeLuca
Miss Olivia Louise
Mobo Doco
Molly Gloss
Nat Rolfe
Navarre Bartz
Noah Buntain
Paige Kimble
Patrick Winifred Archer-Morris
Peter Burt
Rachel Bostwick
Ralph Walker
Renee Christopher
Robert M. Graves
Rose Lemberg and Bogi Takács
Roy Romasanta
S. Qiouyi Lu
S. K.
Sara Norja
Sarah Savage Davis
Sean Pelkey
Shel Graves
Stef Maruch
Steven Saus
Subterran
Suncica

Susan Stockell
Tamara Michelle Slaten
Tammy Luckett
Theeldeltaco
Thomas Matthew Colwell
Ursula Pflug
Vida Cruz
Virginia M. Mohlere
Zacqary Adam Xeper

T.X. Watson
Tammy Jo Crotty
Tamora Tea
Thomas Bull
Tomas Burgos-Caez
V. S. Holmes
Virginia
Yvette Crozier
Zoyander Street

Books by Upper Rubber Boot

Anthologies:

140 And Counting: an anthology of writing from 7x20
    Joanne Merriam, ed., 2011
Apocalypse Now: Poems and Prose from the End of Days
    Andrew McFadyen-Ketchum and Alexander Lumans, eds., 2012
Choose Wisely: 35 Women Up To No Good
    H. L. Nelson and Joanne Merriam, eds., 2015
How to Live on Other Planets: A Handbook for Aspiring Aliens
    Joanne Merriam, ed., 2015
The Museum of All Things Awesome and that Go Boom
    Joanne Merriam, ed., 2016
Sunvault: Stories of Solarpunk & Eco-Speculation
    Phoebe Wagner and Brontë Christopher Wieland, eds., 2017

Fiction:

Bicycle Girl: a short story
    Tade Thompson, 2014
Changing the World: a short story
    David M. Harris, 2014
Heist: a short story
    Tracy Canfield, 2014
Flight 505: a novella
    Leslie Bohem, 2015
Johnny B: a short story
    Phil Voyd, 2014
The Mask Game
    Sergey Gerasimov, 2013
Memory: a novelette
    Teresa P. Mira de Echeverría (Lawrence Schimel, trans.), 2015
The Selves We Leave Behind: a short story
    Shira Lipkin, 2014
Signs Over the Pacific and Other Stories
    RJ Astruc, 2013

The Suicide Inspector: a short story
    J. J. Steinfeld, 2014
The Tortoise Parliament: a short story
    Kenneth Schneyer, 2014
Twittering the Stars: a short story
    Mari Ness, 2014
The Widow and the Xir: a short story
    Indrapramit Das, 2014

Poetry:

Blueshifting
    Heather Kamins, 2011
Floodgate Poetry Series
    Andrew McFadyen-Ketchum, series editor
    (*Vol. 1*, 2014; *Vol. 2*, 2015; *Vol. 3*, 2016)
The Glaze from Breaking
    Joanne Merriam, 2011
    [reprint: Stride Books, 2005]
Hiss of Leaves
    T. D. Ingram, 2012
Marilyn Monroe: Poems
    Lyn Lifshin, 2013
    [reprint: Quiet Lion Press, 1994]
Measured Extravagance
    Peg Duthie, 2012
The Sky Needs More Work
    Corey Mesler, 2014

Copyright Information

Sunvault: Stories of Solarpunk and Eco-Speculation
ISBN 978-1-937794-75-0
©2017 respective authors

Cover art by Likhain
Cover design by Joanne Merriam

Published in the United States of America

UPPER RUBBER BOOT